Off Paradise

Western Literature Series

Off Paradise

S T O R I E S

HART WEGNER

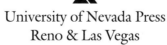

University of Nevada Press
Reno & Las Vegas

WESTERN LITERATURE SERIES

University of Nevada Press, Reno, Nevada 89557 USA
Copyright © 2001 by Hart Wegner
All rights reserved
Manufactured in the United States of America
Library of Congress Cataloging-in-Publication Data
Wegner, Hart.
Off paradise : stories / Hart Wegner.
p. cm. — (Western literature series)
ISBN 0-87417-486-4 (pbk. : alk. paper)
1. German Americans—Fiction.   2. Las Vegas
(Nev.)—Fiction.   3. Immigrants—Fiction.
4. Silesia—Fiction. I. Title. II. Series.
PS3573.E367 O38 2001
813'.54—DC21   2001001405
The paper used in this book meets the requirements of
American National Standard for Information
Sciences—Permanence of Paper for Printed Library
Materials, ANSI Z39.48-1984. Binding materials were
selected for strength and durability.

The following stories were previously published in a
slightly different form. In *New Myths/MSS*: "A Ransom
for Tedek" (1992) and "On the Road to Skaradowo"
(1995). In *Weber Studies*: "Cockshut Light" (1996). In
Ascent: "Following the Nun" (1996).

FIRST PRINTING
10 09 08 07 06 05 04 03 02 01
5 4 3 2 1

For Hildegard Jung Wegner,

who knows the answers

but needs not ask the questions

The book is for the exile

what the Universe is for God.

So any book of exile

is God's place.

EDMOND JABÈS

Contents

Off Paradise

"No, no, Lottel!" Although Mother was speaking into a telephone receiver, her voice was as loud as if it had to carry all the way to the Sahara Hotel. "No! First you drive on Paradise Road. Yes, like *Paradies mit Adam und Eva.*"

From an easy chair in the living room of his parents' house, Martin watched his mother as she spoke on the telephone. Although she was bent with age, the prospect of having guests from home—not just from Germany but from Silesia—was filling her daily with such energy that she had been preparing the house as if nobility was to visit. Though she had known Lottel's family for close to seventy years, she hadn't seen them since five or six years after the war.

How many times had he heard her give elaborate instructions to people from out of town? Her visitors were mostly Germans who settled in America after the war, in Salt Lake City or in Southern California, but sometimes they would come directly from Germany. Mother's house wasn't hard to find, but her detailed instructions made it appear so. It was just that she wanted to help as much as she could; besides that, she had great faith that all would finally turn out well.

Martin could not remember when he had last seen Lottel. He began to figure the years and his trips to Europe. Whenever he was there, he visited Lottel and her family in Bremen.

Could I still live over there? He often asked himself that question, and whenever he did, he reminded himself of an incident in Leipzig. It happened on his first return to Silesia after they had fled in the winter of 1945. He had stopped over at the best hotel in Leipzig. In order even to stay at the hotel he had to prepay in dollars for a package that included a musty room and a cold breakfast. He filed past the laid-out food and took two rolls and some slices of cold cuts. First the cashier looked at him and at his tray, then she took a fork from the breast pocket of her uniform. Poking at his stack of cold cuts, she turned over each of the slices of salami. Martin wondered what she hoped to find. Only then did he realize that she was looking under the larger slices to see if he had hidden a smaller one underneath. She told him in a voice vibrating with teacherly righteousness that he had to pay extra—and pay in dollars, she added—because he had taken two slices too many. He often wondered if this was merely socialist bureaucracy or if it reflected a pettiness that he usually didn't find among Americans. Maybe that was why he could never move back to Germany, because he believed—and he kept this to himself—that it hadn't been communism that accounted for the fork in the breast pocket of the cashier's smock.

His parents had broken more cleanly with the Old Country than Martin had. After their ship landed in Brooklyn, they never went back to Germany and instead committed themselves wholeheartedly to the new life in America. Martin couldn't remember if his parents had ever actually told him that criticizing America was a sign of being unthankful, but if they hadn't said it to him, it had always been understood. In many conversations and in all family prayers it was never forgotten that they were grateful to God for having led them to the Promised Land. To this day, in his mother's eyes any criticism of local or national flaws was clearly a sign of ingratitude to the one who had brought them here.

He often became uneasy when he heard his mother quote from the Bible about the hand of the Lord. She liked Elijah in particular, and the hand of the Lord had been on him when "he girded up his

loins, and ran before Ahab to the entrance of Jezreel." He felt appre
hensive because he had often been called upon to do things because
it had been implied that it was the Lord's desire that he, Martin, do
something like gird up his loins and go alone to America to find a
new home for his family. And he was uneasy because he was also a
Bible reader, and he remembered very different quotes about the
hand of the Lord. It might have been Luke who said about John the
Baptist that "the hand of the Lord was with him." And how had that
turned out for him? Saint Paul was closer to what Martin thought
about life when he said, "It is a fearful thing to fall into the hands of
the living God." But Mother never quoted these lines.

Martin reasoned differently than she did. If God's will brought
you here, it was like being drafted. He himself had been drafted into
the American army during the Korean War, less than a year after he
had arrived from Europe. As a draftee, you could complain about
army chow, your bunk, twenty-five-mile marches, but if you had
volunteered, then it was best to accept quietly what the sergeant
told you to do; otherwise the draftees in the barracks would point
out to you that it was your own fault that you were even there.

Martin was watching his mother as she listened to the voice on
the telephone. He knew that Lottel would be trying to keep his
mother from waiting outside.

"*Aber natürlich,*" Mother insisted. "I'll be standing in the street. I
hope that you still recognize me. Seeing me will help you find our
house. *Auf Wiedersehen!*"

He had noticed that his mother used the German farewell more
and more, even to her American friends. Holding the receiver in
front of her as if it were a microphone and she a singer, she would
say "till-we-see-each-other-again," more loudly and with such faith
in her voice, as if that alone would make it happen. A second phrase
that she always used when Martin was leading her into church, step
by painful step, was an answer to the question "How are you?" Bent
over as she now stood, she would raise her head and look with a
proud smile into the face of the questioner and say slowly and deliberately, "I . . . am . . . here." All she would have needed to add was
"amen," and then she could have offered it up as testimony to God
and the congregation that she was still alive.

Hearing his mother say "*auf Wiedersehen*" to Lottel on the telephone reminded Martin that she had known Lottel since her birth in the same apartment house and in the same year in which Martin was born—and had known her parents even before then. Now Lottel and her husband had both retired and were driving through the American West. Their first stop was Las Vegas, and they were picking up their rental car directly at the airport.

It was the week before Christmas, and Martin was sure that they would enjoy the warm weather more than anything else, especially since Bremen was cold and wet. Martin had visited Lottel in the block of apartments set on a big lawn. The weather was not fit for vacationing, although it was July. Day after day he looked down from the third floor at the rain hitting the seagulls feeding in the lush grass. Through the whole week it kept raining in that sullen, hopeless way that it rained by the North Sea.

While they stood in the doorway, Martin hugged Lottel. She was short and stout, and her gray hair was a carpet of tight curls. Like a doll's hair, Martin thought as he looked over her head and down the steps to the driveway, where her husband was pulling suitcases from their rental car.

She stepped back over the threshold so as to look at him from the landing. It reminded him of his father buying a suit and insisting on taking it out into the daylight to see the true color of the material.

"Do I look real?" Martin joked.

"Every time we meet, you look like a different person." She shook her head.

"I keep changing because I have to adapt. If I had lived my whole life in Germany, who knows, I might have stayed the same." He realized that he sounded unfriendly, and so he decided not to tell her that he would always recognize her because she never changed.

"I don't see a wreath hanging from the ceiling. How do Americans celebrate Advent?" Horst sounded puzzled.

"It's not a big thing here." Martin didn't explain.

"And what about Christmas?"

Mother thought for a while. Martin was sure that she was silent because she never wanted to be thought of as being critical of anything American. "Mostly shopping," she finally answered.

Horst, who usually let his wife speak, agreed. "The same in Germany now, mostly shopping." In the meantime, Mother had thought over her own answer. "But they have Christmas trees everywhere, some of them have them out already in October."

"I think about our Christmases together in Brockau," Lottel said. "They were so different from what we have now. I remember most of all the making. Throughout the weeks of Advent all we ever seemed to do was make things. We cut, glued, and painted, and every December Sunday my mother would light one of the big red Advent candles. All of those sheets of gold and silver paper . . ."

"Did you buy yours at Dudek's?" interrupted Martin. Dudek was the stationer where Martin had bought his first books, those that hadn't been presents from his mother. When he was small, his parents took him to Dudek's, where he could select from sheets of cut-out figures, wild animals, a whole circus, and soldiers. Mostly he picked soldiers because he liked the different historic uniforms.

"Yes, we bought our sheets of silver and gold foil at Dudek's. You remember cutting the paper into strips as wide as my finger is now. Then it may have been as wide as two of my fingers." Lottel laughed good-naturedly. "We would glue the strips into loops and then link the loops into long chains."

"And then we would drape the chains over the Christmas tree!" Mother laughed as she remembered the time when they were all still home. "I remember you two sitting at the kitchen table, bent over your Christmas papers . . ." Mother looked at Lottel and Martin, and then she shook her head as if she couldn't believe what she saw. "A lifetime ago, a whole lifetime ago."

Back home, the first time Martin would get to see the tree, decorated and illuminated, would be on Christmas Eve when the gifts were given. Father and Mother would have been inside the living room behind the closed door for hours, while Martin and his grandmother had to wait outside in the dark corridor. Before the door could open, there had to be the questioning of Martin. Father—standing behind the door—lowered his voice until it rumbled as if he were indeed Saint Nikolaus. He asked in a serious tone how the boy had done during the year. Martin pretended that this was not his father's voice, and he pretended so well that he trembled in the dark. He answered bravely while he clutched his grandmother's hand. His face burned while the excitement went to his feet until he could not contain himself anymore and he began running in place in front of the dark door. The questioning always ended with words of advice: obey Father and Mother, study, be good. Then Father threw his voice back and forth and up and down, while he was saying good-bye to himself. Through the door Martin could hear steps and then the opening and closing of the window. Even then, as he played out being scared and then relieved, he knew that only the inner of the double windows had been opened, because his parents, always concerned about his health, surely would not have let in a blast of icy air just before he was allowed into the room. Often he was sick at Christmastime, and a lawn chaise would be set up for him in the room with the presents.

Finally, when Martin had gone from running in place to twisting around, the door opened, slowly as if no human hand was pushing on the handle, not onto darkness but onto brilliant light. The candles and sparklers on the tree had been lit, and the whole dining table and even the top of Father's mahogany desk were covered with presents, and among those presents were even more candles. Martin never knew where he should look first among all of the presents or whether he should concentrate on the tree or look at Father and Mother, who were beaming with joy.

On that last Christmas at home, the joy was tainted by the coming closer of the war. The first air raid had been in October. At Christmas they were able to hear the artillery fire from the eastern front, which grew steadily louder until they had to flee in January. Even if Martin hadn't known how grave their situation was, the adults in the household must have. When the bombers had struck in October, Martin had walked out of the cellar during the raid. Standing in the garden, he had listened to the explosions of the antiaircraft fire over the city. The older boys had been taken out of school, and it was they who were now manning the guns. While he was standing outside in the night, he heard a strange rustling in the fallen leaves. Bending down, he found a small jagged piece of steel from an artillery shell. It was still hot. Between the explosions in the sky above, he heard the rustling again and again, as if the first drops of rain were falling. He wasn't afraid, but he went back into the cellar. He didn't show anyone the steel splinter he had slipped into his pocket. It had cooled down some, but he still felt its warmth against his thigh. He wondered why his parents had let him walk out during the raid. They all had cowered in the cellar, so close to a pile of winter potatoes that Martin inhaled the sour smell of earth. Their corner of the cellar was dimly lit by a small candle, but its glow didn't reach far enough to shine on the piles of coal and coke, the stacks of briquettes and the barrels in which cabbage was curing. Between the cabbage barrels, Grandmother was hiding under a zinc tub that she had pulled over herself. Martin smiled when he thought about that scene, because for hours they cowered in fear from the explosions of the antiaircraft shells, believing that they were hearing bomb blasts. No bombs fell near them, but they had not yet learned to tell the different explosions apart. Later they would learn.

It was not the last Christmas in Silesia that Martin remembered best, but the one the year before. He had come home by train from Militsch, where he had been sent to be out of the city during air raids. He had taken the two-hour train ride not knowing that he would never return. Although he had been old enough to live in another town—he was twelve—he still underwent the questioning in front of the dark door. When it opened and turned into a white door, Martin's eyes fell first on the tree, but moved in an instant to a glistening line of a hundred—he counted them later—freshly cast tin soldiers. Their rifles, carried at shoulder arms, sparkled in the light of the Christmas candles.

"*Ach ja*," muttered Martin's mother. "*Ach*, Christmas."

"There is so little religion in Christmas. Now, I mean," Horst said.

"Do you go to church?" Martin asked Lottel.

"No, I don't, but Mother goes . . . I mean, she went."

"Why did she stop?"

"When she couldn't ride her bicycle anymore."

"Don't you have a church in your own neighborhood where your mother could walk to the services?"

"She didn't like the pastor in our church, so she began riding her bicycle into Bremen so she could go to another parish."

"You didn't go with her, did you?"

"No, I didn't go with her. As a matter of fact, I don't go to church at all. Does that finally satisfy you?"

"A heathen, that's what you are." Martin said it with a smile, but

Lottel didn't smile back. He knew that she didn't fit into the category of those he jokingly called "heathen," those who couldn't identify a simple biblical reference if it was made in conversation or those who ran their lawn mowers on Sunday morning. He knew that she was Lutheran because he had taken religion classes with her in grade school in Brockau. He and his family were not Lutheran, but it had been his father's thought that any religious instruction was better than none.

As children, he and Lottel had played together, at first almost every day. During the war when the schoolchildren were evacuated from the cities, he and she had been sent to different towns in Silesia. And after the war, when little travel was possible, they had lived in different zones of the divided Germany. Finally, he had gone to America and they hadn't seen each other for many years, but when he went back to Europe at last, he had stayed with her and Horst and they had talked deep into the night.

In that night he learned of Lottel's bitterness. Somehow she still believed, although she had fallen out with her church and bore a grudge against God. Her quarrel with God arose from the same root as her dislike of the German government, because God had been silent when the chancellor had given up any German claim to Silesia and the other territories now to the east of East Germany. She couldn't stay loyal to a government or a church that acted with no higher morality than a business hungering for sales. To her, God was not worthy of prayers because he had permitted a war that first took her father, then her home, all of her possessions, even the graves of her ancestors, and finally even her identity.

"Whenever I can, I mention that I am a Silesian," said Martin.

"Do people here know what Silesia was?" asked Horst.

"No."

"Then what good is it to proclaim yourself Silesian if no one knows what it is . . . was? It's just an affectation, nothing else." Lottel had suddenly become angry, as she often did when the subject of Silesia became part of the conversation. Sitting in silence, she soon gathered herself again. "It really isn't any different in Germany. Nobody wants to hear about it, nobody feels sorry for the people of Silesia. One million killed while fleeing or killed after the war. Shot, clubbed to death, starved . . ."

Martin raised his hand to stop her. "Americans might ask you without really expecting much of an answer to their question, 'What do you expect? After all, you started the war.'"

"We Silesians didn't start the war," Lottel answered hotly.

"But we *are* Germans."

"But *we* are the ones who had to pay the price, not the Bavarians, not the Saxons and all of the others who could go back to their towns. Their houses might have been bombed, but they still had their *Heimat.*"

"But I feel guilty," Martin said quietly.

"Why should *you* feel guilty?" replied Lottel hotly. "You were twelve, thirteen when the war ended."

"Thirteen," he said.

"Not even the *Volkssturm* could draft you. Even at the very end of the war, in the spring of 1945, they only went down to the fourteen year olds. Why should you feel guilty? What did you ever do to anybody?"

"When I came to America, the war had been over for only a few years. Wherever I went to work, I was bound to be the only German, branded by the heavy accent of a newcomer. All around me, in movies, television—which was so new that my aunt had the first set on the block—and in magazines, I kept seeing pictures of German atrocities. Real, as in a documentary, or imagined in the mind of a writer, it finally didn't matter anymore. Faced with pictures of piles of emaciated corpses, I began to feel guilty, not for anything I ever did or didn't do but for whatever my countrymen were accused of having done or having failed to do. Before I was twenty-one I began to feel guilty, and it hasn't stopped.

"Later, I felt guilty for what white America had done during slavery—although my own ancestors had worked in poverty in the fields of Silesia—and for what had been done to the Indians. Then came Vietnam and more guilt."

"But you have to admit, after the war it was us, the Silesians, who were made the scapegoats for the lost war and for the sins of Germany."

"Do you know how the scapegoat was selected?" Martin asked. "In Leviticus, the third book of Moses . . ."

"The Jews," said Horst.

"*Yes,* the Jews," continued Martin. "Two of the best goats were chosen. Then a lot was drawn and one goat was sacrificed on the fieldstone altar. Then Azazel, the other one, was brought to Aaron the Levite, who laid both hands on the head of the goat and confessed to him the sins of the children of Israel. Then the goat was driven away from the camp into the wilderness carrying all the sins between its horns."

"What happened to it?" asked Horst.

"It wandered in the desert, haunted by the demons that inhabit the wilderness, until God took it to Him and with it all the sins it carried on its back."

"Most of the stories in the Old Testament don't turn out too well," Mother said. "At least the scapegoat lived and wasn't sacrificed on any altar."

"Spoken like a true refugee!" Martin laughed.

"It's easy to laugh now, but then, then it was very different. You and I were children. Our parents were the ones who did all the planning and worrying . . ."

"And praying!" Mother added quickly.

"And as for losing, what did *you* lose anyway? Your toys?"

Martin nodded. Lottel was right. What had he lost? He had lost what he should have inherited. Not just the house and the garden but the right to have a family home, a right to the river, the mountains, a language, a past and a future.

"We were talking about religion in Christmas, before . . . this whole story about the scapegoat. Here in America we even have people coming to our door." Mother pointed to the front door. "They stand out on the landing and sing of Our Lord's birth in the manger. And they don't want anything for it. This is nice."

They all nodded, even Martin, who was beginning to feel better about the way his story of the scapegoat had been received. He had felt that either nobody understood the story or nobody cared to hear it. It was good that Mother had mentioned the manger scene. He had always liked to think of the babe in the manger, because he still remembered the smell of straw and hay from the nights they had spent sleeping in barns and stables on their long walk back to Silesia.

"So, you like it here?" asked Horst.

"We have always gone where His hand has led us," Mother answered. "We survived, escaped with our lives. But without Him . . ." She pointed upward and shook her head. Two fingers of her raised hand were loosely folded down while three fingers stood up stiffly in the same silent gesture of testimony and benediction Martin had seen on dark Russian icons. "Without Him, where would we be? We wouldn't even have our naked lives. When we were fleeing from Brockau, God sent us a train, the only one that would carry us to the right destination. Blindly, we stumbled onto it, pushed and shoved by the others who were in a panic because that train might be the last one. As was His will, that train took us to Waldenburg."

"You were born there, weren't you?" asked Lottel.

"Yes, I was born in Waldenburg," Mother nodded. "The train could have gone to Glatz or some other place where we would've been trapped. When the time came to flee from Waldenburg, God sent us a truck. Then He sent us another train, which stopped in the night, and from that train we watched Dresden burning. As a pillar of fire, He led the Israelites. Us He led by the cities burning in the night." She looked straight ahead while the others nodded silently. "And when we were wandering home, on those dangerous roads, he kept us safe in the shadow of His wings."

"You escaped with the clothes on your back," Horst said. "There is something strange about losing everything and grieving about it."

Mother looked at Lottel. "Do you remember the blue spruce by the entrance?"

"I didn't see a spruce." Horst pointed at the window.

"No! No!" Mother laughed. "Not now. Fifty years ago! Here we have palm trees in front. It was in Brockau that we had a blue spruce as tall as our three-story house. The tree was so beautiful that I mourned for the tree but never for the house." Martin waited for Mother to say something more, because it wasn't in character for her to sound somber or to speak so matter-of-factly about something that was sacred to all of them, their houses back home and their memories of them. She had never, not when they were fleeing nor later in Amer-ica, mourned in words their lost *Heimat*. Maybe she had mourned at night when she lay next to Father, but she never had when Martin was near her.

Mother must have finally realized that the others were waiting for her to speak again. "Now, the palm trees are taller than our house," she said.

"It's a consolation," said Horst quickly.

"Cherubim and palm trees decorated Solomon's temple," she said as if he hadn't spoken.

"It's a consolation," repeated Horst. Martin knew what Mother was thinking. The word that Horst had used, *Trost,* could mean only one thing to her, and that was divine comforting.

"He," she pointed again upward at the ceiling, "He was always with us when we were fleeing from Silesia, and He was with us when we were walking back. We were left to live."

"How did the Jews survive through all of these centuries?" asked Horst.

Lottel gave her husband a strange look as if she meant to ask, why bring them up?

"I mean, with someone always persecuting them."

"I know what Horst means," said Martin. "If the Jews survived as a people, why couldn't we Silesians also survive?"

"You've been too long in America with Wall Street and Holly-wood," Lottel said.

"I can think of several reasons," Martin said. "Somebody said, 'Jewish is who eats Jewish.' So, you see, in order to survive as a people, we have to have food that is our own."

"*Schlesisches Himmelreich,*" Lottel said immediately.

"What a grandiose name for a dish made of simple foodstuff— the Silesian Heavenly Kingdom," Martin translated into English. "This way it sounds even more grand." Wistfully he recalled the aroma drifting through the room from the platters of steaming smoked meat, dried fruits, potato dumplings, and gravy that made up the traditional Christmas meal in their household. Not everyone ate the same meal at Christmas. Others had carp or goose, but they, they had their Silesian Heavenly Kingdom. As long as it lasted, he added in his mind.

"And yet, when we tried to make the same dish here, we couldn't get the ingredients the recipe called for. I made a list in German of all the things we would need, and then Martin translated it into En-glish."

"Tried! I *tried* to translate it into English, and then Mother tried to tell the meatcutter in the supermarket what she needed."

"Some things were easy, like smoked ham, except it didn't look at all like what we were used to. But then when we got to the second main ingredient, to *Rauchfleisch,* Martin kept finding strange words in the dictionary."

"'Buccaned meat or boucan,' it said. The meatcutter shook his head. So that was out, and we began to substitute. Instead of the meats we got sausages, three different kinds—smoked, white, and regular frankfurters—and for the complicated dried fruit, Mother threw lots of raisins into the sauce. For the sauce to thicken, she grated gingerbread into it, and instead of the dumplings she made mashed potatoes."

"This is all different from what it is supposed to be," said Lottel.

"And Mother added sauerkraut."

"They don't put anything in it," Mother said.

Martin knew that by "they" his mother meant Americans.

"I enjoyed the apple you cut into the sauerkraut and the juniper berries," he said.

"I never put any juniper berries into my sauerkraut," Mother objected.

Maybe not. Maybe Martin's mind was betraying him.

He remembered the juniper tree of the *Märchen* his grandmother had told him, of the bird singing in the Machandel tree and the wicked stepmother slamming shut the lid of the chest on the neck of the little boy and cutting off his head. And the bird sang from the juniper tree and told the story.

He could've sworn that Mother had put the shriveled black berries into the sauerkraut. It was so hard to remember correctly. He couldn't even remember how the Silesian Heavenly Kingdom tasted when Mother had prepared it the right way at home. What he remembered and what made him happy was the way the adulterated Heavenly Kingdom tasted when his mother had cooked it in America. There had been more and more substitutions, and yet it always tasted of Christmas.

Martin shook his head.

"What are you smiling about?" Lottel asked.

"I was just thinking about Christmas. I'm sorry. We were talking about entirely different matters, like how to keep Silesia alive. There is something else to keep in mind when you want to survive as a people, and once again, Jews offer us a fine example. They, like most other religions, don't encourage marriage with outsiders. If Silesians want to keep on being Silesians even in exile, they will have to find and marry other Silesians, like you and Horst did . . ."

"And not like you, to go and marry a Polish woman!" interrupted Lottel.

"Polish? What does that mean, anyway? Just because she was born in Lemberg? Until 1918 it was Austrian and her father was in the Austrian police. After that, the city was Polish, but only for about twenty years, until 1939, and you know what that meant. Then it was Soviet-occupied for a little while. Stalin even came to Ala's school. A year or two later, the Germans came, and when they were driven out, the Soviet army came back. And when the Soviet Union fell, the city became part of an independent Ukraine. Lemberg, Lvov, Lwow, Lviv, the names changed but the buildings stayed the same.

"Besides that, she is part Swabian on her father's side, from those settlers who went east under Empress Maria Theresa. And on her mother's side she comes from a noble Armenian family. There were a lot of Armenians in Lemberg. Hundreds of years ago, they supervised all of the scales in a town where one of the oldest of all churches is an Armenian cathedral. As I was saying, what does it mean to be Polish?"

"But she speaks Polish." Lottel wasn't ready to give up.

"So does the pope!" Martin's reply made the others laugh.

"This brings us to the next point," he continued. "You have to have a common language."

"We have that!" Horst said triumphantly. "We certainly have that."

"*Ja, gut,*" Martin said. "It would be good if we could at least understand each other. I can't, and I was born there, and if *I* can't, what about anybody living outside of Silesia? When that play about the suffering weavers was performed in Berlin, the author had to translate it from Mountain Silesian into some kind of watered-down dialect that wasn't true Silesian anymore, but if he hadn't done it, nobody would've understood the play. Besides, our language isn't being taught as a matter of fact, never *was* taught in schools. Does your son know how to speak Silesian?"

Horst shook his head.

"Don't feel bad, I don't either. The Silesians would also need a ritual, like Passover, Rosh Hashanah, Yom Kippur, or one of the more personal celebrations like circumcision or bar mitzvah."

"What is that?" asked Horst.

"The ceremony when a boy passes into manhood."

"Just like our confirmation in church. We have that!" Lottel added with enthusiasm.

"But you don't go to church."

"No."

"So we don't have that to unite us. You are Lutheran and maybe half of the Silesians must be Catholic. And the Jews . . ."

"What Jews?" Lottel asked. "I didn't see any Jews in Breslau."

"No, not toward the end. By then they had all been taken away. You knew Edith Stein was from Breslau?"

"Yes, yes," Horst said, "but she was baptized and even became a nun."

"A Carmelite nun. She took the name Sister Teresia Benedicta of the Cross in honor of Teresa of Avila and John of the Cross. It didn't help her. In Auschwitz she might not have lasted even one day."

There was silence around the table. "*God is truth. He who seeks the truth, seeks God, if he knows it or not.*" Martin paused. "She wrote that. And she also wrote that there is a secret history—our own history—that we will not understand until the day it is revealed to us by God."

Martin's mother nodded.

"I'm sorry," apologized Martin, "for getting us away from our conversation. But Edith Stein was also a Silesian and as Sister Teresia Benedicta she will be the newest saint of the Catholic Church. And made so by a Polish pope. Isn't this ironic?"

"It sure is hard to understand what God means with us and our lives," his mother said. "Why did we have to wander so far from home? Maybe it is supposed to make us strong."

"Strong? How?" asked Lottel.

"Because we know that it will all become clear to us. Maybe that's what she meant by 'secret history.' Someone is following our fate and recording it, and one day we will see clearly what it all meant."

"And that makes you happy?" asked Horst.

"That makes me happy," said Martin's mother with a firmness in her voice that left no room for questions.

Finally Mother turned in her chair and pointed at the Christmas tree. "Isn't it a nice tree?" she asked, as she kept pointing at the small artificial tree she had used for years. It stood no more than a meter high, and it had to be put on a small table so that it would show at all among the furniture. Martin imagined what their German friends must be thinking about a plastic Christmas tree, but he didn't care. Although every year he had a tall natural tree in his own living room, he was ready to defend Mother's choice should anyone make fun of it.

"Every year in January, after Holy Three Kings, I take the tree with all of the lights and decorations still on its branches, and I slip it into the box until next Christmas."

Mother's simple words, and maybe even more her single-hearted smile, made Lottel rush over and grasp her hands. Then all fell silent.

"We were talking about staying Silesian." Horst tried to revive the conversation, speaking in his usual mild voice, which made his sentences sound like an apology.

"We never traveled to the Pyrenees," Lottel said, "but to me the Basques sound like the Silesians, forever wanting their own country."

"And to this end they blow up police stations in Spain," Horst objected. "We Silesians just weren't meant to be terrorists."

"But in some ways they are like us," objected Martin. "There is a Basque poem—or is it a song?—that could've been written by one of us: *I pray that God / grant me the grace / of leaving my bones / in my beloved land.* Sounds Silesian, doesn't it? But still, their situation is not like ours. They always had their land on which they've been living forever. They have their own language, which no one else understands because it doesn't seem to be related to any other language. But even those people—strange as they and their customs may seem to us—have their own publishers who put out Basque books, even dictionaries and grammars . . ."

"For a language that nobody understands." Horst laughed.

"There are quite a few of them here in Nevada. Up north around Reno. They came out here as sheepherders."

"How do *they* get along?"

"But don't you see? They aren't like us!" Martin spoke almost angrily. "If any one of them ever wants to go home, he can, because his village would still be there, somewhere in the Pyrenees. He will always have a *Heimat*."

The others nodded.

"They do try to keep their ways alive, and they have books to teach the young, to make them understand what it means to be Basque."

"Yes," said Horst, "we would need books, at least one book to keep us together as Silesians. We do have Gerhart Hauptmann, who was one of us and even won the Nobel Prize for Literature. Everybody learns that in school."

"Everybody *used* to learn that in school," Lottel corrected her husband. "And which of his books should we use, anyway? He wrote so much."

"How about *The Weavers*? It does say much about how we Silesians are. The old man is killed in the street by a stray bullet while he is working at his handloom. He wasn't about to join an uprising, but it was his belief to keep on working. We Silesians are no revolutionaries."

"Horst, this isn't the book we need. A sacred book, something that contains all reasons for living and for which one would be willing to die."

"We have the Martin Luther Bible," Horst offered.

"Do you read it?" asked Martin.

In the silence, Martin didn't look at his mother because he knew that she would be nodding.

"You see, the book has to be important to *everyone* if it is to unite the people."

"So, what else?" asked Horst.

"In order to survive, you need to be persecuted."

"We certainly have that in our favor." Lottel spoke with great conviction.

"Are you being persecuted in Bremen?" Martin spoke softly.

"And you? Are you persecuted in Las Vegas?" Lottel replied quickly.

"Don't be upset," Martin said, trying to soothe Lottel. "I know about some of the things you and your family went through when you went back to Silesia in 1945, but what *was* doesn't count unless you make something big out of it."

"And the one million dead?"

"That was then and now nobody—except us, of course—knows. More or less, we've become the same as the people around us. So there seems no need to cling to each other for mutual support like those who are fearing for their lives in daily persecution."

After a while Horst raised his hand as if he were in school. "And that would leave only food to help us survive."

They all laughed.

"Let me cook you a German meal," Lottel said. "As a peace offering. What would you like?"

"*Rouladen* were always my favorite," Martin answered quickly. "Rolled beef and dumplings. But you shouldn't bother with that. You came to vacation in America, and cooking would just be a burden for you."

"What's so difficult about *Rouladen* and dumplings?"

"It's different here," Martin told her. "We have so much in the food stores, but we may not have the right ingredients for this meal. Mother doesn't have the kind of pots and pans you need because she's given up cooking ambitious fare."

"My age," Mother shrugged and smiled.

"You know what she did?" Martin pointed at his mother. "The year after she had given up cooking—more or less—I got a call from our supermarket that I had won a frozen turkey. I went to pick it up and thought that I would surprise Mother. She looked at me and asked, 'What am I supposed to do with it?' 'Cook it for Thanksgiving,' I told her. When she didn't show any interest in my gift and didn't even want to touch the dead turkey, I told her, 'Even strangers have invited me to their house to eat turkey with them.' And then she said, very nicely and with a straight face, 'Then why don't you go to the strangers?'"

They all laughed.

"What is Thanksgiving, anyway?" Horst asked.

"A harvest festival into which they worked stories and anecdotes of the early immigrants. It's celebrated on the last Thursday of November."

"What kind of crop do you harvest at the end of November?" Horst asked.

"Nothing, as far as I know," Martin answered. "Merchandising has much to do with the date on which the holiday is celebrated. The day after Thanksgiving the Christmas shopping season is supposed to begin with a long weekend to lure everybody into the malls. But even that doesn't really work anymore because by now many Christmas decorations are already put up in October."

"But what about the *Rouladen*?" Lottel asked impatiently. Nothing Martin or his mother said could change Lottel's mind. As a matter of fact, when she had called from Germany to announce their visit, Lottel had hinted at her plan to cook a German meal.

Next evening Lottel and Martin stood on the diving board behind his house. The pool below them had been covered with bright blue plastic for the winter.

"I wish that I could've seen the water," she said.

"When we moved here, Bert was still young, and all of this was new to us. We kept the pool going all year long and we swam even in January, because there are usually a few warm days. But that was twenty-five, no, almost thirty years ago."

They looked toward the west, where the sun was sliding through brownish streaks of cloud hanging over the hotels on the boulevard.

"It'll be a beautiful sunset. Take my word for it. Some dirt in the air creates colorful sunsets. From time to time, I stand up there so that I can look over the tops of the oleander bushes and the olive trees."

They talked about her life in Bremen until the clouds were stained orange and crimson.

"On evenings like this"—he pointed at the clouds—"I often walk along the railroad tracks through the desert, with the sun sinking to my right, while to my left the darkness rises from the valley floor."

"Why are you going into the desert?"

"Most people here don't seem to care for it, thinking it to be gray, beige, and dull. But it has its beauty. After a rainy spring, the desert is green and the beavertail cactus blossoms come out bright magenta. But that isn't why I go. I go because hardly anyone else goes out there."

He never asked himself why he felt the need to be in desolate places, nor did he ask why—out of instinct?—he followed the rails in the same direction of the compass in which his family had fled from Silesia half a century ago. In his true home there had been no deserts, only fields as far as he could see.

"I used to walk with my father," Martin said. "He would take my hand and lead me through the fields, just so we could see the sun go down behind the white birches lining the dirt road. But before we reached the road that the horse carts and the tractors took to the fields, we first had to follow the railroad tracks along that path by Walter Park. You remember that, don't you?"

Lottel nodded. "It went to the pond."

"Walking through the desert isn't as if I were home, except for the railroad tracks and the sunsets. Then, I could step from one wooden tie to the next. Now my stride is longer and after a while my legs hurt and I begin to balance on one or the other of the rails just so that my legs can walk freely."

"Don't the trains chase you off?"

"They don't come all that often anymore. When I hear one, I step off to the side and stand on the gravel bed. A long time ago, my son took a picture of me standing on the tracks with a yellow Union Pacific locomotive bearing down on me behind my back."

"Even as a boy you did a lot of foolish things."

Bert had printed the enlarged photograph twice—once with the negative reversed—and had mounted the two mirror images back to back. Then he had given the framed picture to his father. It was such a large picture—as wide as a doorway—that the only place Martin could find for it in his office, which was crowded with pictures from his life, was above the entrance. Since it hung above the line of sight of those who came into his office, it was his most private picture. From time to time he caught himself looking at it—for no real reason, since he knew it so well.

It had been a cold day on the high desert the day the picture was taken. He could tell by the shapeless hat he wore and the knotted wool scarf bulging out from under the turned-up collar of his denim jacket. The line of the horizon was low, so most of the picture was sky, and out of the blue growing darker, the engine's single headlight flared yellow at Martin standing between the rails. Although Bert had aimed his camera at the swirl of magenta, pink, and purple forming in the sky, the flash of the camera had illuminated his father's face. Surely, Martin had felt the vibration of the train approaching, but standing on the track curving north, he looked as serene as if he were home, as if nothing that happened now would matter.

He looked down at the plastic pool cover, which was a different shade of blue than the desert night had been—harder, brighter, and more intense than the cornflowers that dotted the wheatfields back home. He remembered that the water under the tarpaulin had been turquoise when he used to swim with Bert, chasing him from the diving board to the olive tree whose branches shaded the other end of the pool. Now the water was cold and saturated with chemicals to keep it stable during the winter.

"When you go into the desert, what is it that you hope to find?"

Martin laughed. "It's quite an accident if I find anything at all. Most of the time I find things thrown away by men who worked on the rail line. Maybe a date nail showing the year in which the wooden ties had been put down, or a twisted spike pulled out with great force, a padlock cut off from the handle of the switch because the key for it had been lost. Or from the creosote shrub under the telephone line I'll pick up a glass insulator, blue as the sky or green as the sea near the shore. Those are my treasures."

Lottel nodded.

"One day I was driving out from the southern edge of town looking for wood to burn in the fireplace of the living room." Martin pointed at the brick chimney rising from the gull-wing roof. "I was still close enough to the last subdivision so that people would throw trash out by the side of the road rather than drive to the city dump on the other side of the valley.

"You asked me what I hope to find. Maybe it's what I hope *not* to find. Whenever I go out alone, I wonder if I'm going to come across a body. In the newspapers you keep reading about bodies found in the desert, just thrown from the trunk of a car. There was so much of this that one can imagine the whole desert floor rising up on Resurrection Day. It is in the back of my mind when I go out that someday I'm going to stumble over a body. On the day when I was looking for scrap lumber from construction, I was driving slowly along a dirt road that was dipping and rising as it crossed dry runoffs creasing the desert. Something by the side of the road caught my eye, but only after I had passed by. I had been looking for the end pieces cut from two-by-fours and not for whatever it was I had glimpsed. I couldn't turn, so I backed up slowly, listening for the revved-up sound of dirt bikes that could be on you in a second or two. In my rearview mirror I saw something on my left, more colorful than the dusty creosote shrubs around it. When I got out I saw that it wasn't a body at all, as I had feared, but a large pile of dolls' heads. No torsos or limbs, just heads piled up into a kind of pyramid. They were of different sizes, shapes, and hair color. Some of them looked at me while others lay in the dirt with their eyes closed. I kept telling myself that those faces were just molded plastic, but I felt as if I had stumbled on the site of a massacre. When I held one of them in my hand I began to brush the sand out of its hair. When I tilted the head back, the lids would slide open in the doll's face. Then the head looked at me, and it was as if my hand had grown a head.

"I didn't know what I should do. Finally, I picked up a few heads—maybe five or six—and I set them carefully on a towel in the trunk of my car. I did it gently, because I thought that they had suffered enough. At home, I cleaned them as best as I could and then I set them, here and there, between the books on my shelves. One of the heads I put on my desk, a large one with curly pink hair. The lids are always open, and every day the bright blue eyes look straight at me."

"Aren't you scared out there?"

"Never."

"Do you still go out into the desert?"

"At first I walked with my son, then with my dog, and now I'm walking alone."

The sky above them had turned the darkest of blues.

Lottel shivered. "But you do have beautiful sunsets over the desert."

When Martin went next to his mother's house, he found no one at home. A note on the kitchen table told him that they had gone to Smith's Food King on Sahara, the biggest supermarket in the valley. He knew that Mother would want to show off the large variety of food, especially how they could buy so many different vegetables, and the kinds of fruit that could be bought in the middle of the winter.

When Martin saw the car pull into the driveway, he went out to help carry in the bags. He was just in time to hear Mother recite, "*I brought you into a plentiful country, to eat the fruit thereof* . . . dadada . . . and *the goodness thereof.*"

It always surprised Martin how well his mother remembered. When they were fleeing, their Luther Bible had been everything to them, the schoolbook from which his father gave lessons to Martin and a book for daily readings. To the family wandering through Germany, it had been what the Ark of the Covenant was to the Israelites in the desert. In the morning, before they would pull their handcart out on the road back to Silesia, Mother would let their Bible fall open on its own and pronounced from it their divine sign and the parole of the day, which they needed to pass through the battle lines of the devilish enemy.

"We found everything!" Lottel called out from the steps. "Didn't I tell you that we would find everything?" She stayed in the doorway to make sure that Horst carried the bags with the greatest of care. "We found the right *Rouladen* meat, red cabbage, sauerkraut, and potatoes for the dumplings. We got it all."

That night, they sat down to dinner together. It was awkward not only because the oval table was really too small for them, but also because in those sixty and more years they never had sat down to dinner together. The dining area, really part of the living room, was so narrow that one side of the table was pushed directly against the kitchen counter. Mother's chair was, as always, the one at the end of the table closest to the kitchen. Martin sat opposite her, in the chair where his father, like a true patriarch, had presided over festive family meals. Although Martin felt comfortable at the head of the table, he had never settled into the role of head of the family. Thinking about it, he had come to the conclusion that this must be because he was really unaware of his age. He always held open doors for others, male or female, old or young. He would have thought of himself as being prideful had he gone first. Now he sat in his father's chair while Lottel and then Horst were to his right. Beyond them, at a spot that at any other table would have been a corner, sat Ala.

Although more than a quarter of a century had passed since their divorce, Ala somehow had stayed. Although the reasons were not quite clear, it may have been because her background and early life had run vaguely parallel to that of Martin's family. She had begun her journey farther to the east than Martin, but the war and fleeing west from the Russians, air raids, and refugee trains had formed a loose but more durable bond than that of a marriage.

Mother began to serve. Ala, as always, did not eat from the main course, because she had given up meat long before it became fashionable. She asked only for a dumpling and some red cabbage. In the meantime, Martin waited eagerly to taste this rare treat, of which he wanted to eat every last bite. After all, this was the dish that he had enjoyed so long ago, and then only on the feast days of his childhood.

And so they ate and talked, and when they had finished eating they sat in silence. This isn't what I remembered, thought Martin. Maybe between then and now he had eaten too many meals in too many restaurants in different countries, but he also knew that this couldn't be the reason why it hadn't worked. True, they were happy being together at the same table after half a century away from Silesia, but the food that was to have reminded them of home didn't have the flavor of the past.

"Everything here is sweet," said Horst. "I don't mean to criticize, but the sugar shoots right up into your teeth."

"Most of the desserts are made with the taste of children in mind," said Mother, choosing her words carefully.

"And so the adults keep the taste of children?" asked Horst.

It was then it came to Martin that what Americans seem to remember about their childhood is how sweet the things were that they had eaten as children, while just thinking about Silesia made him taste such tartness that it made his mouth pucker. Fruit in Silesia hadn't been sweeter or bigger.

"But the blueberries look very nice." Horst pointed to the plastic box they had brought from the supermarket and which now stood in the middle of the table.

Martin looked at the berries sitting in orderly rows in the clear plastic tray like buttons sewn to a card.

"It's amazing how big they are." Horst took one of the berries from the box and held it between thumb and forefinger as if it were a jewel. "As big as our cherries at home. Do you remember how sour the shadow morellos were that we used to grow in our gardens? They were really sour, not even faintly sweet like other cherries. Near where I was a child, they even grew grapes, green grapes. They pressed wine from these Grünberg grapes, but it was so sour that it darned the holes in your socks."

They all laughed because they had heard that saying before about Silesian wine. Martin had been too young when they fled to have ever drunk the sour wine from home.

Everyone reached for the blueberries, and the guests tasted them carefully, as if they were biting into an exotic fruit. Martin had gone berrying in the dark, dense woods near his father's village by the Bartsch River, where the blueberry bushes grew low to the ground and bristly as if to hide and defend their fruit. Martin gathered the berries into a small bucket, but every second or third berry he ate on the spot, right there in the murk of the forest.

Nothing had ever tasted quite like that again, and the blueberries in front of him—Canadian, he thought—might as well be a different genus from those that had grown on the sparse shrubs of his childhood.

Lottel looked morosely at her plate. "I don't know what went wrong. It just didn't taste right. The red cabbage was too young and so it wasn't spicy enough. And the potatoes were too new to keep the dumplings from falling apart."

Horst held up his hand to stop his wife from saying more. "Now, Lottel, you have to be honest, at home it isn't any better. We have Thai restaurants and even African ones, but where do you get German food?"

"I remember what happened the last time I was in Bremen," Martin said. "It was Sunday and you asked me what I wanted to eat. Never even for a moment thinking that this would be a problem, I said dumplings. And where did we have to go and eat that time just so that I could have dumplings?"

"In a German city we had to go to a Czech restaurant to find dumplings for our visitor from America. I am ashamed to admit this, but that's how it is back in Germany now." Horst smiled sadly over something that surely could not be changed.

Lottel picked up the dishes and set them on the kitchen counter. "*Reinen Tisch machen,*" she said when she took away the last plates.

Yes, we are a neat and tidy people, Martin thought. Then he remembered the other meaning of the German phrase for clearing the table, which was to tell the truth, the whole truth. But what truth lay between them that needed to be told?

By then Ala had left, slipping out almost unnoticed because she didn't want to interrupt the dinner. She had to leave, she said, because she had the early shift in the casino buffet where she worked.

Relaxed by the meal, the others sat back in their chairs, which were not as comfortable as the sofa, but nobody wanted to leave the table where they could sit so close to each other that each of them seemed to touch the person sitting in the next chair.

Mother looked around the table, pausing at each face as if her sight and memory were worse than they were, or as if she wanted to see below the skin of the faces she had known so long ago.

"Who could've thought fifty, no, sixty years ago, that we would be sitting around this table in Las Vegas?"

Martin looked down at the table. He knew that it had been inexpensive, meant for what decorators call a "breakfast nook." Its legs were gold-colored metal tubes and its top was laminated orange plastic. Of course, the guests didn't know, because a fine white tablecloth covered everything. The table was bringing them together, and because of that, Martin felt ashamed that he hadn't bought his parents a proper dining table made of some noble wood, even if it could not be seen.

He tried to remember their dining table at home, which had always been covered by a tablecloth. Mahogany, that had been the wood. When he saw 1930s Hollywood films set in Germany, everybody lived surrounded by heavy oak furniture and sat on crudely carved benches under antlers decorating the walls, as if all German apartments were ski lodges in Bavaria.

"This may sound strange," Lottel began after a long silence, "but in many ways you were fortunate that you fled in 1945. As you know, we went back to Silesia after the war, but in 1947 the Poles drove us out. The night before we were herded onto a train, they put us all into a school gymnasium. We had taken with us everything we could carry. Next morning, it was Sunday, we heard them conduct a religious service above us. We could hear their singing. Then the Poles came down and went through everything our people still had left and stole it all. They took so much that the loot, piled up, reached all the way to the ceiling of the gymnasium. Even small personal things that had no value and couldn't possibly mean anything to them, like photographs, were taken.

"When a militiaman asked my mother if she had any photos, she held out a small picture of my father. The man tugged at it, but Mother didn't let go. I watched her thumbnail getting red and white, that's how hard she pressed down. 'My husband,' she said, 'dead in war.' The man looked up from the photo and into Mother's face. Then he turned around and walked away. My mother had this photo till the day she died, and now I have it."

Mother excused herself and got up. When she came back, she put a small photograph in the middle of the table. "From home," she announced.

"It's your garden!" Lottel exclaimed. "But how can this be? You didn't bring any pictures with you."

"True. When we left we thought that it would be just for a few weeks and then we would be allowed to come back home. We locked our house door as if we were going to the mountains or to visit relatives in Militsch. I don't know how we thought all of this would go when we left. It was late in January of 1945, and the Russians had attacked everywhere across the German borders. Did we believe that Germany could win the war? Anyone looking at a world map could have said that it isn't possible to win against the whole world. We took what we could carry, and when we left we didn't know that it would be farewell forever to Silesia."

"That's right," Horst said. "You never did go back to Silesia."

"After we came to America, we never went back, not even to

what was left of Germany. For the longest time we couldn't afford it, and then it was too late when my husband's health grew worse."

Lottel kept looking at the picture. "How did you get that photo if you weren't able to take any pictures with you?"

"During the thirties we sent snapshots to a relative in America. After the war, when he heard that our family had lost everything, he sent us some photos, saying that we should have at least a picture by which we could remember home." She looked across the room at the front door. "Not that we need a picture to remember."

They crowded around the photograph and moved in closer to each other, as if it were a healing relic, a splinter of the true past.

Like the others, Martin looked at the picture, although he knew it by heart. Mother is wearing a flowery dress that is so long it nearly touches the tips of her white shoes, and she stands on the walk leading up to their garden house. Little can be seen of the *Laube* except its window, but Martin knows what the green wooden house looks like. He looks again at the little boy she holds by the hand, who is dressed in a white suit with short pants. His hair is cut in bangs and seems still light, not black as it would be later.

Martin looked at the boy with the objectivity of an observer but also with cordial familiarity. The woman in the flowery dress is in her early twenties. This always shocked him because this is the age of many of his students, most of whom seem to him mere children. She holds her chin up and with a confident smile looks over the top of the camera and so over the head of the photographer, who was surely Martin's father with his Agfa.

Martin looked down at the picture and then quickly at his mother sitting at the other end of the table. It was as if in this fraction of a second, time-lapse photography had aged her. Although she was now bent and stooped, her eyes were still filled with curiosity and smiled as they always had when Martin entered the room.

She nodded at him. "*Mein Junge,*" she said.

At that moment he knew that against all nature and the preordained order of things, he could not bear losing her, his last companion of the long trek that had taken them ever farther away from home.

"When we lived in Silesia, we didn't even know what we had," Lottel said after a while. "You have to be away . . ."

"And hurt," Horst added quickly.

"Only then do you see what had been hidden," said Martin's mother.

Lottel was still looking at the picture of the young mother proud of her firstborn son.

It was so silent in the room that they could hear the faraway sirens of a police car.

"Tonight is like being back in Silesia," Lottel said.

"Tonight, Silesia is where we are," Mother replied.

They reached for each other and held hands, although the circle stayed open.

"And Silesia will be forgotten," Martin said.

"Might not some of us be remembered?" asked Lottel.

"Maybe two. Manfred von Richthofen, who wasn't quite twenty-six when he was shot down over the western front at the Somme, and Edith Stein—whom many Silesians don't even claim as one of theirs—a Jewish-Catholic nun who was killed in Auschwitz. On the eastern front, so to speak. Those two are remembered, one as a now-comic character, the Red Baron, the other as a martyr, but neither one of them as a Silesian."

"Maybe it would've been better to have been born Jewish," Horst said.

"Hush! We are what we are," his wife objected.

"But look at them!" Horst said. "So many of them died, but as a people they survived and still are God's Own. We Silesians suffered, not as the Chosen People, but as the Forgotten Ones."

After a while, others began to speak and Martin closed his eyes. When he opened them again, the light was suddenly burning too brightly. Abruptly he got up from the table.

"Are you all right?" his mother called after him as he walked the narrow corridor to his parents' bedroom. Inside the open door he stopped, but he didn't turn on the light. He was still close enough to hear their voices.

Lottel spoke first. "He is getting older, too. Is there anyone in his life?"

Although he couldn't see her, he knew that she must be asking about him. He wondered how his mother would answer.

"He is still so busy at work and with his writing and taking care of me."

"What about Ala and him?"

"They are friends. They've known each other for such a long time."

"But you, you should come and visit us in Bremen."

"Not in this life," she said. "We had to wander too much, and now I want to rest." Her voice didn't sound regretful or tired, but was as firm as her handshake. "From Brockau—and I wasn't even born there—to Waldenburg, to Rehau in Bavaria, Mengen in Württemberg . . ." She began to recite the way stations of her own life and that of her family. "The years in Erfurt under the Russians, then back on the road again, through the Iron Curtain and on to the coal pot of Westphalia. Over the sea and across America to Salt Lake City, and then when Martin moved here, we packed up once more and followed him, but we are no gypsies."

"Hm, hm, hm, hm, hm," hummed Lottel. "*Lu-stig ist das Zigeu-ner-le-ben . . . ,*" she sang softly, and Horst joined in the refrain. "*Fa-ria, fa-ria, ho.*"

"We sing it in the choir," he explained. "It always makes me happy when we get to sing it, because it's not only from Silesia but from my part of it."

"It's hard to believe." Mother shook her head. "*Happy is the life of the gypsy,*" she recited, "but I don't even remember gypsies coming through our town."

"*Merry it is in the green woods where the gypsies stay,*" the visitors sang, now louder, as if a conductor were urging them on.

"*Fa-ria, fa-ria, ho,*" murmured Martin in the darkness.

"It has a nice last verse. I enjoy singing it," Horst began to sing alone in a pleasant tenor voice. "*Even if we don't have a featherbed, faria, faria, ho, we'll dig a hole in the ground, faria, faria, ho, put in moss and twigs, faria, faria, ho, and that'll be our featherbed.*" Horst halted, waiting for the others to join in. "*Fa-ria, fa-ria, ho,*" they sang softly.

For a while there was silence, as if the singing had brought them too close to each other.

"That was more like Silesia, my Silesia, to dig a hole in the ground to lie in," Mother said. "And all we wanted out of life was to be left alone, so that we could live where we wanted. Even the children of Israel were cursed to wander only for forty years. For us it has been longer, and we still haven't found home."

It was the Lord's hand, thought Martin, the Lord's hand coming down again and again. And their carcasses shall fall in this wilderness until finally all of their bodies will lie in the desert.

He sat down heavily on the corner of the bed. With one hand he tested the hardness of the mattress. This was where his father and mother had lain and where, one sunny afternoon, he had found his father bleeding unstanchably as if the blood running from his mouth and nose was the living water Jesus had promised at Jacob's Well.

Martin turned on the small lamp by the bed and reached for a book lying on the nightstand. It wasn't Father's, but one of Martin's own that he had brought over when he had stayed here for a few weeks. It was a thin book, and he remembered that he had taken it from a shelf above the poor box at the Church of the Servites in Vienna. On the cardboard of the book's cover, a cross had been drawn crudely on the plaster of a broken wall. Over it all, someone had scrawled red wiry loops and twists, as if to annihilate the cross.

How appropriate, he thought as he held the book, a fellow Silesian as a companion in the night. Leafing through it, he couldn't settle on any of the quotes until he came to the last page, where he stopped at a paragraph entitled "Testament." He read the few lines in German. He felt tired, and he wanted nothing more than to lie down and read. Today had been too much, as if he needed an excuse to be tired, but he didn't lie down. Instead he read the paragraph again, and, as had become his custom with anything he read in his mother tongue, he began to translate it into English.

Already now, in full submission to His holy will, I joyfully . . . No, he stopped himself, that was still too German. Maybe that had been his problem all along, he simply was too German and not enough of anything else. *I joyfully accept the death God has intended for me.* Maybe even then, when the Jewish nun wrote these lines, she was able to see what would happen to her. *I pray for the Lord to receive my life and my death to His honor and for His exaltation so that His kingdom may come in all of its magnificence* . . . No, *glory.* What is the difference? *Lastly, I pray for my relatives.* As I do, mornings and nights. I name them all, as if I could hold them to me by pronouncing their names. *The living and the dead.* No, those who died since Silesia, those I have given up in my prayers. They don't need any help from a weak and struggling earthbound human being. *And I pray for everyone God has given me, so that none of them be lost.*

Amen, he added, as if once again he was kneeling with his father and mother by the side of the bed, as they had done whenever they were together.

"What about *him?*" Lottel's voice was insistent, as if she had asked before and Mother hadn't answered her. "What about him?" had been Peter's question about John the Beloved, asked at the end of the Gospels after everything had been done and said. And Jesus had answered, "And what is it to you?" Indeed, what was his life to anyone, although he did wonder how his mother would answer a question he himself could not answer.

For a while there was silence. "He is still a wanderer," she said, speaking very slowly.

At the last sound of his mother's voice—which had the finality of the clap with which she closed the Bible after her fingers had blindly found God's word for the day—he reached to turn off the lamp. Now the room was dark, except for a dim streak of light falling onto the bed from a small draped window high under the ceiling. As he stood up, he supported himself with one hand on the edge of the bed.

That afternoon, when the room had been bright and sunny, he had picked up his father from his bed, bleeding, his father had lain in Martin's arms as he carried him out of the house, down the stairs, and into the car. He couldn't save his father. Nobody and no thing can be saved, only memories.

As if he were listening to voices, Martin stood with his neck bent in the streak of light that fell from the window above. "Still a wanderer," she had said.

As if Aaron's hand were pushing him away from the light of the campfires, Martin stretched out his arms as he balanced on an invisible rail between the fading glow of the sun and the coming night. Step by step he left behind the city that had never been his, yet he had given it what he had to give. He would walk through the wilderness, however long he would have to walk, because he knew that one day he would come upon a field of magenta blossoms covering the desert after a spring rain. Maybe then he would be home.

The Stone Girl

Why, when I lay sick as a child, was my room always kept dark? Would light have hurt me? Did they really believe that darkness was good and that light was bad? When Dr. Kasprzycki came to tell me a story, my room was bright—but only when he was entering—and then, as he leaned against the door frame, the dark shape of his body blocked the light falling from the hall into my room. As if to make up for taking away the light, he would tell me a story.

"Ala, let me tell you about Pan Mundzio . . ."

"We call Uncle Zigmund 'Mundzio.'"

"That was not quite the name of the young man with long blond hair . . ."

"Uncle Mundzio is bald."

"The young man with the long blond hair rode on a white horse and carried a sword, the only one of its kind in the world. It could cut through the armor of any knight. He also wore a magic ring that let him understand the language of the animals."

"Not even cats and dogs speak the same language." Although I strained to be heard, whispering as loud as I could with the hoarse voice of a sick girl, he, like most adults, didn't listen to me.

"One day Pan Mundzio slew a dragon that was guarding a treasure. His sword cut through the armor plate of the dragon, and the blood gushing from its wounds filled a deep pit. A talking bird told the hero to climb into the pit . . ."

"Full of hot blood?" I interrupted him.

"He took off his clothes to bathe in the blood of the dragon."

"In the hot blood? I hate it when the bathwater is too hot."

"He did bathe in the hot dragon blood to make his skin hard like horn."

I began to breathe in short, rapid puffs.

"Ala, take a deep breath! Just like me!"

I began to breathe deeply, and soon I was breathing in Dr. Kasprzycki's rhythm.

"Pan Mundzio could feel his skin hardening."

"How could he feel with skin like horn?"

"I guess he couldn't feel, but what was more important, he couldn't be hurt."

"Nettles couldn't sting him?"

"There are things that can hurt you worse than nettles."

"Nettles blister my legs up to the hem of my skirt."

"Now that he had a horned skin he became a true hero: unyielding, unbending, unfeeling. Nobody could hurt him anywhere, except on his shoulder where a leaf had fallen from a linden tree. There the blood of the dragon hadn't been able to harden the hero's skin."

"Telling horror stories to the child?" Mother's voice was floating to me, coming from behind Dr. Kasprzycki's back. All I could see of her were her shadowy hands on his shoulders.

"Opera, my dear." He turned away from me and toward her. "Just opera."

"And what happened to Pan Mundzio?" I called after him, wanting him to finish his story, but he kept walking away on Mother's arm. He had to speak to me over his shoulder as if he were drawn away against his will.

"Where the linden leaf had fallen, he was pierced by Hagen's spear. . . . The Black Knight . . . with raven wings on his helmet."

And again the room of my memory grows dark.

Now my room lies in shadows except for the light cast by the lamp on my nightstand. From time to time—as I do tonight—I look at an album that is small enough to fit into a lady's handbag. As a matter of fact, that is exactly how it was saved from *then* and *there*. The first picture, taken on the sidewalk in front of the Hotel George in Lvov, is not of us twins but of Mother, wearing a tailored suit over a white shirt and a necktie. She wore a hat that Schwadronowa on the Rynek must have modeled on a man's fedora. With her usual confidence Mother strides diagonally past the camera of the street photographer.

Some of the pictures show my sister Zofia and me visiting the Warsaw Zoo during one of our summer vacations. In one photo I sit cradled in the crook of a camel's neck while its head is raised high like a hammer about to strike. Of course, being me, I ride uneasily, while Zofia in *her* picture is sitting as comfortably on the broad back of an elephant as if she were on a throne. It is true that in order to avoid jealousy each of us had been photographed on an elephant and each on a camel, but since we looked alike and were dressed alike, someone had thought that these pictures were identical and they had been thrown away as "doubles." In this album as well as in my lifelong memory, I am never safely riding on the elephant and she never had to ride shakily on the camel.

In one picture both of us are together. Zofia sits on the left of the park bench. Since we are wearing the same ankle socks, our naked knees look as if one knee had been copied three times. We look so much alike that I actually had to think before I could really say *she* is the one on the left, the one whose lap is pawed by a tiger cub. It has to be her, because my hand is on the back of the tiger, and I remember how soft the fur felt, like Mother's coat. In winter, when I was walking next to her, I would hide my face in the wide sleeve of her fur coat that always smelled of snow.

As usual, we didn't want to share ourselves with the photographer, whoever it might have been. From under straight brows shaded by the turned-down brims of our school hats, dark, somber eyes are looking up at an angle, giving an indication that the photographer was taller. Against the black straw of our school hats the Nazaretanki badges gleam like metal crosses.

Looking at these pictures in the precise circle of light cast on my nightstand, I see no sign of the "weakness" that the eyes of our parents constantly searched for and found in my sister and me. The only peculiarity is that neither one of us ever smiles in the photos surviving from our years in Lvov. In the pictures from the zoo, both of us look healthy in our pale linen dresses. What doesn't show in the small ivory and sepia photographs—but I remember it was there—is the thin, bloodred line of trim around our throats.

My eyes hurt, so I set my glasses on the nightstand and turn off the light. That is the time when I remember best. Tonight it is the old section of the Lyczakowski Cemetery in Lvov, on the day when the funeral was held for Rudolf, the son of Pan Bonk. It must have been in the mid-1930s—I was still wearing the school uniform of a Nazaretanki girl—and surely, after the death of Marshal Pilsudski in 1935; most likely even later, after the coronation of the Gypsy king in 1937. It definitely was summer, because only then were we allowed to wear a white blouse with our uniform instead of the navy-blue middy traced with black trim braid.

On the day of the funeral Zofia and I had been excused from school, although being kept home was in itself not memorable, because our parents considered us frail and susceptible to all illnesses. Our parents may have worried more than necessary about us, because they had eagerly wanted children and tried everything possible, until, after many years of marriage, we were born. While our parents feared constantly that we might become sick, they never tired of upholding Lala Kajser as a model of robust health. She was a snub-nosed girl in our class whose thick braids hung down on both sides of her face like limp sheep's ears.

"*A hunter, a deer he did shoot . . .*" Our maid, Pazia, sang in Ukrainian, as she did every day while she was braiding our hair and getting us ready for school. Although today was special because we didn't have to go to school, she still sang. Even when Mother came into the room, Pazia didn't stop singing. "*She tumbled, the poor one, her end she did meet.*" She even kept singing while she left our room and walked into the kitchen.

"Turn around!" Mother ordered. Her command made us spin in front of her like two identical tops. She examined us closely to see if our maid had not dressed us secretly in Ukrainian blue and yellow. It didn't matter to her if it might have been an accident or if Pazia might have done it out of some primitive nationalism, as Mother would have worded it.

"*To struggle with death was not her intent,*" Pazia sang loudly in the kitchen. "*But struggle she did until ni-i-ight fell,*" and in protest she slammed the door of the oven.

When my mother was young she had a deer that was her own. Sliding occasionally on the hardwood floor, it walked through the house, its hooves clicking and clattering on the parquet like Uncle Tedek's fingernails on the ivory piano keys. When Mother played the zither, the deer would come to her and lay its head in her lap, but in the spring the deer returned to the forest and it never came back.

After Pazia had dressed us and we still didn't look sick to our parents, they took us to the funeral. We were told that it had to do with Pan Bonk, who was my godfather. It was he who had given me the emerald ring that I always wore.

"A *szmaragd* for Ala?" Mother had chided him when he gave it to me.

"It's just a child's ring," he had soothed Mother. "As long as she wears it, it'll protect her chastity. Like Angelica who was chained naked to a rock by the shore and a sea monster came. Was she . . . ? Did she have to . . . ? No, a knight came and gave her a magic ring to protect her chastity. And then the knight might have killed the monster, but I'm not sure about this." Setting me on his knee, he pushed the ring on my finger. "Besides, the stone will cure epilepsy, dysentery, weak eyesight, *and* ward off evil spirits."

Mother laughed. "I shouldn't really laugh. As sickly as my girls tend to be, they can use all the help they can get." Both of them had laughed.

When I was able to read novels—and that came very early because I was always an old child—I linked my emerald ring to Esmeralda, the Gypsy girl in Hugo's *Notre-Dame de Paris,* who suffered much and made others suffer.

On the way to the funeral, Pan Bonk, my father, and some others were walking ahead, while Mother and I were the last to follow along the pathways of the cemetery. Mother was constantly pointing to the left and to the right as if we were sightseers. For me the crypts became houses in a foreign country and the *katakumby* with its round-domed chapel the cathedral of the necropolis, as Mother called the cemetery. Lvov had other cathedrals—Armenian, Roman Catholic, and Eastern Orthodox—but this one was the cathedral of the dead.

Mother stopped when we came to a row of urns, each of them taller than I.

"Here lie the Orlatka."

"Who were they?"

"The Young Eagles, those who fell during the *Obrona Lwowa,* the defense of our city during November 1918 that winter and even after that."

"Wasn't the war over and the Russians had lost?"

"On the first of November 1918, Ukrainian nationalists occupied Lvov until, on the twenty-second, the Orlatka freed us."

"So many names by the urns."

"Two thousand. Officers, women, and boys. The blossoms of our youth."

The largest number of people that I had ever seen at the same time had been at Easter services at the church of the Dominicans, and that certainly hadn't been two thousand.

"They were heroes."

When I was eight I had written a poem about Thermopylae, so I thought that I knew about heroes, but I still asked.

"How do you become a hero?"

"With heroes and saints it's the same, you have to be killed."

Looking down between the points of my patent leather shoes, I imagined the congregation of the dead kneeling under the long summer grass.

"Later, when Marshal Pilsudski came to Lvov, he said that the whole city deserved the Cross of the Order Virtuti Militari . . . but this was before your time."

By the tall urns I saw a metal vase shaped like a miniature urn. Wilted roses had dried into brownish weeds smelling sweet and rotten at the same time.

"It's a shame," Mother said, pointing to the right. "He was a captured revolutionary who had been held prisoner in a fortress." Her head was turned while she spoke and I couldn't understand everything because she was murmuring. "They tortured him and he lost his mind."

I walked around Mother so that I could see her face and watch her lips.

"His parents ransomed him and brought him back to Lvov, where he lived another three years in an insane asylum where he died."

"Was he an Orlatko?"

"No," Mother laughed sharply. "No, *he* fought in the Second Polish Revolution of 1863 against Alexander II, the one they called 'Czar Liberator' because he freed the serfs. Being a liberator, though, didn't keep him from torturing Poles."

"Is this the grave of the *tortured* man?" I hardly dared to pronounce the word while pointing at an eagle whose powerful talons gripped a large rock monument. The eagle strained as if he was trying to lift the rock off the grave.

"No, that is not a tortured man, that's a general." She leaned down to read the inscription on the tombstone.

"From these bodies . . ." She still talked in a muffled voice.

"Which bodies?"

"The Orlatka. From all the dead bodies they selected one and took him . . . no, *it,* to lie in the Tomb of the Unknown Soldier in Warsaw." She wasn't talking to me but to the tall urns. "It might even be a woman." We were walking slower and slower, as if she had forgotten that we had to go to a funeral. "Imagine, the Unknown Soldier might be a woman warrior, an Amazon from Lvov."

"What is an Amazon?"

"A woman warrior."

The only woman warrior that I could imagine at that time was Mother.

"There used to be a tribe of female warriors who often went to war. When they had girl children, they would burn off their right breasts so that they could shoot bows like their mothers."

I shuddered.

"Ah, there's Dr. Kasprzycki," she cried out while she smoothed down her silk dress over her hips.

His white summer suit made him look exotic, as if he had just walked out of the jungle, although he was merely stepping out of the shadow of an overgrown mausoleum.

"I managed to escape from the others and took a shortcut to you." He kissed Mother's hand. "And to Ala, of course." He didn't kiss my hand. Zofia and I didn't like him and it was not only because he was our dentist, but also because Mother spent too much time with him. Now I regret that as a child I hadn't liked him because he told interesting stories, painted well, and was a ski champion, but I wanted Mother to myself.

"I was just teaching her about the Polish heroes buried all around us."

"*I lay, with lead in my breast,*" he recited in a soft voice, "*my deep wound still steaming.*"

"You know how much I love the words of Lermontov, but the words of a Russian seem hardly fitting here, where we stand surrounded by dead heroes with *Russian* lead in their breasts."

"Dearest Zofia, surely it was *blue and yellow* Ukrainian lead that accounted for most of the Polish heroes lying under the grass."

Although they argued, neither Mother nor Dr. Kasprzycki seemed angry with each other. Bored with them, I walked a few steps ahead, stopping when I came to a large churchlike building with pillars in front.

"This is the mausoleum of the Dunin-Borkowski family," he explained.

"A whole family is in there . . . together?" I imagined Father lying there, looking gray, and Mother stern. Zofia and I would surely be in a double coffin, forced to be together for all eternity.

"Up there on the gable is the family's coat of arms."

I couldn't see more than a bird with a neck shaped like an *S.* "They have a goose on their shield?" I asked.

"A swan," he corrected me. "A nobleman doesn't put farmyard animals into his coat of arms."

"A swan is supposed to sing beautifully before it dies," Mother said softly to Dr. Kasprzycki.

"But they sound ugly!" I protested.

"See the man by the door?" He pointed to a statue of a nude man, who was shielding his face with a corner of a robe he had drawn up from the lower part of his body. "This is Apollo, the god of the sun, and the swan is supposed to be the bird sacred to him."

I shook my head about a god with such taste in birds. Although swans looked beautiful, they were just like geese: they sounded awful, and what was more important, they scared me.

"And this man on top of the building?" I pointed to a statue that had to be another Greek god. During my childhood I read the *Odyssey* five times and the *Iliad* five times, so I had become adept at spotting gods.

"This is Charon, who rows you across the dark waters into the world of the dead." Putting his hand on Mother's shoulder, he pointed with the other at a tangle of trees and bushes that had grown into each other like sisters. "Over there are several monuments, all designed by a woman sculptor. Since we came early, there is still time to view them before the service."

"Ala, do you want to come?"

Why would Mother even ask me to go into a wilderness where nettles surely grew waist-high?

"No. You go, I'll wait."

I watched Mother disappear with *him* behind a rearing horse pulling a chariot. When they had been swallowed up by the green wilderness, I examined every detail of the monument as if it would provide a clue to their disappearance. The warrior threatened me with his spear, but the wheel of the chariot made me feel safe again. It looked like the spiraling grooves of a puzzle game that I jiggled in the hollow of my hand until all the steel balls dropped into black holes.

For a while I continued along the road, until, off to the right, I saw what looked like the entrance to a temple. Two pillars, one on each side of a bench, held up a gabled roof. Only after I had almost reached what I took to be a temple did I notice the young girl on the stone bench, sitting as erect as if Mother had told her, "Sit up straight!" By her size, I judged her to be my age. When I came closer I saw that I had been fooled because the girl had been sculpted very lifelike out of stone just like the bench. Sitting down next to the statue—so close that my hip was touching hers—I wondered if she looked at all like the girl buried under my feet.

I began to think about Dr. Kasprzycki, who had taken Mother away. Soon after Christmas, I had to visit him. Mother didn't send our maid to accompany me; instead she dressed carefully and walked with me along our street, the Kurkowa Ulica. The name means Cock of the Gun Street because it led to the shooting range. "He has an elegant office, you'll see," she said. With a toothache brought on by the holiday candy, I didn't much want to think about his office.

While I waited for my mouth to become numb, he talked to Mother about the picture that hung across from the dentist's chair.

"*The Death of Sardanapalus*. A copy, to be sure, but a good one; the colors are close to the original painting that I saw in the Louvre."

Dr. Kasprzycki painted much, mostly in shades of green. His canvas world was as if I were peering through my emerald ring. The women in his pictures looked drowned, their bodies entangled among reeds and water lilies.

While my lips were turning to stone, I listened to his soothing voice tell Mother about the people that were being killed in the painting. After I noticed that all those being killed were women, I let my eyes escape the slaughter to a horse in the lower left-hand corner. Its whiteness was peaceful after the turmoil in red, brown, and gold that threatened the pink female bodies.

He put a tray in front of me with gleaming chrome instruments laid out in a row, from a harmless-looking mirror to picks and hooks.

"The whole composition is focused on this woman." His slender hand may have been pointing at a rosy body in the foreground, but he was looking at Mother. "I know that you can appreciate the forward-arching of her body bent like a bow of flesh."

Mother's handkerchief muffled her cough.

"She was Greek and her name was Myrrha. We know that much." His voice sounded as professional as it did when he told me how to brush my teeth.

I refused to obey his pointing hand, staring instead at the white horse, whose headstall looked like that of the camel I had ridden in the zoo, except the horse's was golden and studded with jewels.

A tall, beautiful woman walked into the room as if she had stepped from the painting. Dr. Kasprzycki introduced her as Jula, his assistant. He had a homely housekeeper—whose name also happened to be Jula—who sometimes visited Mother. One day the housekeeper had cried while telling Mother that she loved Dr. Kasprzycki, but that he didn't show any interest in her at all. Mother had smiled. Mother didn't smile at beautiful Jula, who handed me a heavy ruby-red tumbler, cut like crystal. Turning to spit into a bowl, I saw that it was also made of ruby glass. Zofia had told me that everything in the office was red so that your blood wouldn't show, but she always said things to scare me and I didn't believe her. I thought that the ruby glass looked like it came from a treasure in a *Märchen*.

While Dr. Kasprzycki was working on me, his shoulders were blocking out the horse, which made me look again at Myrrha. Her naked body was bent forward like a bow about to be shot, and I wondered about the arrow for such a bow.

It was spring before Mother took me back to the dentist. Eagerly, I peered over his shoulders as he hunched over me. Outside of the lighted circle cast by the lamp, there was little I could see in the darkness, so I tried to remember the bodies in the painting that had reminded me of the girls in the gymnastics class at the Nazaretanki—from which we were soon excused because of our weakness but which we nevertheless were forced to watch—except that the women in the painting were bending without order and rhythm.

He spoke to Mother, who sat hidden in the dark. When his probe slipped and hit a nerve, I bit his hand. He jumped back with a cry, knocking the lamp askew.

"Tadeusz!" Mother called out from the darkness. "Are you hurt?"

"*Your* daughter . . ." he exclaimed angrily. Without adjusting the lamp, he held his hand close to the light. On one of his fingers glistened a drop of blood. He looked as closely at his finger as if he were examining a ring with a red gem. "Just a little bite," he said in a voice that once again had become soothing. The circle of light, now twisted into an oblong, illuminated the lower left of the painting where the horse's head stood out ghostly white like a carousel horse in the night.

"Ala, apologize to Dr. Kasprzycki!"

He washed his hands, while I stared at the horse, which had

thrown back its head. As if pain had opened my eyes I saw for the first time what I had not been able to see before. I cried out when I discovered the sword that a naked black arm was thrusting into the chest of the horse.

Through my thin summer dress I felt the coldness of the stone girl seep into my thigh. Holding up my ring I gazed at angels, gods and warriors, lions, eagles, and grieving women. The world in my ring was even greener, as if I had drowned in the thicket behind the statues.

"Ala! Ala!" Mother called from the path. Now alone, she was looking in all directions but couldn't find me because I was sitting quietly just like the stone girl. While she was walking, Mother kept brushing her hands across her shoulders. Just then, my sister, who also had heard Mother's voice, came walking across the grass, but Mother didn't see her. Zofia wanted to sit next to me, but I silently pushed her away because I wanted to sit alone with the stone girl. Mother was walking in our direction, but she didn't see us, because we didn't push each other anymore and Mother had her head down and kept brushing her hands across her shoulders. When she was only a few steps away, we broke into snorting laughter.

Mother jumped back as if one of us had hit her in the face with a ball. She was so angry that she just stood in the grass as if our laughter had turned her into a monument.

"You monsters!" she shouted and ran the last steps toward us and then lunged at our wrists. "What are you doing to me?" Pulling us off the bench, she screamed in our faces. "Heroes lie all around us, and you savages defile this sacred place!"

She quickly decided to keep Zofia and me together, although usually at functions we were kept separated from each other. After threatening us with more severe punishment at home, Mother calmed down. Again she looked at gravestones on either side of the path. Walking behind her I noticed a green leaf between Mother's shoulder blades.

"Do you see this?" Zofia pointed at the statue of a woman who in one hand held an upside-down torch, while, in a gesture of grief, she pressed the other to her forehead. "You monsters! What are you doing to me?" Although Zofia had spoken in only a whisper,

Mother whirled around ready to hit her, but my sister dodged and ran to catch up with the others while I dutifully followed Mother.

Without transition in my memory, I am standing close to Rudolf's grave, and my foot is nudging a clod of black earth into the hole. The thump on the coffin makes me jump back.

"But I would not have you to be ignorant, brethren, concerning them which are asleep." The priest, a pale young man, looked extremely ill at ease, as if he feared that at any moment someone might come and order him to stop the service.

Mother made me stand behind her so that I wouldn't fall into the open grave. I kept my eyes on the leaf, whose stem had threaded itself into the loops of her summer knit dress. In the sunlight, the leaf shone bright green like an enameled brooch that, accidentally, had been fastened to the back of my mother's dress.

"Kyrie eleison, Christie eleison, pater noster." Half-listening to the prayers I had heard so often, I sniffed the incense. I made up my mind not to tell Mother about the leaf on her back; instead, I bowed my head like the grown-up mourners. As I was looking down I remembered—and I swear it was only then that I remembered—that the boy who was being buried had once saved my life. I couldn't have forgotten, but my child's mind might have refused to believe that Rudolf, who had saved *me,* now lay dead himself. Maybe I thought that my guardian angel had died.

It was at a family outing in Turka that Rudolf—Romek to us— had brought me back from death. I had been stretching my arm as far as I could toward a water lily until I toppled headfirst into a pond. Dressed in white, Romek threw himself into the dark green water and pulled me ashore. I don't know how he saved me, but what I now see is Pan Bonk bent over me as I lay in the grass spewing water the color of bile from nose and mouth.

I remember Romek the way I had seen him that day on the mountain meadow, dressed in white trousers and a white silk shirt with sleeves that flowed and fluttered like wings.

Seeing Romek in my mind like this made me think of Lermontov before his duel. What I knew about the poet I had heard from Mother as she had stood on our balcony with her back to the three convents on our street: the Franciszkanki, the Marianki, and the Josefitki.

"Fallen in a duel at twenty-seven in the Caucasus." Then, standing as she was under the flowering branches of the acacia tree, she recited Mikhail Lermontov: "I lay, with lead in my breast, my deep wound still steaming, as my blood oozed out, drop . . . by . . . drop."

Mother was still reciting when Father came.

"What is this love affair with Lermontov, he, a Russian guard officer and you a Polish patriot?"

"I don't *hate* Russians. Besides, Lermontov was a Scot."

"A Scot? Dressed in a kilt and playing a bagpipe?" Father was mocking her earnestness.

I laughed, but Mother stared at me with such anger blazing in her eyes that I blushed and fell silent.

"They say that he was of Scottish ancestry," she replied stiffly, as if not only her idol but she herself had been insulted.

I went back into the apartment to look at the book with the picture of Lermontov before his death. The painting was crowded by two immense mountains; the flank of the bigger one glowed pink like snow in the morning, while the other—shaped evenly like a casket—was dark brown. A white horse stood off to one side as if it wanted nothing to do with what was about to happen. A small black figure at the edge of the abyss pointed a pistol across the void.

I was sitting on my bed with the book in my lap when Father came into the children's room.

"What are you studying?"

"Lermontov falling," I said, proud of my learning. "In a duel."

He examined the picture.

"No, no. Mikhail Lermontov *painted* the picture. Besides, the reproduction is so small that you can't tell what's happening." Then he left.

I didn't believe him, but I cried, consoling myself only by telling myself how much older he was than Mother. He could easily be my grandfather. Maybe his eyes didn't see clearly anymore.

Father came back with a large book under his arm.

"The atlas is old and all the names are in German, but I hope that the mountains are still in the same place." He laughed and pointed to a brown throat of land between two bright blue ponds. "Here is the Caucasus. The Black Sea and the Caspian Sea are to the left and the right. This is where the sturgeon swims, a big fish with a pointed snout. Cutting it open you get caviar from its belly and isinglass from its bladder. Ala, look at the stove over there! The little window in the door where Pazia checks on the flames, that's made from isinglass."

I watched the orange tongues licking behind the yellowed window of the stove until I could imagine a fisherman tearing the bladder from the belly of a long-snouted fish.

"This is Mount Elbrus, the mountain in your painting." Eagerly my eyes followed Father's nicotine-stained finger. "And this over here is Mount Mashuk, where Lermontov died."

I swallowed hard, feeling sorry for Lermontov and the fish that had been slit open, but not only for them. When Father heard me drawing deep breaths as if I were about to sob, he quickly took my finger and pointed it at the map.

"Now we journey through the Pass of the Cross into Ge . . . or . . . gi . . . en." He pronounced each syllable separately. I imagined the syllables to be camels carrying precious bales in a caravan following the route our fingers were traveling across the map. "And on to Tiflis, where the houses cling to the rocks like swallows' nests hanging from the eaves of a farmhouse."

"Were you ever there?"

"No, not me." He sounded sad. "Uncle Tedek told me about the houses." He dropped my hand on the map. "Here, keep the atlas and lie down with it."

I pressed my hand so long on the brown land that I thought my moist palm could feel the ribs of the mountain range rising.

For weeks I didn't look at the painting of the mountain with the black figure by the edge of the abyss. My sister and I were busy collecting tinfoil for the parish of Swietego Antoniego, hoping that, by the end of summer, we would have enough money to ransom a black slave in East Africa. We gathered candy and chocolate wrappers and, when Mother wasn't looking, empty cigarette boxes from the gutter of our street.

Mother had invited Dr. Kasprzycki to dinner. Zofia and I were in our room smoothing out squares of foil before pressing them between the pages of our encyclopedia. While we worked, we sniffed each foil, searching for the vanilla aroma of chocolate or the leather smell of tobacco, and if we found very nice sheets of foil we traded them with each other.

Dr. Kasprzycki came to our room to bring us a teddy bear with eyes the color of real amber stones like those that we had found on a beach by the Baltic Sea. I ought to have liked the bear.

"What are you studying?" he asked.

"Ge . . . or . . . gi . . . en," I answered, pronouncing the camel-syllables as carefully as Father had.

"Poles call that Gruzia," he corrected me. To me, the new word didn't sound like precious cargo of a caravan. Then he aimed the glowing end of his cigarette at the slender brown throat of the mountain range.

"The Caucasus," I volunteered.

"This is where a Titan named Prometheus . . ."

"Like the insurance company?"

"It is a good name for one, since in Greek it means *forethought*."

I laughed, relieved that I hadn't embarrassed myself.

"Prometheus was chained—naked, mind you—to a rock in the Caucasus with an eagle feeding on his liver. All day long and every day."

I gasped.

"Don't worry, Ala. At night his liver grew back."

I was used to adults giving happy endings to the stories they told us, so I had become suspicious that everything they told us was nothing but the children's version and not the real story.

"What happened then?" Because I thought that I knew what his answer would be, I began to cry.

"Every morning the eagle came back. That is the way of divine punishment." He stopped as if he wanted to draw out the cruel story. "*But* . . . sometimes there is a solution even for such a hope-less situation. Zeus himself gave Hercules permission to unchain Prometheus."

I sighed with relief, thinking how the chained man would mas-sage his ankles and his wrists.

"But Hercules had to kill the eagle."

I wept again, now not knowing anymore if I wept for the tor-tured man or the slain bird.

"Don't worry about Prometheus; you are more like 'After-thought,' his brother, because you always ponder things that have happened."

"I want to be Prometheus," I replied angrily. "I don't want to be anyone's brother . . . or even anyone's sister."

"You are probably right not wanting to be Epimetheus. Life couldn't have been easy for him being married to Pandora. They say that he even helped her open up the urn . . ."

"Urn?"

"Some call it a box, but it was an urn. In the meantime, Prometheus, in order to remember not to anger the gods, had to wear a piece of stone from the Caucasus on an iron ring."

The moment I heard this, I held up my hand with Pan Bonk's emerald ring. He shifted his cigarette to his left hand before he pulled off my ring. Rolling it between thumb and forefinger like a gooseberry that he was about to eat, he held it up to the lamp on my nightstand.

"Light shining through the stone will reveal the mystery of life to you." He spoke in a strange voice as if this were a seance of Mother's. *Tajemnica,* he had said, the mystery. "This emerald will ward off demons and ghosts."

I wanted to ask him a question, but Mother came to lead him to the dining table. I didn't eat but sat at my place at the dining table and watched the eaters turn the hare into a small skeleton until, at the end, only ribs stuck up from the serving plate like a cage of twigs.

The praying stopped and the mourners moved slowly away from the grave. The priest tried to dump out the smoking incense that had caked the insides of the censer. He shook it, and when the old incense wouldn't drop out, he knocked the golden vessel two or three times against the corner of a gravestone. From the top of the stone, an owl stared at me with eyes set deep into discs of stone feathers, like marbles that had rolled into pits in the dust when we played *kulka*. Squatting by the grave as if I were peeing, I bent over the smoldering heap of incense and sucked in the blue smoke like I sometimes did with Mother's perfume, which made me feel like licking her skin.

"There is a leaf . . ." Father said, standing behind Mother.

"Where?" she asked sharply without turning around.

Still squatting on the ground, I had to crane my neck so I could see what was going on.

"On the back of your dress. It's hooked . . ."

"Don't, Albin! You'll snag it."

"Here." Father handed her the leaf. "A souvenir of today."

Mother raised the leaf to her face and, for a moment, I thought that she was going to kiss it. Father stared at her as she held the leaf between thumb and forefinger until she finally sniffed it as if it were a rose.

Father looked at her in a way that made me think that something had happened. Suddenly it came to me that whatever it was was my fault, because I hadn't warned Mother about the leaf on her back. I sank down as if my knees thought that we were in church. Somebody picked me up and carried me to a stone bench.

"Let the child have some air!"

Father pushed away the men and women crowding around me.

"Air!"

They must not have listened to Father, because when I again opened my eyes their faces were hovering over me. Since they weren't talking to me I closed my eyes and I listened to their murmurs, which weren't about me at all. It was from what I heard that I learned why Rudolf had been buried in a corner of the cemetery, scratched into the ground like a dog run over by a horse cart. He was fourteen when he saved me from drowning, and now only a year later he had taken a rifle when he had gone walking with his friend. At a field that had been harvested early, he stopped and said: "I always wanted to know how it is over there." Then he shot himself.

Father slid his folded coat under my head. The faces moved away from me.

"So that you won't lie there like a little . . ." He didn't finish, but I knew he had begun to say "a little corpse." As I lay there, propped up by Father's folded coat, the graves around me seemed as if I had never before seen them: lashed to the earth by tendrils of wild ivy, the stone monuments had become an army of angels who would never fly again.

Wet from the lush grass where I had fallen, my shoulder blades shivered against the clammy marble of the bench. Lying there, I was sure that I had fainted not from the summer heat but from the stench rising from the ground around me, as I had smelled it first from the vase that held the dead roses for the Young Eagles. I thought that sniffing the same smell of death on my clothes and even on my own body had made me faint.

During the walk from the cemetery I was silent. After we arrived at home, I felt like being by myself, and so I went out on the balcony. It was cooler now and a breeze blew the sweet smell of the acacia tree across my face.

Without thought, I picked up the teddy bear that we had never named because for us it had stayed Dr. Kasprzycki's bear. That night, when he had given us the bear, I had picked up the empty cigarette box he had left on the dining table. Pulling out its foil lining, I tilted the tobacco crumbs into the ashtray and lit them. Then I held my nose close to the brief wisp of smoke and I inhaled. Later I smoothed out the green and silver foil with its delicately embossed design and named it the "Turkish." It became my favorite, but I was never certain if it was because of its design or because the smell of his tobacco still clung to the foil.

Standing on the balcony, I played with the bear, pressing and kneading its chest, the way I had probed the tiger's baby fur for its ribs that had been thin as twigs.

The ministrant's bell from the funeral kept ringing in my head, and I heard the priest knocking the incense from the golden censer. Pressing the chest of the bear more urgently, my fingers searched for and did not find ribs under its fur. My elbows were resting on the iron railing of the balcony, as I was facing the three convents of Francis, Mary, and Joseph, which dominated the street of my childhood, when the bear slipped from my hands. Watching it tumble toward the granite cobblestones of the Kurkowa Ulica made my stomach heave. I even sucked in my breath as if I had dropped the bear by accident.

On All Saints' Day of the same year, I was lying with a fever on our brown ottoman. While I idly traced its Persian patterns with my forefinger, I listened to the broadcast of Adam Mickiewicz's drama *Dziady*. With the ghosts moaning from the radio, I decided to look through the album in which I had glued the most beautiful pieces of my tinfoil collection. The faint aroma of vanilla and tobacco made me think of leather suitcases standing by the tracks in the steam of a locomotive. Was that the smell of Daghestan or Georgien? Was it incense? I wasn't sure if the inhabitants of the brown mountains were even Christians, but why else would they have a Pass of the Cross? My fingertips, tracing the dales and ridges impressed on the green and white "Turkish" foil, searched for the notch of the pass that would lead me into Tiflis with its houses clinging to the mountains like the nests of swallows.

My whole family had gone to the cemetery to light candles for the souls in Purgatory, while through a wintry window I watched the sky turn from lead to fire and then to smoke. Fatigued by the fever, I dropped the album, and falling back against the pillows, I raised up my emerald ring and peered through it at the fire glowing in the window of the stove. At that moment I imagined that I could see everything. "*Tajemnica, tajemnica,* the mystery, the mystery of life," I whispered to myself. Maybe it was because I was feverish that I didn't feel foolish for saying such an important thing that surely was not meant for children. But I was not hallucinating when I saw Father, Mother, and Zofia as small figures wandering in a single file through the overgrown cemetery. It was difficult to tell the people from the shrubs. Dr. Kasprzycki had told us on the day of Romek's funeral—after Mother had complained how ill-kept the holy place looked—that the souls of the dead change into trees and flowers, even into birds. So that was why they didn't prune the trees or even mow the grass, for fear of hurting the souls of the dead. I didn't know what to think of this when he told me about it, but I thought about it now as I tried to "see" my parents. I finally made out our maid straggling behind the others, because she was loaded down with baskets of food for the dead. The candles of the small procession were lighting up the edge of the wilderness. They were passing a pale figure that might be a marble monument guarding a grave or even Dr. Kasprzycki in his white suit. The same dank smell that enveloped the temples of the dead rose again around me. It made me float like an angel—I thought then—high above the cemetery, so that I could look down on the flickering lights of my family walking. Watching Zofia walk behind Mother was like seeing myself. Were they all dead? My sister too?

A crash made me jump up from the ottoman. My heart beat fast while I listened, fearing that the *dziady* were hacking through the door to our apartment. Only when I heard the briquettes settling in the tiled stove did I breathe a little easier, but not much. As if I were hypnotized, I kept staring at the lighted window in the cast-iron door of the stove until the aureole of my sister's candle grew bigger and finally swam through the dark of the room like a fiery ghost fish.

I screamed and ran into the kitchen, as if I too were a lost soul, flinging open cupboard after cupboard until I found matches. Then I ran back into the living room to light a candle before Our Lady of Lourdes. I didn't turn on the electric light, because then the candle wouldn't be able to do its work of saving me. After it flared up, I sat down in front of the statue. The yellow light was spread in a circle around my legs as if it were the pleated skirt of my school uniform. While I was watching the Madonna for any sign of saving me, I didn't dare to stick even a toe out of the circle of light. The white Madonna from Lourdes was Mother's favorite. Even the roses that her feet were crushing were white.

Fever chills shook me as I sat half-naked on the parquet floor. I held out my emerald ring to the illuminated white statue and kept repeating "*tajemnica, tajemnica,*" as if this litany would save me from the fury of the Night of the Dead.

Then in the darkness, beyond the circle of the saving light, the *dziady* were rattling their chains at me, rattling them so loudly that in fear I pulled off my clothes and thrust out my belly toward the door. A dog with fiery eyes circled around me and I screamed, but then it was only Zofia taunting me: "Naked belly! Naked belly!" My sister had run ahead of my parents. Then Pazia carried me back to the sofa and covered me with a blanket.

"She fetched her death from that stone bench," she chided my parents while she piled more briquettes on the fire.

Again I was in darkness. Did they believe darkness was good and light was bad? After a bed rest of I don't know how many days, I felt well enough to sit up and write a poem about heroes. Maybe it was because I wanted to be like Mother, who loved heroes. In my poem, the Young Eagles died once again. At first I thought that a celebration of Polish heroes should not mention Lermontov, who, after all, had fallen in the wilds of Daghestan, nor did it seem fitting to celebrate the boy in white who had thrown himself into a pond to save a girl reaching for a water lily, but without them my poem would be incomplete.

Sister Columba at the Nazaretanki asked me to recite my poem as part of the patriotic celebrations on November 11. But on that day, Mother decided that my sister and I were too ill to go to school. Instead Lala Kajser—who surely must have looked like a bleating sheep in her navy-blue middy—was called to read my poem. In honor of the patriotic holiday she might even have worn red and white ribbons in her sheep's-ear braids.

While she was reciting, something strange happened to her, something that I didn't think she was capable of doing: she cried. For years I was angry with her for bawling over my poem. It was not until I was a grown woman and only after I had learned to cry over my own dead, that I realized that it had been right for Lala Kajser to cry.

Darkness crowds the circle of light falling on the small album of pictures on my bed. Yes, it had been Dr. Kasprzycki who photographed us in the Warsaw Zoo, just as he had painted Mother's picture, which hangs down the hallway from my bedroom. Day and night, a red light burns underneath Mother's picture that *he* painted, making her look as if her body was caught in a strong green current. From my bed I can see the red glow on the picture down the hall.

No, I had not fetched my death from the stone bench, but, like the "Afterthought" that I am, I ponder how it can even be. Can one *fetch* death? Is it like when as a child I ran to the corner store to fetch a herring that Barachowa's red hands pulled from the murky brine of a fish barrel in front of their store on the Kurkowa Ulica in Lvov?

Sometimes I am convinced that my life is quite useless, were it not that I remember. Every single day in this country eats away at my past, but when I lie awake in the long nights and see the red glow from my mother's picture, I feel my past growing back.

The Blue Line

When Martin parked his car behind the privet hedge, he could see that his father had already driven the Toronado out of the carport. It stood on the wet driveway, where Mother was drying a fender while Father, from a lawn chair, pointed his walking stick at a spot Mother had missed.

"We'd best go inside," Father said when he saw Martin walking over from the street.

Mother gathered up the wet rags and dropped them in a green plastic bucket. "Come inside and have breakfast before you go."

His parents went in ahead of Martin while he stopped on the porch for another look at Father's car. How old was it now? Seventeen, eighteen years? The Toronado had been the best of the cars his parents had been able to afford in America, and they had taken good care of it. The golden metallic paint glowed in the spring sun as if it were a car waiting for a king.

"You . . . look handsome . . . this morning." His mother shouted from the kitchen over the clatter of the juicer.

"How do I look on other days?" Martin dropped the morning newspaper on the sofa by his father's side and bent down to kiss him.

"Other mornings . . . you might not . . . wear a tie." When Martin cocked his head, she shouted, "In a moment . . . I'll be finished with the juice."

"You didn't have to wash the car. I looked at it yesterday and I didn't see one speck of dust on it."

"*Ordnung muss sein.* You know how much we like things to be orderly."

"Papa isn't even taking a driving test, just a reading examination." Sitting down in an easy chair, Martin propped his legs on a footstool.

"Somebody from church might see you driving in a dirty automobile." Mother set a breakfast tray in his lap. "Besides, the car should look beautiful on such an important day."

For at least two weeks they had talked of Father's having to renew his driver's license. Mother was worried that the authorities wouldn't give a license to a man whose eighty-sixth birthday was coming up next month. "We really need this license. You think they would understand that we have to go to church and that we want to buy groceries on our own, get our checks cashed." Although Martin kept correcting her, now and then she still pronounced it "grosheries."

"And be free," she added. "We still want to be free."

"Why don't you stop polishing your shoes?" Martin asked his father. "They are already gleaming like chestnuts."

Bent over his shoes, Father wiped them gently with an old woolen sock. After a while he folded the sock carefully and put it on top of the shoeshine kit. "Ah, the chestnuts," he said, looking over at his son eating breakfast from a tray in his lap.

Martin remembered when the wind shook the chestnut trees lining the road near their house in the Old Country. Bouncing on the ground, the spiky green shells split open and the chestnuts rolled sleek and moist into the dust. He gathered them into a pillowcase. Then, at the round table in the living room, he made chestnut men, chestnut animals with legs made from wooden matches, chestnut boats, and heavy chestnut necklaces. It didn't matter how beautiful the things looked that he had made because every year the sleek shiny chestnuts always shriveled into dull brown stones.

Father stood up and put on his jacket.

"You don't have to do that yet," Mother said. "You'll be sweaty even before you leave the house. Martin is still eating. But since you have your coat on, let me look at you." Walking around Father, she inspected his shirt collar, slid the knot of his tie up, pulled his jacket down in back, then brushed the shoulders of his dark blue blazer.

"Take off your jacket, your hair's too long. People will think that you're Ben Gurion."

"No, more Old Testament," Martin said. "More like Moses on Mount Sinai."

From her sewing box Mother took a pair of scissors and clipped some of Father's white locks from the back of his neck. "Don't move, I have to cut over the ears too." Then she brushed his hair once more. Stepping back, she looked at him and shook her head. She licked her fingertips and smoothed back a wisp touching the top of his ear. Then she helped him back into his jacket. "Just one more thing." Not knowing what to expect, Father obediently stood as if at attention. Mother tiptoed up to him, with a pink can of hair spray hidden behind her back. When she squirted twice at Father's neck he sneezed and pulled his head into his collar like a threatened turtle. "Don't touch your hair," she said. Standing behind his back, she waited until he raised his head and then squirted him once more. "This way you'll look tidy and orderly for the photographer."

As his father waited by the door, Martin noticed that both of them had dressed the same way for the trip to the Department of Motor Vehicles: gray trousers, blue shirts, striped ties, and navy-blue blazers. To Martin, it made sense that Father had dressed this way. He refused to wear his blazer to church, where only a dark suit would do, and the jacket was too nice for grocery shopping, so a visit to a state office seemed the proper occasion for the blazer.

Mother stood in front of Father and smoothed the shoulder of his jacket. "My green-eyed hawk."

As his father aged, his nose had grown to dominate his features, not with the arrogance and mercilessness of the Hapsburg hook that Dürer had drawn in the face of Emperor Maximilian, but to resemble the curved point of a raptor's beak.

When Martin saw that Father kept glancing at his wristwatch, he took his breakfast dishes into the kitchen and pulled on his jacket. He hadn't finished eating his breakfast, but he didn't want Father to worry about time and he wanted his mother to see how he looked by Father's side. At the door he stood next to him. Although his father was a head shorter than Martin, both men looked very much alike, even down to their gray mustaches, except that Father trimmed his until it lay flat against his upper lip.

"Why do you cut your mustache so short?" Martin asked, although he knew how their church felt about facial hair.

"I want to look orderly."

"The beautiful sunshine we have in America." Mother looked around from the porch. "And the car shines too, as if it were the chariot of Israel . . ."

"And the horsemen of Elias," Father added with a smile.

"You are so *Bibelfest*," admired Mother.

"Elijah," Martin wanted to correct, but didn't. Both of his parents could quote readily and correctly from the Bible—as long as it was the German Luther translation—verses that they had learned by heart when they were children in school. The English Bible had never taken with either one of them. Even now Mother still followed the Sunday school lessons in her German Bible.

She kissed husband and son as if they were setting out on a long journey. "You drive," she told Martin, "so he can save his strength for the examination."

Martin drove slowly past the privet hedge so that they could wave at Mother from the open windows of the car. Father pointed back at the hedge.

"You saw that the *Liguster* wasn't cut evenly?"

With nothing more than a yardstick, a ball of string, and hand clippers, Father used to sculpt a sharp-edged wall from the privet bushes. Now, the man who mowed the lawn also took a few minutes to go over the hedge with an electric trimmer. When Father complained that the hedge wasn't evenly cut, the man looked at him with incomprehension, as if Father talked to him in a language of aliens.

"I saw it. The privet is sloping toward the right." Martin nodded. "I noticed it." He used the German expression "it fell into my eye." His father had taught him to let things fall into his eye. As a child, Martin had often been taken to construction sites where his father's company was building apartments for the railroaders in town. It was then that Martin had learned to spot anything that wasn't straight, level, or true to plumb. Father would ask, "How long is this wall?" and Martin would sight along the edge of the concrete foundation and guess. Then they both paced off the distance, Martin having to stretch the steps of his shorter legs as best he could. When Martin's estimate was close, they would both laugh and walk on. As he thought about it now, night always seemed to have fallen quickly so that they hurried home where Mother waited with supper.

When he stopped at the first intersection, he glanced into the rearview mirror and saw that his mother stood in the middle of the street, still waving.

He took St. Louis Avenue because its broadness reminded him of a grand boulevard in a city with real history. Here in Las Vegas, the only old building had been the icehouse by the Union Pacific tracks until someone had set fire to it. There had been talk of arson. In this town, it was almost as if anything old made people uncomfortable.

Buckled up, Father looked straight ahead at the road as if he himself were the one who was driving. Martin was always surprised how easily the big car handled, so easily that he could steer it with his index finger. Out of the corner of his eye he saw his father motioning to him with his right hand, telling him to slow down. He glanced at the speedometer drum revolving vertically and saw that his father was right. Obediently he eased his foot off the gas pedal, and out of the corner of his eye he saw that his father smiled when the car slowed down. Father had always driven with élan or, as he himself put it, "I drive briskly."

As soon as Martin turned into the parking lot he saw the long line.

"Look at all of these people."

From the end of the line Father counted the people between them and the olive tree standing in front of the double glass doors. "There are fifty people ahead of us. We should have left earlier."

"It's not so bad." Martin tried to soothe his father. "When they open the doors, people are going to line up at different counters."

When they got inside, Father shook his head when he saw the

long lines of people snaking in different directions through the big hall. "We should have left earlier."

"This is like Ellis Island," Martin said.

"What do you know about Ellis Island? You never had to go there."

"True, but I've seen pictures, and I know what it looked like."

Father walked to the end of the nearest line.

"Wait!" Martin kept pointing to a large overhead board.

"Black, blue, green, red, and yellow lines. This reminds me of the control panel at the railroad, of the office in the shunting yard."

"Let's see if we can shunt ourselves in the right direction." Martin kept pointing at the overhead board. "The lines are color coded. Yellow line, information; black line, truck plates; red line, license plate for the first time; green line, license plate transfer. Here. Blue line, drivers license renewals."

Martin began to read aloud the placards posted on the buff-colored walls. "Thumbs-Up to Seat Belts," he read from a poster showing policemen in different uniforms. "Give a Chance at Life—Be an Organ Donor."

The line moved slowly and stopped altogether in front of a corkboard displaying special license plates.

"This is for a state legislator, that one for former prisoners of war, and this over here is for soldiers who were awarded the Medal of Honor. I wonder how many people in the state of Nevada are eligible for that plate?"

"How about this one for me?" Father pointed at one of the silver license plates.

"'Disabled Veteran,'" Martin read aloud. "You certainly are that, but they may say that you fought on the wrong side." When his father was hit by shell fragments during a French artillery barrage in World War I, how old had he been? Nineteen? Twenty?

"Maybe this one?"

"No. 'Old-timer' is for old cars, not old people."

"And this? I can't see what's on it."

"It's a scenic plate. You can get it for an extra ten dollars. It shows a mountain with a Joshua tree. You must have seen them when you and Mother used to drive down from Salt Lake City, before you moved here. After you pass through St. George, you must have seen a whole field of Joshua trees. With their arms raised up, they always made me think of an army surrendering in the desert."

"Under Joshua the children of Israel never surrendered to anyone, not at Jericho or when they were on the midnight side of Ai."

"I didn't mean that. . . . The other items on the license plate are the usual Nevada stuff, like a bighorn sheep, our state animal. I think that it's the same as Aries, your horoscope sign."

"It is?" Father smiled. "But of course this horoscope thing is nonsense."

At the counter, more windows were being opened. To pass the time, Martin speculated which would be theirs. Finally, a woman waved to them to step forward from the end of the blue line.

"This nice lady will help us." Father shook hands with the examiner, an older woman who wore her dyed black hair in a beehive. Looking from one to the other, she smiled at the two men dressed identically in jackets and ties as if they were aliens from another world who happened to be stranded in a colorful crowd wearing T-shirts, halter tops, and shorts. She was still smiling when she dropped the card with the reading test into the machine.

Martin squeezed his father's shoulder, although it wasn't necessary. Already thirty years ago his father had known all the road signs when he taught his son how to drive along the loop of Liberty Park, and he hadn't forgotten them since.

His father drew himself up and stood with his eyes closed, as if he were praying, then he bent down to peer into the machine. As he called out the signs, he saw the woman's powdered face turn sad as she checked the list in front of her. Then she glanced again at Father's application on the counter.

"All of your answers were wrong." She didn't raise her eyes from the application.

"Did you understand everything?" Martin asked his father in German. He nodded. "I'll translate for you." Martin looked apologetically at the examiner, as he always did when he spoke German in front of others.

"Take your time." The examiner flicked to another row.

"It's going to be all right," Martin said in German.

Clearing his throat, Father began to read. He spoke slower now, as if he wanted to make sure that he would not be misunderstood.

"Wrong again." The examiner gave Martin a reproachful look, as if she wanted to say, "Martin, why are you putting your father through this torture?" "Everything is wrong again."

His father stood alone, although only an arm's length away from his son. Martin could see the perspiration beading among the brown spots on his father's forehead.

"He is nervous because he has to take this test." Martin spoke softly to the examiner so that his father wouldn't hear that his son was making excuses for him.

The examiner clicked in another row of signs. "Tell your father to take a deep breath and to read more slowly what he sees."

Martin translated the examiner's instructions, although he could see by the look in his eyes that he had understood.

"He's nervous. His English is usually much better." The moment he had finished speaking, he knew that he had betrayed his father by apologizing for him. Martin put his arm around his father's shoulder. The wool of the jacket felt warm and moist to his touch. He kept his arm on his father's shoulder while he read the signs as he had been told to do in two languages.

When he stopped reading, the woman looked pleadingly at Martin. "I don't know how to tell you this."

Martin took his father's arm as if he were leading an invalid. It has come to this, he thought. Finally it has come to this. The beginning of the end.

"No," Martin said aloud.

His father looked up at him with a face that was serene, not nervous or sad. Martin dropped his father's arm. "I am going to check the machine," he said in German, while his father stepped back to the end of the blue line.

The red, green, and yellow road signs stood out from the dark depth projected by the machine, sharply defined, as if they and the darkness were part of a memory of home.

"Is *this* what you see?" The examiner's eyes were filled with such sadness as if she were about to cry. "All of your answers were wrong, too."

Martin straightened up from the machine. "No, I had no difficulty recognizing the signs." He spoke louder than before. "All the answers should be correct."

As Martin's voice rose angrily, Father looked at his son and pulled at his sleeve. "Don't make trouble because of me."

Martin gently drew his sleeve out of his father's grip.

"No, this is wrong." Now he spoke English to his father.

Puzzled by the challenge in Martin's voice, the woman looked first at Martin, then at her fellow workers at their desks, and finally down at her machine. She pulled up the card with the road signs and read aloud its title and number, reassuring those at the desks that she couldn't possibly have made a mistake. Then she slowly re-read the card. As if it were a close-up on a movie screen, Martin watched as her lips began to quiver. Then she looked with relief at the two men on the other side of the counter.

"I'm sorry. This was the wrong card." She waved to Father. "Please, step to the counter and look into the machine. It was a mistake."

This time Martin didn't translate the instructions. Instead he stared angrily at the woman, ready to tell her what he thought, when out of the corner of his eye, he saw that his father was smiling.

"Press your forehead against the pad."

Martin didn't dare to breathe as his father obediently pushed his face into the machine. Then he called out the signs in a clear voice as he calmly pronounced each foreign word.

"Perfect! Congratulations. You don't have to read anymore."

Father straightened up, and Martin wondered how his heart was bearing up under the strain of the examination. He remembered him in the hospital bed after his first heart attack. Martin had flown in from Denver to find his father in the intensive care unit of a Salt Lake City hospital. Tubes were coming out of his father's nose. Martin was sure that he was dying. That had been fifteen years ago.

"Put your signature on your new driver's license."

Martin watched over his father's shoulder as he signed with the old fountain pen he had brought to America. Writing his name clearly and evenly, he filled the assigned spaces without going beyond the borders set for him.

Martin had to look away. His eyes wandered along the counter until they came to rest on the black machine that had tested his father. Martin imagined that it retained an imprint of his father's face when he had pressed it into the machine, so eager to answer all questions correctly. At least it would be able to keep his father's high forehead, his eyebrows, which he trimmed back so that they would be orderly, and his lids, folded and creased with age. It would remember all the ridges and grooves of his features, but it could not recognize the flare of Father's gooseberry-green eyes, reflecting a fire that he kept banked, and so it could not preserve the real face.

They followed the blue line to the photographer's station. When Martin put his father into the low chair in front of the yellow backdrop of the booth, he saw that the woman behind the camera was the one who had examined him.

"The photographer is taking a break, and I didn't want your father to wait any longer than necessary." She smiled at him. "No, that won't do! Smile a little, but not too much. We're not supposed to take smiling pictures."

The camera flashed twice, and his father got up.

"How long will it be until we get the license?" Martin wanted his father to sit down and rest, although he looked slim and fit in his navy-blue blazer and not tired at all.

"It won't take more than five minutes to develop the picture and laminate the license. You can take it with you and you don't have to come back."

"Are you sure that you don't want to sit down?" Martin asked his father.

"No, we should go home. Mother will worry."

They walked slowly back and forth as if they were on a promenade at a European spa. When they came to the end of the blue line, they stopped. From there they could see the Toronado parked close to the entrance. Almost playfully, his father peered along the blue line, as he used to do at his building sites. "How far do you think it is to the doors?"

Martin also looked along the line, but he shrugged. He had never been as good as his father at estimating distances.

"Thirty-five meters," Father said.

Martin expected him to take out a pad and a pencil stub from his pockets and jot down the distance, not as estimate but as fact.

Martin watched his father stride along the blue line with a stretch to his steps so they would give exact measure. He had drawn himself up, and he walked with exaggerated steps, as if he were marching toward the sunlight behind the glass doors.

When they picked up the license, both men shook hands with the examiner. Martin didn't bow, but his father did, and the woman smiled at him as if he were a Continental gentleman calling on her.

As they walked toward the exit, Father stopped and pointed toward the golden car parked under the olive tree with two trunks and the sunshine and the blue sky. With his circle of white hair, he might have been Moses on a rocky ledge of Mount Nebo gazing into the land of promise.

"Look at that golden background behind your head," Mother said. "Something special for Papa."

Martin didn't have the heart to tell her that everybody in the state would be photographed for a whole year in front of the same yellow background.

"You could have smiled."

"I did. When they were through with me."

"Look at him! Now he smiles."

They laughed as if with one voice.

"I'll lie down for a while."

Martin embraced his father.

"Either you're still growing or I'm getting smaller."

Martin didn't answer, but he kissed his father and watched him walk down the corridor to the bedroom. Then he picked up the plastic card from the kitchen table.

"Be careful!" Mother warned. "The license might still be wet."

"I'm just checking for mistakes. Height: five-ten," Martin read aloud. "Hair: gray; eyes: green." He examined the picture more closely. "You know, his eyes don't really show green in the photo." But for some reason he couldn't put down the card from which his father's eyes were looking at him, not unkindly but without any lightheartedness. And under the mustache that looked so much like his son's, the line of his mouth ran straight and level to its corners.

"That's it, I guess," Martin said, but he still didn't let go of the card. He was shocked when he saw how deep his father's head had sunk into his shoulders. Had his father declined so much, unnoticed by his son, who saw him every day? Although his neck may have shrunk into the collar of his jacket, the bent of his nose made him look even more fierce. It was as if his shoulders had been frozen in the upward motion of a defiant shrug that said, "No, I will not." And then, of course, there was his signature, which moved evenly along the line under the old face, as if the letters were soldiers drilled to march in formation.

"I guess that's it," repeated Martin as he turned toward the door.

He stopped in the carport by the Toronado. For the drive home from the test, he had asked his father if he wanted to take the wheel. He had driven smoothly and swiftly, so much so that the speedometer had rolled above the speed limit. Martin had tapped his hand in the air in imitation of his father's cautioning motion, but he had pretended not to notice. Martin stroked the sloping rear deck of the car. He could see how the metallic paint had faded in the desert sun.

"*My father, my father,*'" he said, recalling the quote that neither of his parents had been able to remember fully. "*And Elisha saw and cried, 'My father, my father . . .'*" Then he too faltered and all he remembered was the last line: "*And he saw him no more.*'"

A Ransom for Tedek

"Listen to this," Ala said. "In 1937 Wanda, my aunt, allowed her fifteen-year-old daughter, Cesia, to live with a cavalry officer serving in the Fourteenth Uhlan Regiment stationed in Lvov. Maybe she actually *sent* Cesia to him? My mother said that he was as handsome as if he had been painted, but they said that about all uhlans. When war threatened, his regiment, together with the other units of the Podolska Cavalry Brigade, was transported by train to the German border. Of all the Polish cavalry it was the Fourteenth Uhlan Regiment, the Jazlowiecki, that received the assignment to strike through the German lines and ride on into Berlin. After three weeks of war—and probably much sooner—this plan had proved to have been a dream.

"By then the Fourteenth Uhlans had taken part in the battle at the Bzura River and were fighting their last major engagement by breaking through the main line of the Germans at Weglowa Wolka. Riding eastward, in the direction of Warsaw, not westward toward Berlin, they fought through the Kampinos Forest, carrying their lances—with pennants furled—in a horse-drawn baggage wagon, which followed another horse wagon with the radio equipment.

Warsaw was already burning when they rode in to defend the capital with other uhlans, infantry, and artillery units until its surrender on September 27, 1939. The 120,000 soldiers who survived the bombardment and the shelling were taken prisoners of war."

"You really have a marvelous memory," Martin said, "and you know how bad I feel about my own forgetfulness." He stood in the shallow end of the swimming pool at what he called his "summer desk," two overturned drawers stacked on top of each other on the edge of the deck.

"Jan told me all of that, because you have asked me so much about uhlans," Ala said.

"You were staying with him in Warsaw?"

"With Cesia and Jan. They keep a room for me. Imagine, my own room in Warsaw. In the evenings we would sit together, talking and drinking. Jan is quite a collector of military history, especially the first few weeks of the last war, when there still was a Polish army. He told me about the Fourteenth Uhlans. It interested me because they were stationed in my hometown. Jan told me that their official motto was 'Hey, girls, lift up your skirts, here comes a Jazlowiecki uhlan.' So Jan told me about the uhlans while Cesia tried to get me to smuggle gold out of Russia."

"What if they would find it on you at the Soviet border?"

"That's what I said to her, 'What if they find it?' She said with a shrug, 'Gold is cheap in Russia, and I'll teach you how to hide it so that they never find it. I know how.'

"Then she told me about life in Auschwitz.

"During the war they caught her on a train while she was on a courier run for the Polish underground. For most of her time in Auschwitz she worked in barracks called Kanada."

"Kanada?" Martin asked.

"Some say that it comes from '*Keiner da*,' 'no one there.' It was a place nobody was supposed to know. All the clothing that was stripped from the prisoners when they came in to Auschwitz was brought to Kanada. Cesia worked there for two years.

"'We undid all of the seams,' Cesia told me, 'and then we made piles according to what it was that we found hidden: rings, diamonds, dollars, gold coins. Mostly in the overcoats, where there are more places to hide things.

"'Then,' Cesia said, 'I had to carry the bags to another part of the camp and when I passed from one section to another I gave the ss guard a little bag. They became used to me passing through with the little bags.'

"By that time Cesia had another glass to drink and she kept talking. 'The black ones didn't scream.'

"'Black ones?' I asked. 'Sephardics?' Cesia didn't listen to me and didn't answer, but kept talking.

"'Men, women, and children. The black ones walked slowly as if a spell had been put on them. We screamed, the red-haired ones, the blond ones, we screamed, but the black ones walked in silent columns.' If Cesia hadn't been drinking with me, she wouldn't have told me, because never before did we talk about that place.

"You know that I always go to Auschwitz when I'm in Poland," Ala said. "It's strange, but from the outside the place reminds me of Fort Douglas, the layout and the old brick buildings."

Martin remembered Fort Douglas. In graduate school at Utah they often had lunch at the officers' open mess, sometimes every day of the week, and they had gone to the crowded happy hour on Friday nights.

"The first pavilion in Auschwitz that I saw is the hardest for me, with pictures of children from Polish villages. The boys have their heads shorn, the girls have small kerchiefs. The children—" Ala stopped, trying to hold herself together. "They had such . . . such potato faces. Scared potato faces."

Hunched over his summer desk Martin happened to murmur "mussulman, mussulman," repeating it as if it were the refrain of a song stuck in his mind.

"Why are you saying this?" Ala asked sharply. She was sitting submerged to her waist on the steps leading into the pool.

"I don't know. Maybe I was thinking of another word. Maybe 'muscle man,' which might have led to 'mussulman,' I don't know."

"Mussulman, in the camps they used to call a walking corpse, the emaciated . . ."

"Let's not talk."

"Last week at the hotel this happened during breakfast rush. A man sat down without first handing over his ticket. At a table for four yet and he, he was just a single. When I asked him for his meal ticket and wondered aloud how he had gotten past the cashier, he gave me his ticket, telling me that he himself had picked out this table. He was already eating when I talked to him. A bowl of cold cereal. He should have waited at the door—you know that—then given me his ticket and then I would have shown him to the right table."

Things like that happen to her, Martin thought, because she takes her job so seriously.

Ala took a sip of wine and put the glass back down on the deck. She sat where she always did when she was in the swimming pool, on the steps in the shallow end, by the tall cypress. Martin stood in the shade of the olive tree where he always stood when he was in the pool. Today he had picked up Ala after work and brought her over to his house that used to be their house until they divorced years ago.

"I wanted to make him move to a smaller table, because we had a line of people waiting to be seated for breakfast. While I was talking, I looked down and I saw *the* number tattooed on his forearm. I don't think that it was from Auschwitz. Must have been a different camp, because the Auschwitz numbers I have seen were smaller."

"Maybe just another number tattooer?" asked Martin.

"'Because of this,' I said, pointing to his arm, 'you can stay at this table.'"

"'Yes,' he said with a really long drawn-out *yes*, 'this is my zip code.'"

"Then I smiled at him and asked, 'Do you want to sit by the window?' I mean, it wouldn't have been easy for me to do that, but I would have tried. He could have sat by the window and looked out at the pool, the palm trees, and the women tanning on the chaises.

"'No, this is fine,' he said. 'I'm finished.'

"Walking back to the hostess desk by the door I looked over my shoulder and saw him pick up another small bowl of cereal and carry it carefully from the buffet to his table. He could have had lox or even omelets, but he took cereal. The people next in my line were an elderly couple. Although it was a busy morning, I smiled at them."

She let her legs float to the surface and reached forward to massage her toes.

"Who knows, I might not have smiled at them otherwise."

"On *that* day they served herring. Everybody in the whole *Gasthaus* ate herring."

Ala was talking about another time and another place. Martin knew if he listened patiently, the connection would be revealed to him because there always was a connection in Ala's history.

"When I had enough ration coupons, I went there almost every night. To cut out the proper coupons, the waiter had a pair of scissors dangling from a cord tied around his waist as if he were a sommelier and they were the keys to the wine cellar. Sometimes they even had a dish that you could buy without him snipping a coupon from your ration card, like herring salad. Maybe in 1945 they had more fish in Düsseldorf than in other cities in Germany because it wasn't that far to the North Sea, although I never got to go and see it until years later." She stared down in front of her as if she were looking for something on the bottom of the pool. "The restaurant stood on a corner of the Karlsplatz, near the underground air raid shelter where they had put me up . . ."

"Down. They put you *down*."

When she was talking about the past, she didn't appreciate interruptions, as if they might break the spell.

"The place was called Puff."

"Puff?" Both of them laughed.

"The owner's name was above the door: Karl Puff."

She looked down into the pool again, and he knew that it wouldn't be a lighthearted story she had begun to tell him. "One day, they had smoked herring. For that you needed coupons, although the herring salad was free. The waiter, who knew me, brought me a good-sized fish, lying on one of those heavy plates they have in places where they worry about breakage."

He listened to her voice over the humming of the pool motor. Looking at a stand of bamboo by the edge of the pool, he noticed that the ends of the light-green leaves were beginning to turn yellow and to curl. He would have to fertilize it.

"Over by the window, in an alcove, sat a couple that I noticed whenever I came in. The same waiter who knew me and brought me a bigger herring told me another time that the Americans had freed the couple from a camp. That day, the woman didn't begin to eat immediately like everybody else—people were hungry all the time—but she first looked at the herring and then turned her head slowly to look out the window. She had big blue eyes. They might have seemed bigger to me because her face looked shrunken, as if her hair had been pulled back too tightly."

Ala took a sip from her glass on the edge of the deck.

"I was observing people in those days all the time because I was painting for a living. Herr Cybulski was selling everything that I drew or painted. Money wasn't worth much and people bought what they could get." She shrugged.

"After a while the woman with the blue eyes looked down at the fish as if the waiter had just set down the plate in front of her, but it had been there for a while. She looked down as the sun reflected golden from the scales of the herring on her plate and then her big blue eyes filled with tears."

She stopped talking, her head now turned away from him, in the direction of the side gate, as if she expected someone to come along the path.

"It made me angry. Can you understand that?" She didn't look at Martin and couldn't see that he nodded, but she didn't seem to expect an answer. "Here I was living underground in a strange city, thinking that my parents and my twin sister were dead, sleeping in my clothes for fear that someone would come after me. The war was over, but the conditions were still terrible. During the war we had gone from Lvov and the Russians, to Warsaw, and finally in 1944—days before the Polish Uprising—from Warsaw to Austria. During the last months of the war I traveled from there—by myself—all the way through Austria and up into North Germany. I was sixteen and a survivor." She looked up and pointed at a hummingbird sitting on the lowest of the wires. They both watched the tiny bird in silence until it flew away.

"That woman made me angry. When you're bad off, you hate the people who are worse off."

He walked back to his papers and wanted to pick up the book

that he had been reading, but he couldn't. He looked out from the shadow of the olive tree at the dark red oleanders along the fence that had become almost invisible behind the bushes they had planted together after they had bought the house. Ever since then they had used the shallow end of the swimming pool as an extension of their living room. During the long hot summers she would sit by the cypress while he was standing at his summer desk under the olive tree.

They were talking in the pool even before the sale of the house had become final. The swimming pool was still empty and the overgrown garden very quiet. It was never as quiet after that once the pool pump and the air-conditioning motor were running. They had driven to town just to take another look at their new house, and they had sat, shoulder by shoulder, on the narrow steps. They had eaten hearts of palm with their fingers from a can and drunk cold duck. They talked about how life would be once they had moved. That had been more than twenty years ago. Since then they had moved in, were divorced, and he had stayed on in the house. She now visited.

"In Tbilisi . . ."

"You've never been to Tbilisi."

"I had an uncle, Tedek, who, as a soldier under the czar, was sent to the Caucasus, to Georgia. Years later, when he was happy that Zofia and I were visiting, he would tell us, 'In Tbilisi . . .' and then he would pause and smile, 'the houses hang on the mountainside like swallows' nests.'"

She put on her reading glasses to look through a large manila envelope stuffed with photos that she had been bringing with her for the last few days.

"You remember that Tedek was sent to a concentration camp?"

Yes, he knew, but he kept confusing the foreign names of her various relatives. Maybe it was not so important to remember detail, he told himself whenever he forgot, so long as you remembered at all.

"Here." Ala pushed a photograph over to Martin. "This is Tedek, the husband of Stefania, my mother's sister."

He forced back the serrated edges of the snapshot—of different size and proportions than American pictures—that, with time, had curled inward. It reminded him of pressing his thumbnails in along the seam of a pea pod and gently prying it open. He hadn't done it since he was a child in his parents' garden, but right now—standing up to his knees in his swimming pool—he could taste the sweetness of the line of shiny young peas.

The photograph showed a man and a woman huddling under an umbrella. He held it up for Ala to see.

"That was a mountain party at Turka. I don't remember the year, but I know it was the earliest that Easter was ever celebrated. On the twelfth of March. There was an argument among the relatives having to do with Stefania's hair. She finally said, 'Only very intelligent women wear their hair like that. Wally Simpson, for example,' and then, to make sure that all understood, she added, 'the Duchess of Windsor.'"

Ala pushed an album at him, not much larger than a wallet and also made from leather. A blue flower had been painted on it—a gentian, he guessed—but it was almost worn off. He had seen the album before and remembered the hand-painted flower. Standing behind him she opened the album to one of the first pages. He looked down at two pictures that, side by side, had been glued on coarse wartime paper. The photo on the left showed a man and a woman standing next to each other in the sand. Neither of them was dressed for the beach.

"Where was this taken?"

"At the Baltic."

The woman wore an expensive-looking flowery summer dress, belted at the waist and closed tightly at the throat. The man had turned toward his wife and not toward the photographer as she had done. He wore suit pants and a white dress shirt with a tie. His round shaven head glistened in the sunshine. The sand lay flat under their street shoes, and the sea, without the slightest scrawl of surf, lay like a smooth, dark band between the white sand and the white sky.

The picture on the right showed the couple on board a ship, maybe even on the same day, because both are dressed in the way they were in the other picture, except the man now wears his suit jacket. They have been joined by another woman, and the man stands between them—under a lifeboat hanging from its davits—his arms linked with each woman. In the distance Martin could see a city.

"Where is this?"

"It says right there." Ala sounded irritated.

"I don't speak Polish. You know that."

"What does it say? Read what is written."

Looking at the faded pen markings on the porous gray paper, he slowly pushed his reading glasses upward on his nose.

"Don't bother with your glasses. It's Gdynia. Gdynia is the harbor . . ."

"I *know.* I know it's near Danzig."

"Gdansk," she corrected him.

He looked down at the picture again. Underneath Gdynia he deciphered "1939" in faint blue pen markings.

"What did he do for a living?" He looked at the stout, well-dressed man in a series of pictures she wordlessly had put in his hand.

"He was a treasurer, maybe a comptroller? I think that he was the head cashier at the Franco-Polish Bank in Warsaw."

Standing at his desk, he jotted some quick notes on his yellow pad. He knew that it irritated her when he wrote while she spoke, but he also knew that she secretly wanted him to write down what she said, to record what would be lost without her and might even be lost in spite of her. Their children didn't seem to care for the past, neither the past of their parents nor their own.

Last Friday—Ala's day off from the hotel—Martin had decided to stop by to see how she was, although he kept thinking about the list of things he had to do, which lay on the passenger seat. She stood on the landing in front of her door, dressed in an olive-colored jumpsuit, whose legs were stained black up to her knees from watering her garden.

"Come in and sit down," she said, throwing the hose into the ivy on the other side of her walk.

"No, I really can't."

"Last night and early this morning I've been reading one of the books I brought back from Warsaw. I wish that you could read it too. Stories about country life, written by Roman Turek."

"I've never heard of him." He worried that Ala was at the beginning of a lengthy story and that it would make him late.

"Roman Turek worked as a furnace man in the brandy distillery of Count Potocki. During the years he worked he didn't have time to write. It wasn't until after he was pensioned that he began writing down the tales he'd been telling for years to the people he met."

The front of her house had become so overgrown with cypress, oleander, and especially ivy, whose runners had grown as heavy as tree branches, that her landing looked like a tree house jutting out into a forest thicket.

Martin looked down at the book on the small round table.

"Why is there a chair drawn on the cover?"

"Roman Turek's room was very small, and all he had was that chair. In order to write he knelt down in front of that chair and wrote on its seat."

"He didn't even have a table?"

"Real work you do on your knees. That's what he used to tell people."

A cat came up and rubbed against Ala's legs, but shied away when it felt the wetness of her suit.

"He wrote for survival." Her face had become very intense, her eyelids blinking rapidly. "He *had* to write." After a moment she added, "I want to write." She sounded wistful and defiant at the same time.

"You don't have the patience."

She walked with him to his car, stopping only to pull the watering hose out of the ivy. While he was backing out of her driveway he thought how insensitive his remark had been. She stopped on the landing by her wicker chair and her small round table with the open book and waved good-bye as he drove away.

"I remember one night Tedek realized that he hadn't locked one of the safes in the bank. Worried, he walked down to the taxi stand, but at this time of night he couldn't find a cab, and so he began to run and he ran through all of Warsaw to the bank. Such a conscientious man."

Ala was forcing the "recording" now, Martin thought while writing as fast as he could to keep up with her and not to forget what she had told him.

Yesterday Martin had been so exasperated that he had compared his own task to that of Clemens Brentano's. He admitted something like that only to himself. He hadn't thought of the poet for a long time—maybe since a Romanticism course in school—but he remembered that Brentano for years wrote down every word spoken by a stigmatized nun. That night Martin had looked up Brentano's life. For five years Brentano, somewhere in Westphalia, had transcribed the sayings and visions of Anna Katharina Emmerick while she bled from the wounds in her hands and feet.

For whom did Ala want him to write? For her or for him? He put his pencil down and the block of art gum he held in his other hand. It had to do with time. Maybe she wanted what she remembered to stay undiminished by time, which now was overtaking both of them. Who after them would know the stories? Who would remember the heroic run through the night of the conscientious head cashier of the Franco-Polish Bank in Warsaw?

"In a way it was Stefania's fault that Tedek was sent to the camp. In the evenings she would tell him at five o'clock, 'Tedeczek, do your duty.' Then she made him carry out the pamphlets of the underground. Every day he went at the same time, through the same little doors and narrow gates. He would cut through the gardens that connected all of the villas and he may have been observed for a long time, we never knew. They caught him once in a *razzia,* a street raid, taking him first to the Paviak, where they sorted out everyone they had caught in their dragnet, but they didn't keep him. My parents used to say—even then—'It was she, Stefania, who sent Tedek into battle.' Then he was arrested in winter, taken away in his pajamas, shaking nervously. Thinking of Tedek's bald head, my mother said, 'Surely, they beat him on his head.' You know Mother's wild imaginings.

"One day when I didn't feel well I was sent home from school. It was a humid day in Warsaw and from the windows of the streetcar the whole city looked gray. Although I sat by an open window and the wind blew in, I was becoming sick.

"When I opened the door at home, I saw that our whole family sat in the living room. Something serious was happening. Our *whole* family, even uncles and aunts. Not Zofia, of course, because she was still in school, nor Broniu, who was in a German prisoner of war camp for officers. Did I show you the postcards they let him write home? Nor Cesia and Tedek, who at the same time were both in Auschwitz."

Ala took a net from the deck and scooped up a cluster of dried olive leaves, each one sharp as a dart, that drifted by on the pool's current. Then she sat in silence.

"Why was the whole family together?"

"Oh, yes. When I think of that day, what I see is the greenery outside threatening to press into the living room through the big windows. On that humid day, they were all together, talking about Tedek, because the night before Stefania had received a visitor who brought an offer from someone at the camp, an offer of ransom for her husband.

"It wasn't Stefania who had called the family together. All she had done was talk to one of her sisters about the offer, and everybody came. Stefania mentioned that the woman living across the street, Madame Adrianowicz, had bought out her husband from Auschwitz."

Ala pointed to a large dragonfly shimmering bluish in the sunlight, clinging to a piece of bamboo as thin as a wire, right by the edge of the pool. When she continued to speak, it was very softly, so as not to scare the dragonfly away.

"I still see them all in the living room," she whispered.

"What was decided? What did she say?"

"'Tedeczek will survive.' Then Stefania took a deep breath. 'If he doesn't survive, I'll be a hero's widow.'"

The pump motor sounded loud, as if it had to work harder to push the water through the pool.

"I still see them, sitting on their green leather chairs drawn in a circle around Stefania."

Ala pulled the visor of her white cap down to shade her eyes.

"Stefania was a romantic person. This whole underground thing was romantic for her, while Tedek was a down-to-earth person. Maybe this went with his occupation as a banker.

"She was a hard woman. There were to be no pets at the dining table, that's what she decreed, but Tedek was feeding the dogs under the table, furtively dipping down first one shoulder and then the other when he fed the second dog.

"The messages on the pamphlets that Tedek carried out and laid on the doorsteps of the houses in his neighborhood were copied down from BBC broadcasts. Many promises, no practical purpose. Maybe it was good for the morale of the underground, but nothing more than that."

"That was worth something," Martin said, although he didn't know how much it was worth.

"He did like his piano. Before he sat down Tedek would sort through stacks of yellowed sheet music piled high on both ends of the piano, as if he were searching for something very special, but when he began to play it was always the same: gypsy romances and Ave Marias.

"His nails were too long. When he played his nails went *krch, krch, krch* on the ivory of the piano keys, making it sound like a dog on the parquet floor.

"Zofia and I, we also played piano. Four-handed most of the time, and most of the time we were fighting, pushing and hitting each other. One day when we were visiting at Stefania's house, we were rummaging through the sheet music in the piano bench and found many bank notes inserted among the pages of the gypsy romances. In triumph we carried our find—large bills, unfamiliar to us in color and size—to Stefania, telling her that we had uncovered a treasure. She yelled at us. We didn't understand why they had hidden away money, but we didn't ask.

"That's when Mother attacked her sister. 'You ought to scold and educate your *own* child, but, ah, you aborted it.' That wasn't the only time this matter came up. Once both of them sat on the sofa and talked. They didn't know that we could hear them, when Mother asked Stefania: 'Should I get rid of mine the way you got rid of yours?' Even then we knew what Mother meant. And she didn't have any more children after us, but you know that.

"Then they argued which one of them had suffered more.

"Maybe all of the arguing over the years between Mother and her sister began when my father didn't marry Stefania as had been planned. She was the older of the sisters, but one day when he was in the house, my mother came running in, her face flushed from playing outside, and my father became interested in *her*. She was fourteen at the time."

Ala picked through the manila envelope.

"Right here is a photo of Tedek at his piano."

It was a small photo that seemed to have been glued down at one time. Martin examined it carefully. Judging by its back, it had been torn from an album. He was sorry that it was so small, because he wanted to enjoy the ornate details of a period living room. At first he didn't see Tedek at all, because his eyes were drawn to the brightly lit woman in the left foreground. She poses on the sofa, holding an open book in her hands. She is not looking down at the book but straight ahead, past the camera. It would be a somber room were it not for the bright panels of curtained windows in its center. Far over to the right, out of the light and in the background as if he were a small statue decorating the room, Tedek sits at the piano. His banker's suit blends into the darkness of the corner and only his shaven head keeps him from being invisible. His head is turned away from the sheet music propped up on the piano, and he gazes directly into the camera, as if he is saying, "I'm here too."

"Then the telegram came from Auschwitz. . . . They wanted to sell Stefania an urn with Tedek's ashes."

"Did she buy it?"

An olive plopped into the water from a branch hanging low over the pool. He curled his toes around the olive and lifted it out of the water.

She didn't continue immediately.

"They wanted six hundred zloty for the ashes if they were delivered in a wooden container, eight hundred zloty for a metal one. Of course, metal was rare during the war. Did you have scrap metal drives at school too?"

He nodded.

"Again the family deliberated about Tedek. Even Marian Rybicki was there, a distant cousin, an intense, tall, square-faced Communist, maybe twenty at that time. Nobody in our family seemed to mind that he was a Communist. Zofia and I didn't like him for other reasons. Once we found love letters written by his fiancée. My sister read them aloud to me, doubling over laughing. Then we squeezed his toothpaste out and filled the empty tube from the bottom with Vaseline."

"What happened to Marian?"

"After the war he became minister of justice until he lost his position because his son was involved in some *machloykes*."

"What did he do?"

"Maybe theft, a stolen automobile, I don't know. My father loved his stamp albums. When he worked on his collection Marian sat with him and they would argue about anti-Semitism."

"Dangerous in the middle of the war."

"I can't even remember which side of the argument my father took. . . . It was such a valuable philatelic collection. In 1945, when my parents had made it to Vienna and Father was already getting weak, my mother traded the stamp collection for three loaves of bread.

"But on this day, when the air weighed heavy in the room and one of the women sobbed and wailed, 'What remains? What remains?' Marian sat with the family, muttering, '*Zemsta, zemsta,* revenge, revenge.' Once more the members of our family sat in the green leather chairs, and they all surrounded Stefania."

"And?"

"She didn't buy the ashes."

Yesterday morning, having come earlier than usual to take her to work, he had time enough to sit in the wicker chair on her landing. As always in the mornings her door stood wide open—"letting the house breathe," she said—and he could hear the music she was playing. Most of her records were Polish or Russian, brought back from her trips to the east, but what he heard this morning was a man and a woman singing in English. The song was a sad one, played softly, of a sprig of lilac placed on a coffin and a bird singing from the swamp.

Over the music he heard her footsteps on the wooden floors as she walked from room to room, readying herself for work. In a quiet moment she had told him what she was thinking as she walked through her house. "I'm having my morning devotion." Walking past her icons—glowing in brass, copper, and silver from the dark paneled walls—her statues of saints and peasants, a large painting of her mother that somehow had survived the many moves, Huzul axes and bowls wound from straw rope and filled with carved wooden eggs, she silently remembered the faces of those in her family who had perished in the war or who had died since. Even Martin's father and grandmother were part of this ritual. "I do this every morning," she had said, "instead of going to church."

"After the war, long after, it was actually through Stefania that I found Cesia again. On my first trip back to Warsaw I had gone to the cemetery, to the family plot. I wrote a note—'Who is taking care of this grave?'—and slipped it under one of the four iron rings used to lift up the granite slab whenever another one of us was to be buried beneath it. Two days later I heard from Cesia."

"How did Cesia survive?"

"She was young and beautiful."

"How old was she when they sent her away?"

Ala figured silently.

"She was in camps from the time she was nineteen till she was twenty-three."

"That's when she was liberated?"

"When I was in Warsaw last May, we were sitting one night, drinking and talking, she, Jan—her husband—and I, when she told me how she came home in 1945. Toward the end of the war she and a group of other inmates were moved from Auschwitz to a camp near Hamburg." She turned toward Martin. "I've forgotten its name. A double name with a hyphen? Maybe it was Ravensbrück. They marched the inmates. Those who were too weak . . . For some reason they had a lot of *Panzerfäuste* in that area . . ." She didn't go on.

He remembered, as a boy at the end of the war, the *Panzerfäust* and how some of the older boys were being trained in the use of the hand-held antitank rocket.

"They had many of these *Panzerfäuste,* and since there were no enemy tanks to crack open they shot those who couldn't walk anymore with these antitank rockets. 'It went *poof,*' she said, and then the gray stuff flew out of their heads like balloons. They kept shooting and it went *poof, poof, poof.*

"'Before that I enjoyed eating brains with scrambled eggs,' Cesia said, 'but after I came back I couldn't do it again. I never dream of the camps, except after I see something on television,' and she gestured with her cigarette at the set. 'Fifty years and they still go on.'

"'If it gives you nightmares, why do you watch it on television?' I asked her.

"'There's not much to choose from,' she said."

The metallic-blue dragonfly skimmed across the pool. They followed it with their eyes as it darted, hovered over the surface, and darted again.

"When they were freed nobody bothered to give them any transportation. Cesia said it was more like somebody had forgotten to lock the gate. So she talked to some that had walked from Auschwitz with her, and they decided to walk back to Poland. She was in terrible pain at that time. From the train where she had been caught she had been taken to the Paviak and held for a year in Warsaw. They had beaten her on the kidneys. In Auschwitz she'd had a second heavy beating. As she was walking, the deep, open wound on her back was draining and pus was running down her back and her legs.

"They took their time walking home. Stopping along the way they looted, breaking into the houses of people who had fled. I can't imagine where you would flee from North Germany. You wouldn't want to go east where the Russians were. You couldn't go west into Holland or Belgium, because they weren't fond of Germans at that time. You couldn't go north to Denmark. Same reason." She shrugged.

"When they broke into houses, they took food and whatever else they could carry, burning the rest. Somewhere along the way they found a bale of tobacco. Tobacco leaf was like money in those days, so they 'liberated' a handcart and loaded the tobacco in the cart, pulling it along as they kept walking east.

"One day they broke into a house. They thought it was empty, but when they walked into the dining room they saw a well-dressed couple in their sixties, sitting motionless with elbows propped on the table, their faces buried in their hands." She stopped, looking straight ahead.

"The inmates, *former* inmates, I guess they didn't have a new identity yet, were surprised, even stunned by what they saw. Looking at each other they went out to their cart and carried the bale of tobacco to the dining room table. Then they left without saying a word.

"We were talking about many things that night. It was my last night in Warsaw and we stayed up. I've been going back over to Poland more often. One never knows when it is the last time. Cesia talked more, confiding in me. You know what she looks like?"

"You've taken enough photos of her," Martin said. "A dignified lady with gray hair."

"Did you ever notice that in every picture her left eyebrow is raised?"

"You mean like Gustaf Gründgens playing Mephisto?" Martin said, but Ala didn't reply.

"As Cesia and I were talking she became thoughtful and stopped before continuing: 'Who knows, if I hadn't been sent to the camps I might have become the biggest whore in Warsaw.' After a while she said, 'I lie awake in the dark and when I think of some of the things I did, I feel myself blushing.'

"Then Cesia told me something strange: 'Dr. Mengele operated on my crippled thumb. They were going to send me to the quarries, and friends of mine—you may be surprised that in Auschwitz you could have friends, but I had people who protected me—they told Mengele that I had bone cancer. The truth was that while I was still a child I had broken my thumb and it had grown crooked. By then there was more wrong with my hand than just a broken thumb, but I didn't know what. I was taken to Block 11 to Dr. Mengele. He told me that it wasn't bone cancer at all, and then he operated on my thumb and it was normal again and I didn't have to go to the quarries anymore.'

"I don't remember what I told Cesia, but when I hear Mengele's name I get sick. All I have to do is think about the research he did on twins.

"'You know,' Cesia went on, 'one isn't supposed to say things like what I'm going to say. Some things are too holy to speak about and some things are too gruesome, while others are just unpopular. You know what they say about Dr. Mengele, but he did more good than evil.'

"While Cesia was talking to me, she kept looking down as if she was too ashamed to confess to me what she thought and felt.

"You know, Pan Adrianowicz, the man across the street who had been bought free, he was strange too after he was brought out from

Auschwitz. A tall, ruddy-faced man. I remember seeing him on the street, although not often after he came home."

"I imagine that such suffering might make a man strange," Martin said.

"He never mentioned his suffering in the camp, because he never spoke to anyone again, except for saying 'good morning' and 'good-bye.' Even if he wanted to tell them anything, because nobody talked with him about anything that mattered."

"Why?"

"They didn't trust him. He had come home."

Again he picked up the photo of Tedek and Stefania under the umbrella, taken at the earliest Easter ever. It reminded him of a work by a nineteenth-century French salon painter whose name he had forgotten. He last saw it on the cover of an expensive hardbound journal featuring the rediscovery of sentimental art.

The painting showed a boy and girl—Arcadian shepherds?—fleeing from an upcoming storm. They are sheltered by a copper-colored cloak flapping over their heads. The boy has dark, tousled hair, and his arm encircles the fair-haired girl's waist, with his right hand resting lightly under her left breast. Martin was surprised how well he remembered the details of a picture that when he was younger, he had dismissed as kitsch. Actually, he was surprised that he remembered the painting at all, because, as of late, he was forgetting much. At that moment he remembered that her gown had been diaphanous. In his mind he added defiantly, *and always will be.* How inane of me, he thought before he could not help but remember another detail of the painting, the lightning that flashed sulphur yellow over the heads of the lovers.

"I remember Stefania in her gardening dress and sun hat bending down to embrace me. She was startled to find me unannounced at her gate. My parents had sent me ahead from the streetcar stop to surprise my aunt. Her astonishment and then the happiness on her face, I still remember today, and the sunshine while we were in her garden.

"She had created this truly beautiful garden. I always think of Stefania's garden as the garden of paradise. In the morning she went to count her trees. One hundred and twenty-three, she told me with pride. Birches, firs, and pines, with wild strawberries—the tiny ones—growing under the pine trees. Of the fruit trees all I remember are the cherries. She had planted many berries too, gooseberries, raspberries, beds of the big strawberries and currants, red, yellow, and black ones. Under the firs and pines grew mushrooms. Roses, larkspurs, snapdragons, and all colors of dahlias."

The garden grew before Martin's eyes. What Ala had forgotten he filled in from the German garden in which he had grown up: plum trees, apples, pears, peaches, and morello cherries. How could she not have had *sour* cherries in her garden or *black* raspberries?

"*Wunderschön,*" Ala said in admiration, putting emphasis on the first syllable. "You know, for me the real wonder is that Stefania after all that had happened to her had her garden as the fruit of her life. *Her garden was the fruit of her life.* This just came to me as we were talking." She seemed surprised and awed by her insight. "In Tbilisi . . ." She stopped and he waited in silence. She shook her head. "For Tedek I bought a tree in the Martyrs' Forest. Remember? You were there that day in Dornbusch's delicatessen."

The certificate that the tree had been planted in Israel arrived a few weeks later in the mail, picturing a steep hillside with a row of blue-and-white flags at the bottom. The name typed in had not been Tedek but Tedeczek. The certificate—in a thin black metal frame—had hung in their house.

"And in the mornings . . . as I walk through my house, I'm now including Stefania, because who in the whole world thinks of her? The last time when I was in Warsaw I didn't even visit Bohdan. I didn't want to stop by. Although he lives so close to the cemetery he lets Stefania lie under weeds. And it was *she* who made such a beautiful garden.

"Stefania's garden was paradise, but her house was Gehenna. There was always something bad in the house."

Ala had fallen asleep on the water chaise, which drifted slowly away from him until it rested against the diving board.

Martin propped open a book of war paintings on the pool deck, to a double-paged spread showing the cavalry charge at Weglowa Wolka in mid-September of 1939. The work was less than ten years old and its painter unknown to Martin. Looking like a heroic nine-teenth-century painting, it seemed anachronistic to him—like much of the art produced in communist countries—and of no particular interest. Nevertheless, he kept staring at it, because his mind had become trapped by something, except he wasn't sure what it was.

The riders charge from the left across the clearing of a birch forest until the noses of the lead horses touch the white frame on the right. A saber flashes through the gritty air like a moon sliver through torn clouds. A single white horse, its rider blowing the bugle, races to the front of the attack. The bugler's horse is crowded—in full gallop—by another uhlan who is holding high the yellow-and-white swallow-tailed pennant with the regimental colors.

Martin tried to hear the tinny bugle. How did the uhlans sound attack? Probably differently from what he had heard in films, after all, they were riders in a foreign army.

He kept examining the picture, although everything seemed as it ought to be in a painting of horses and men at war. It reminded him of one or the other of Frederic Remington's cavalry charges—although *he* might have painted a diagonal line of attack—or of Henry Fonda under a fluttering flag with his saber drawn, leading a suicidal charge into a box canyon. There was even the same dust cloud, although it wasn't the alkali of the Apache country but dust raised from the brownish grass of a desolate forest clearing in Poland.

He walked out of the pool to get a magnifying glass. Padding along the deck, he left dark footprints on the porous stone. He hated to track water onto the living room carpet, but he had to take a closer look at the picture.

Not a painter of men, Martin concluded, but of horses, which seemed to have been constructed from muscle clusters. The horses were featured in different positions of the gallop, some with two, others even with four legs off the ground. He wondered if the number of legs in the air meant what it did on monuments of riders, denoting if the hero shown was wounded in battle or had fallen. Which of them had died? The longer he looked at the painting, the more he became disturbed by the lack of proportion between the large, finely detailed horses and the smallness and insignificance of the riders, who seemed like jockeys except that they didn't wear flashy racing silks. But the horses were as detailed as the thoroughbreds in the English hunting prints he had seen in a prime rib restaurant in town.

He examined the cavalrymen, but only briefly, because he could not find anything at all in their faces. They reminded him of the tin soldiers that he, as a boy, had cast in a mold, a Christmas present from his father. Whenever he used lead and pewter in the right proportion, they came out shiny with perfection, each newly cast soldier looking exactly like those already lined up in marching formation on the kitchen table.

There was no enemy in the painting. The forward-directedness—a force he couldn't find anywhere in the olive-drab bodies of the men but *did* see in the definition of the leg muscles of the cavalry horses—found no opposing force in the painting. Everything slanted forward toward the white border on the right, where it found no resistance.

Then he saw something for the first time: the bright fan of an artillery shell exploding under the belly of a dark brown horse, the force of which lifted the hindquarters of the horse high off the ground. The painting was so busy with motion that he hadn't noticed the stumbling horse, its neck twisted toward him as its head hit the ground.

Studying the background more closely he saw the puffs of exploding shells hanging in the birch trees like white blossoms too large for their branches. A chain of small white fans crossed the foreground, settling in the grass like shuttlecocks batted behind the boundary line, coming from a machine gun firing low, somewhere to the right beyond the frame of the painting.

An uhlan breaking out of the middle of the squadron was flinging up his lance. Martin noticed that he was the only cavalryman to carry such a weapon. Moving the magnifying glass, Martin saw why the rider was throwing his lance like a spear at the enemy: the uhlan had been hit. He was clapping one hand to his face as if he didn't want to see what lay ahead to the right, while with the other he tried to keep his grip on the heavy cavalry lance.

Martin's eyes traveled once more across the scene—reading against its grain of motion—until he finally saw something else he hadn't noticed before: None of the uhlans wore a *czapka,* the lancer's cap he had seen so often in such paintings; they wore steel helmets instead. The helmets, tiny in this painting, looked exactly like those worn by the French infantry during the war of 1914. Painted by a clumsy artist, the ridge running along the top made the helmets look like Magritte bowler hats crowned with broad cockscomb.

Why had he become trapped by this painting, which had little or nothing to do with Tedek and the others in Ala's story? Had Tedek ever even ridden a horse? What difference did it make if the riders wore *czapkas* or French steel helmets, maybe bought in France as surplus from another, an older, war?

Before closing the book, he backed away from it, looking at the picture from the distance of the one step he had taken toward the deep end of the pool. He squinted at the painting through the reflections flashing up from the rippling water into the dark green canopy of the olive tree.

All the horses were gliding past him on a cloud of white dust, illuminated from within like a Baroque ascension. He heard the bugle bleating faintly, as if calling already from another clearing, and the kettledrums thumping as they had when he was a boy. The horses now moved—some higher, some lower—as if impaled on the platform of a carousel. Then the calliope began to play "Old Comrades," and he half expected—stepping closer because of this—that the horses nosing into the white space on the right would return on the left, their nostrils bellowing out from the exhilaration of the ride, but now their saddles would be empty.

"I dreamed that I had something in my eye," Ala said drowsily. "Touching my finger to it I pulled out what was hurting me. The blue dragonfly had drowned in my eye."

She sounded as sad as a young girl.

"What are you reading?" She slowly paddled the chaise over to him.

"I was studying a painting of the charge of the uhlans at Weglowa Wolka."

"I think that the Polish Legion had a song, *'Jak to na wojence'*: 'It's beautiful in battle . . .' I'm translating, I'm still half asleep. 'When an uhlan falls from his horse, the others don't pity him as their horses trample his body.' My father used to say that this was the dumbest war song he had ever heard."

"I remember standing on the balcony of the house in Lvov next to Mother with my sister on her other side, when we saw the first Polish soldiers retreating down our street. Their uniforms were already in tatters and they looked exhausted. Many had dirty, bloody bandages, hanging loosely on them as if their bodies had shrunk from the bitter but brief war.

"Mother gripped our hands and murmured, 'They look as if they've been fighting for three years, not three weeks.' We watched for a while, then Mother—I'm sure without thinking about it—began to sing a few lines from a song about the uhlans: 'What kind of lady are you, that the painted boys run after you?' Then she pulled us into our living room as if it were too dangerous to stay outside. With her back already turned away from the street and those on it, she said bitterly, 'The last of the Grand Armée.' This sounded strange to us, because the only pictures we had seen of Napoleon in defeat showed him riding through snow up to his horse's belly, but this was a hot day in September. It didn't make sense, but we didn't ask any questions."

"What became of Cesia's uhlan?" Martin asked. "The one she loved when she was fifteen?"

"Cesia's uhlan disappeared forever."

Ala drifted on the current to the last sunlight floating over the deep end of the pool.

Looking through the stack of pictures she had left on the deck, Martin found a photo that Ala hadn't shown him, an overexposed view of a terrace. The walls are bled white with a black rectangle rising in the center of the picture, a door leading into the house.

Tedek—his plump outline by now unmistakable to Martin—plays the violin in the darkness of the open door. One of the twins stands awkwardly in the lower left-hand corner as if she had run into the shot and after seeing the camera had stopped in mid-motion wherever she happened to be. Maybe she had been charmed by the violin music.

Looking closely at the door and the shuttered windows, barely visible in their outlines, Martin realized that this was the reverse of the photo of the living room. He estimated where Tedek's dark corner would be with his piano with the mahogany bench and the bank notes hidden among the pages of gypsy romances and Ave Marias, where he sat in darkness, his shaven head turned toward the camera.

Now he plays the violin, smiling down at the girl in the white dress, who would surely disappear into the blinding brightness of the wall were it not for her suntanned face, arms, and legs and the bow that sits on her head like a small crown.

The way she threatens to disappear—were it not for her dark face and limbs floating disjointedly in a pool of brightness—reminds him of the icon Ala had brought back for him. The details of the Virgin's robe had been pounded out of silver-plated copper, except for her face, hands, and feet, which were cut out of the metal, exposing dark colors painted on the wooden panel underneath.

Tedek's white shirt stands out against the doorway, which is so black that the violin bow is a ghostly white line. In none of the pictures Martin had seen does Tedek smile as he smiles here, playing in the darkness, for the girl in white, but she has raised her forearm across her chest and stares down at the ground as if she doesn't want to see, hear, or follow.

Cockshut Light

"You were elegant." Mother was talking to Father while she dragged a wicker chair to the foot of his bed. Martin wanted to help, but by the time he had lifted the sleeping dog from his lap, Mother was already cranking down the hospital bed. After the amputation of Father's left leg, Mother had ordered an electric bed for the living room rather than leaving him a single day longer in the hospital.

"Before you get comfortable, help me slide him up. But don't hurt yourself. He looks thin, but he has a heavy skeleton."

Martin winced. He didn't like it when she talked about Father's heavy skeleton, although she'd done it as long as he could remember, usually in men's clothing stores when they had gone shopping with Father. When Martin slipped his arm under his father's back, it felt moist and warm where it had lain on the egg-crate pad. Like lifting up a hen, he thought and remembered how, when they had kept chickens — he had been a child — he had carried them around by putting his hands in the pit between feathered body and wing. That is how his father's back felt. With his left arm Martin clasped his father to his own chest, while supporting himself with his right hand in the warm hollow that his father's head had made in the golden-yellow pillow. Mother liked bold colors, and when she saw something dull or gray, she would ask, "How can I bring some life into it?"

She unbuttoned Father's pajama top. "Can you hold him for another moment?" Together they pulled his jacket off. The flesh of his arms had shrunk so much that his elbows were large knobs. She toweled him and shook baby powder over his bent back and held on to him with one hand while she plucked with the other a freshly laundered jacket from the sofa. When they lowered him onto the yellow pillow, Father smiled at Mother and Martin.

"That's done," she said and smiled at her son. Every morning when he came by on his way to work she proudly presented Father to Martin, alive, cared for, and doing as best as one could expect from a man who had celebrated his ninetieth birthday and had been disabled since the first of the big wars. Martin knew that in spite of all she was doing for Father the coldness was rising from his swollen foot. Not only was it chilling his one remaining leg but it was also moving upward until his whole body would lie cold.

Martin kissed his father and turned away. His father patted Nini, who stood upright, resting her forepaws on the rail of his bed.

"Ah, that's done." Mother sighed while she propped a pillow for her back into the wicker chair. It wasn't comfortable for her, but she wouldn't give it up, because it had been Father's favorite chair before his illness. When he still drove, she had picked out carpet squares in colors she liked from samples bins at a builder's store and had sewn two flat pillows for him. Then he had to give up driving. Now the sun was fading the golden metallic paint on Father's Toronado, which had been parked too long in the same spot. While Father lay sick she refused to accept rides to go shopping, just as she hadn't left Father's room during his six weeks in the hospital. When the surgeon—who was to take Father's leg—had asked Martin why his mother stayed day and night in the hospital room, Martin had apologized that his parents were "Old Country people." And so am I, he should have added, but he had just stood there in his fine American suit and had said nothing. When he later thought that he should have done it, he wasn't even sure that it would have been the truth. Was he an Old Country *mensch* or a man of the New World or possibly something entirely different?

"Today's mail is right by your elbow." When Mother mentioned mail casually yet deliberately, there was bound to be something important in it. Usually it wasn't good news and this was her way of trying to soften the blow.

"Anything?"

"Some bills . . . and a letter from Germany."

From the bottom of the stack protruded an envelope in the wider European format, rimmed with a black border. Martin weighed the death notice in his hand before turning it over for a look at the return address. He found none, and so he tried to decipher the round stamp. Meppen. Herr Friedeler must have died. Although it was more than forty years since he had seen him last, Martin could still hear his thick-soled boot scraping on the sidewalk. Sometimes Martin had seen Herr Friedeler, slight of build and wearing thick glasses, as he rode by on his bicycle to work at Father's office. Although people talked about him, saying that he wasn't a well man, he was not bitter, not then. They were surprised when he married a strong blond woman much younger than he. The picture of health, people in Brockau said about her, meaning he had married her as a sturdy nurse and she had married him for his pension.

From among the pencils and pens of Father's orderly desk tray Martin took a pair of scissors and carefully slit the envelope, knowing that his mother would save the announcement. Reading the black-rimmed card, he saw that it was *Frau* Friedeler who had died and not her husband, who had always seemed much closer to death's door. When he picked up the envelope once more he saw that it was addressed in *Herr* Friedeler's hand. Martin should have recognized the handwriting from his letters as his mother must have done, letters that almost always complained about the boring life in the town on the moors. After the war he had been sent there as a refugee, but he was still considered an outsider by the locals. In every letter he discussed his illnesses, but that was true of many of the people who wrote to Martin's parents. He wondered how Herr Friedeler would cope without his nurse to look after him, living in a town among the peat bogs, where no one wanted to know him and where he did not want to be.

Pushing the card to the end of the table, Martin thought that Mother was doing the right thing by keeping the death of Frau Friedeler from Father, who might never again ask about his former cashier and his wife.

"Yes, you *were* elegant." Mother talked toward the bed. Pushing her shoulders back against the hard pillow, she turned to Martin. "It keeps going though my mind. When we first met . . . on the stairs, he wore a tailored suit. Very fashionable. Midnight-blue with a handkerchief in his pocket, as white as blossoms. It was during a weekend conference at the Elisabet Gymnasium. The next day he wore a different suit."

"What color was the other suit?" Martin had always liked to hear about the church conference where his parents met.

"Dove-blue."

"Dove-gray?"

"Dove-blue."

"I remember that he had three suits made all at once," Martin said. "The next time I'm in Europe I think I'll have a suit made in London."

"When you go away what will we do without you?" The pillows muffled his father's voice.

He is right, Martin thought. What would they do without me? But they have little reason to worry. How often do I plan to travel and how often do I actually go to Europe? Once every ten years?

"I want just *one* suit." Martin laughed. "You had three of them made at once. I was with Papa when he ordered three suits, one of them dark-red, maybe burgundy . . ."

"How would you know?" Mother asked. "You were just a child."

"*I* was the one he took to his fittings. You two are not the only ones who remember. I was old enough to have eyes." Martin pointed toward the bed. "He stood tall and straight while the tailor knelt on the ground with pins in his mouth. His tailor shop was on the second floor. I still see us walking up the steep, narrow steps."

"Maybe they just seemed steep because you were a child. How old could you have been?"

"On the big day when the suits were ready, *I* was with him, but I can't remember if we were still living in the apartment on Pulststrasse or had we already bought the house?"

"Don't strain yourself, it doesn't matter," Mother consoled him. She often told him, "Remembering is hard work, so don't try so hard to remember."

"I *was* with him that day, but how could he have carried three suits? We didn't have a car, not until America when you bought the dark-blue Plymouth. Maybe the tailor delivered them. What was his name?"

"Janek!" Father called out before Martin could even begin to search his mind. Although his father's voice was dulled by the pillows enclosing his face, he sounded eager, like a schoolboy wanting to answer first. Since he didn't speak much anymore, Martin was startled to hear his voice.

"The druggist on the corner . . ."

"Duvineau," Mother answered triumphantly.

Duvineau, the small cluttered drugstore, that's where Martin got the pictures of wild animals for his collection. He had finished the first album, gluing the pictures onto the stiff cream-colored pages, and had begun to collect toward completing the second volume before they fled from the Russians. As long as Mother bought Chlorodont he would get a new picture with each tube. Every day he looked at his second album, which was filling up with pictures of wild birds. The empty toothpaste tubes he melted down in a ladle to cast lead soldiers. Duvineau. Martin was stroking Nini's hair, and although her hair was soft, he thought that for just a moment he could feel the rougher texture of the crepe paper wrappers of Palmolive soap. They had always bought that brand in Germany, even during the war, but when he came to America he was disappointed when he found the same brand wrapped instead in glossy slick paper.

"Next to Duvineau was the Engel butcher . . ."

"And across the street was the bridge to Tschansch." Martin spoke quickly so he could better the others at remembering.

"We took the bridge when we had to go to the . . ." Mother stopped in the middle of the sentence.

When we had to go to the cemetery, that's what she was going to say, Martin thought.

"On the footpath curving from the top of the bridge to Bahnhofstrasse below, we rode a sled. Not often, maybe only once . . ." It was the same sled that they packed, with everything it would hold, when they were fleeing. The sled stood in front of the door, waiting for Father to come back from the office. Mother, Grandmother, and Martin were ready to walk toward the west, away from the artillery fire of the eastern front, which was growing louder every day.

Mother and Grandmother had planned to walk and pull the sled. When Father came home he was angry and argued that they would freeze to death or die from exhaustion in some snowdrift by the side of the road. He made them unpack the sled and take only what they could carry to the railroad station. "Coming down from that bridge to Tschansch on the sled, I had my arms around whoever was sitting in front of me. I don't know which of the boys it was. All I can see are my mittens . . . brown mittens, that Grandmother knitted for me." How long ago did Grandmother die? He couldn't remember the day when they buried her in the sunshine under the big tree, the first of them to die in America.

"And the Dietrich baker. . . . Now, that's all of the houses between Duvineau's and the railroad station. We remembered them all." She sighed as she settled back in her chair.

With eyes closed he listened to his mother as she shifted in her uncomfortable chair while she tried to keep the wicker from creaking.

"What are you thinking about?" Martin asked without opening his eyes.

"*An die Heimat.*"

He didn't ask which mountain, or house, had been in her mind, but he knew that she had meant Silesia and not Germany, although one had been part of the other. Years ago, when he was learning English, he had made a file of definitions. He had to file *Heimat* in German, because he couldn't find a fitting translation. *Home* seemed to mean something else, *back home* reminded him of a Frank Capra film and seemed fitting only for America, while *homeland* was a word for immigration and census forms only. After a few years he had also given up trying to explain the meaning of *Heimat* to his American friends. How much sense did the meaning of such a word make to people who moved every few years after having a garage sale of what it wasn't worthwhile to take along? He was shocked when he noticed the coincidence that in his file index the *Heimat* card came directly between *heaven* and *hell*.

"What was I wearing when I met Father? It doesn't come to me right now." She bowed her head as she concentrated on a night almost sixty years ago. "It used to be that I could ask Aunt Bertel and she would know because in those years she tailored everything that

I wore. After she was gone, I could still ask Aunt Lydia, because we were always together, even on the night when I met Papa. Now I'm the only one left of those who remember.

"When Aunt Bertel saw Father, she said to me, 'This man is of nobility.' Just like that. Not, this man *looks* like a nobleman or *acts* like one, no, he *is*. That humpbacked little woman knew, the way she knew many other things." With her head lowered, she drifted again into the past.

"He asked me to dance." Laughing softly, she reached under the blanket to pat Father's foot. "And then he came back and asked me for a second dance."

Through the years he had heard about the meeting on the stairs, when Mother saw Father for the first time. After reading the story of the Nibelungen, he had imagined the meeting on the stairs as having been of the same importance as that of Kriemhild and Brunhild on the steps of the cathedral in Worms. Even as a child he had understood it to mean that great things would happen, but he had hoped for his family's sake that they wouldn't be all blood and fire as they had been for the Nibelungen.

"Ah, the stairs," Mother said, as if she had read his mind as she so often did. "It was a church conference with a Saturday night dance. Hat in hand, Father was walking upstairs, while my mother, Lydia, and I were going down. Midnight-blue. Now I remember." She laughed with satisfaction. "My dress was made of midnight-blue velvet, and the stairs were as wide as those leading to the ballroom of a palace."

Martin remembered the stairs well. When he was nine years old his father had enrolled him in that same school, Elisabet, and he had told his son that it had been in operation since 1292. Martin knew that Father wouldn't have enrolled him there because of this or because he once had danced there with Mother. As a practical man he had selected this college preparatory school over others in Breslau, such as Holy Ghost or Zwinger, because its location behind the main railroad station would make it easier for Martin to commute. But Father's planning had been in vain. Soon after Martin began going to this school, it was turned into a military hospital—at the beginning of the Russian campaign—because it was so close to the railroad station.

"He had such masterful green eyes."

"Ah, yes . . ." Father sighed.

"Don't you make fun of me." She patted his foot under the blanket. "Next day in church he wore his dove-blue suit." She lowered her head. "I have never forgotten."

Dove-blue.

Leaning his head against the high back of the chair, Martin remembered a rainy day in New York. It hadn't been on his last trip, but on an earlier one. Passing the jewelry counter at Bloomingdale's, he had looked across the rectangle of glass cases and had seen a woman standing at a table full of hats. Unaware that he was watching her, she tried on hat after hat, posing in front of a mirrored pillar with each hat for a few seconds; then she would take it off and pick a new hat from the table. One of them was so wrong for her face that Martin instinctively shook his head, and, as if someone had slapped the woman's hand, she dropped the hat. It was then, just for a moment, that Martin caught her eyes in the mirror. After that she picked up and put back three or four hats without trying them on, as if she had tired of the game. She didn't look at him at all. Finally she picked up a hat, but she shielded it with her back from his eyes as if she were hiding a surprise. Only after she set it firmly on her head did she turn around. With a thrust of her hip she struck a model's pose for him. As if he were a critic at a fashion show, Martin nodded—without a smile—at the rightness of the match. The round crown and turned-down brim of the hat continued the curve of her oval face. She thanked him with a slight nod. When she had faced him, waiting for his approval, it was as if she was standing naked before him. No. He shook his head. That wasn't it. But, no, he corrected himself. That *was* it. He hadn't done anything, and she hadn't looked back after she had turned up the collar of her raincoat and walked out into the drizzle. He had never thought about the color of the hat because it had been its curve that had mattered to him then. The hat had been blue, and for a while he imagined that it had been dove-blue.

Shivering in its dream, the dog whimpered on Martin's knees. He gently shook her awake, something that he would have done for anyone who cried in a dream.

"Poor Nini." Mother patted the blanket of the sickbed. "Ah, yes, after that Sunday service he waited two weeks before he came running." She gave Father's leg a squeeze and he laughed among his pillows. "Listen to him," she said proudly. "Laugh! It's good for you. Yes, he came running all the way to Waldenburg, where I was living with my parents. Two hours by train . . ."

"What did you do?"

"We walked together."

Father *did* like to walk, Martin thought, in spite of his leg wound that he had brought home along with other wounds from the First World War. The few photos left from home were mostly walking shots. On an outing Father would mount his Agfa on the tripod, set the timer, and then at his cue the three of them would smile as they strode in measured steps toward the ticking camera.

When Martin was old enough Father took him on walks at dusk. Every evening they walked along the edge of the wooded Walter estate. Between a hedge and the rail line to Breslau, the path led to a pond where they often turned around to go home.

One evening they heard shots.

"They are hunting birds," Father said.

"So late?" Martin asked fearfully. "It's almost dark."

"The birds fly at dusk." Father took him by the hand and they walked on.

After a few steps they heard rustling in the dry leaves. Crouching down, Martin saw a big bird huddled under the hedge. From one of his toothpaste pictures he could tell that it was a pheasant: the feathers of its back were iridescent and the reddish wings were flecked with gold. What hadn't been in the picture was the crimson stain on one of the wings. Martin was kneeling by the hedge with his face close to the wounded bird, when a boot came down and forced the pheasant's body against the wire fence. Pressed into the mesh, the bird's shiny feathers had become square golden pillows. The bird was stretching its neck toward Martin and opened its beak to crow. Its eyes glowed yellow in the fading light, when, without warning, the hand of the beater reached down and twisted the pheasant's neck. Once more its wings tried to fly, but only a few feathers twitched among the golden pillows shiny with blood.

Martin couldn't get up. He told himself later, that he must have heard the fragile, white-banded neck snap, but what he remembered most sharply was the whir of wings above his head. He kept kneeling while he listened as the sound of the wings grew faint, and he listened to the silence afterward, until his father pulled him up and drew him along the path toward the railroad crossing and the pond. The hedge along the path bore snowberries, that glowed white in the dusk like lanterns during the Night of the Dead. Martin stripped off a handful of white berries and threw them on the hard-packed earth. When he stomped on them, each berry exploded with a crack.

"They won't shoot anymore. It's too dark." Father pulled him along. When Martin didn't stop crying, his father walked up the railroad embankment and picked a sorrel leaf. From his breast pocket he pulled a handkerchief, blindingly white in the near darkness, and rubbed the leaf on both sides. Then he held it out for the boy. Martin put it in his mouth and began to chew.

Their house was dark because Mother had already pulled down the light-tight black shades so that enemy planes couldn't spot the house. The blackout badge in the shape of a magpie that Martin wore spread a greenish glow on his lapel. At their front door Martin spat out the sorrel juice that had formed a sour pool under his tongue. At the dinner table he couldn't get himself to swallow any food. Before he went to his cold bedroom he unpinned the magpie badge from his jacket and took it with him. Father had brought it back from Bad Elster, a spa where his doctor had sent him for a cure. Martin thought it strange that a spa where invalids bathed in waters that were supposed to make you well should be named after a carrion-eating bird. Shivering in his bed, he pressed the pin in his cupped hand against the bulb of the lamp on his nightstand. The bird, with its wings spread, glowed brightly like an angel, but when Martin sniffed it, the magpie smelled like sulphur on the head of a match.

He leaned back in his chair, his mouth puckered as if he were still chewing the sorrel leaf of long ago. Mother looked up when he cleared his throat.

"My mind drifted. On one of our walks Papa and I went to look at the new palace. My grandfather had worked there as secretary to the prince. In the new palace they had built a hall of mirrors especially for the emperor, but it wasn't finished in time for his visit. The Silesian prince had married Daisy, a girl from England with long golden hair, blue eyes, and beautiful skin. She was a real princess, although her father had been just an officer. Daisy always wanted to go back to England. She knew what it meant to be homesick.

"Long before I met Papa, Grandfather had been invited to a birthday party celebration of the princess. Daisy, the greatest beauty of them all, drew the winning numbers of the raffle and Grandfather won a painting of Eve under the apple tree framed in *Ebenholz.*"

Ebony wood. Martin hadn't heard that word since Grandmother's fairy tales of princesses whose long hair glistened in the moonlight like ebony wood.

"When the prince proposed to her at a ball in London, she told him that she didn't love him. Her family needed money and there was talk that Hans the Magnificent, as they called the Fürst von Pless behind his back, bought Daisy for a string of pearls six yards long."

Folding a pillowcase, she kept smoothing the yellow linen in her lap.

"I had pearls of my own." Taking off her glasses, she rubbed her eyes. "They were almost real, but I never cared about jewelry. When we had to flee, I didn't even take my amethyst pendant because we barely got away before Breslau was declared a fortress. When our refugee train finally arrived in Waldenburg, Aunt Lydia immediately asked me: 'Did you bring your amethyst?'" Mother shook her head. "We were still sitting on our suitcases, and Lydia asked about the amethyst, while I was sick with worry about what might be happening to Papa, who stayed behind in the fortress."

A mighty fortress is our God, Martin thought, a good armor and weapon. And they were still fighting in the ruins of Breslau on the sixth of May 1945, after everybody else in Europe had given up on the war.

Behind the pillows Father breathed faintly. Was he asleep or was he listening to the stories from the past?

"It *was* a beautiful violet stone. So clear."

"I remember your amethyst." Sneaking into his parents' bedroom—he wasn't supposed to be there at all—Martin had pulled out the drawer of Mother's table, but only far enough so that he could peer into it. With a pounding heart he watched the amethyst shoot purple rays from its cave in the drawer.

He shook his head like Nini when she climbed out of the pool. Most of the time he tried not to think of Silesia and their losses. "And Daisy?"

"For the sake of the pearls she moved as a very young woman into a strange country. When she married Hans Heinrich the Magnificent she was just a little younger than I was when I married Papa. She was eighteen and I . . ."

"You were twenty."

"Moving to Brockau was for me like going to a strange country. Waldenburg, where I grew up, was surrounded by hills, mountains, and forests, while Brockau sat in potato and sugar-beet fields, flat and gray as a slate board. We still wrote on slate in the first grade."

"I did too."

"Before your papa took me to Brockau he gave me a colored brochure, like a travel agent might. It described Brockau as "the Garden City," while it was in reality a town railroaders built around the shunting yard." She laughed. "Not an ordinary railroad station, but the biggest freight yard east of Berlin. But you know all of that anyway."

"I was so young when we had to leave . . . and that was a lifetime ago."

"The people in Brockau were proud of their freight yard, except during the war; then they worried that it might attract the bombers. Most of them rented apartments from Papa's company. I still remember the day when I went for the first time to your father's office. Every man behind the counter and those behind their desks looked at me, including Herr Friedeler." She nodded in the direction of the table with the mail. "They stared because I was new in town, the one their boss had married. Father was the comptroller and sat on the board of directors. I was proud to be married to Papa. Men pulled their hats when they saw him walk by, even if he was walking on the other side of the street. But I did feel alone in the new town. Daisy von Pless must have felt like that too. But one day the empress befriended her when she heard Daisy play the piano in a distant room of the palace. . . . We too had a piano. Too bad you didn't learn how to play. Do you know that the empress I am talking about was the mother of Kaiser Wilhelm II?"

Martin shook his head. "But I do remember pictures of him with his mustache upturned like the horns of a bull."

"Although no empress befriended me, I had Papa, and later I moved my mother down from Waldenburg and she brought her father with her, but we soon buried him in our cemetery."

"I went with you to the graveyard. When you weeded his grave and watered the flowers I played near the back wall, by the heap where they threw the old decorations."

"You knew Herr Else, who sat on the board of directors with Papa?"

"I remember him as a stout man in a Bavarian suit with green piping around the lapels and pockets of his jacket and also along the seams of his pant legs."

"To me he seemed formal, but so were the others on the board of directors. After twelve years together they still called each other *Sie* and by their last names."

Visiting Father at work, Martin would stand outside of the double doors of the conference room. Although he never heard a sound come through the padded doors, he imagined the three stern men deciding who would get an apartment, how much rent should be paid, and where the next apartment houses were to be built.

"After 1945 Herr Else was living in his old apartment. The only reason the Poles had not taken it away from him was that parts of the walls had been blasted out during the bombing raid."

"In January of 1945."

Their own house wasn't hit in the raid. In the same night, Martin went with his father to check his office for damage. There was rubble through the streets, but his father kept drawing him along, as he had done on the footpath by the railroad tracks. The office building stood dark and looked the way it always had, but when Father unlocked the front door a heavy skylight fell and crashed down at their feet. If his father hadn't pulled Martin back, he could have been killed. This had been their last walk together in Brockau, except, of course, the very last one to the refugee train.

"Herr Else starved to death. Sukale, who rented one of the apart-

ments from the company . . . You know that they had more than sixteen hundred apartments?"

"I know."

"Sukale buried Herr Else. He sewed the body that had become
so frail that its bones were sticking through the nightshirt into a
sheet of field-gray canvas from an old army tent. It didn't cover all
of him, his head and his feet stuck out from the tarpaulin. Sukale's
son helped him to carry the body down the broken stairs and load it
on a handcart in which on other days Sukale carried his rake, spade,
and bucket to his small garden by the tracks. Although Herr Else's
head and legs hung out of the cart, nobody in the street paid attention because the load that was trundled past them was a familiar
sight. Sukale went alone; maybe he wanted to keep his son from
harm. It was a hard pull to get up and over the railroad bridge to
Tschansch. On the way down, the body on the cart pushed Sukale.
At the cemetery he dug a grave by the heap where they threw the
old ornaments and the dead flowers and where you used to play."

It had grown dark in the room.

As a child he hated nightfall. At dusk he was called in from the
garden, where he liked to play all day. Often his parents made him
sit with them in the living room without turning on the lights.
When Martin asked why he had to sit in the dark, Mother answered
by calling it "our twilight hour." His parents wanted him by their
side and to be as quiet as they were while night was falling. He
looked longingly across their big garden toward the highway and
the rail line into Breslau. In better light he would at least have been
able to watch the big storage tanks of the municipal gas company
and tell which one was rising and which one was sinking into the
ground. Father and Mother put up their legs while they were listening to the radio that played softly in the twilight. Caught on the
glass doors of the bookcase was the last gleam of reddish light, like
the fire in the kitchen stove when it was about to die out.

For Martin darkness came too slowly. If his parents would just let
him twist the light switch so that he could read. While they made
him sit in the deepening dark, he welcomed even the yellowish
glow of the radio dial, as if it were a porthole in the brick walls. If he
could just see if anything was happening in their garden—but
Father's large mahogany desk kept him from standing close to the

window. He knew that by now all of the chickens were in the henhouse, although he wondered how they knew when it was about to get dark, because they certainly weren't very smart in other ways. Before the fading of the light most of them filed quietly through the door, while some dodged through the open hatch and flew up to their perches. They all knew, the old ones that couldn't fly anymore and had to wobble up the slanting board with the cleats nailed to it as well as the young ones, they all knew when it was time.

One night he asked if he could leave the room.

"Why can't you sit quietly with us?" his father asked.

As if he had always known the answer to this question, Martin answered immediately, "Because my heart beats too fast."

On another night he finally couldn't wait any longer and he turned on the light. In the glow of the overhead lamp filtered through a large disk of gathered silk he saw that his father and mother were holding hands.

"Too early," was all his father said. Guiltily, Martin switched off the light, as if he knew that he had broken a spell.

Sometime after he had seen the killing of the golden pheasant, Martin became ill. As an unusual favor, he was allowed to sleep in the living room because it had the best stove in the house. An even greater favor was the permission for a light by the makeshift bed his mother was making for him on the sofa. He had asked that Father's brass desk lamp be put on a chair next to his head. Father grumbled, "You are pampering the boy," but Mother won and put the lamp by Martin's side.

Because his throat was so sore that he couldn't eat, Mother put a jar with strawberries from their own garden under the lamp with the green silk shade. From time to time during the night he would spoon some strawberries from the glass jar. Even now he could feel the strawberries in their cold, sweet juice sliding down his aching throat.

In the middle of the night, when he was sure that no one would come into the living room to check on the patient, Martin opened his book on wild birds. He didn't turn anymore to the picture of the red-and-golden pheasant, but instead to the page with the black-and-white magpie.

When his lips were forming the Latin words *pica pica* he laughed because it sounded like a chicken pecking. Although the laughter hurt his throat, he hoarsely kept muttering "*pica pica.*" Because of the food rationing, they had fenced part of their garden as a chicken run. Among the brown Rhode Island laying hens, he imagined the black-and-white magpie, its head tilted as if it were eyeing a kernel. After Martin had fled with the women of the family from Brockau, Father slaughtered the chickens and ducks and took them to his aunt in Breslau, who stayed in the city after it was declared a fortress. Friends last saw her walk out of her burning building, and then she was lost forever. The magpie was pecking away at them all.

Nini moaned, her belly resting on Martin's thighs.

"How can a dog sleep so much?" Mother asked.

"Maybe, it's with her the way it is with Father."

"I guess she is getting to be an old dog." Nini an old dog? He couldn't think of her that way. True, a grayish cast was dulling her big black eyes, but it was only noticeable in a certain light. At home they had a saying for finally getting a task done that kept being put off, *alte Hunde totschlagen,* to slay old dogs. He never liked to hear Mother say that, just as he didn't like her talk about Father's heavy skeleton. Stroking Nini, he entwined his fingers in her pale curls as if he could hold on to her and keep her forever.

He was back on the sofa in the glow of the silky green light, looking at the bird book that said magpies mate for life. He liked that, because it sounded like Father and Mother, who were never separated for any length of time, but another part of the description puzzled him. Within a day after one bird of a magpie couple has been killed, all the other magpies flock together and the survivor selects a mate from that group. How do they tell each other that someone has died? How do they know? Propped up by extra pillows so that he could breathe easier, he imagined the silent council of birds. At the center of the circle stood the magpie with its head tilted, looking at each of the birds and choosing solemnly, as if it were a meeting on the stairs.

When he was too tired to keep the large book from closing, he would hold the magpie pin to the bulb. Watching the bird glow brightly, he wondered why he liked its phosphorescence, because everybody knew that these birds were thieves. But the secret glow made up for the many silent dusks in the living room.

"Do you want me to turn the lights on for you?" Martin asked softly, so that if his mother should be asleep he wouldn't wake her.

"No."

"Whatever happened to Daisy?"

"She was paralyzed and the prince divorced her. At the palace they never finished the hall of mirrors, not even by 1914 and what wasn't finished by then . . . And by 1918, after the war had been lost, all the horses were gone. The prince had been proud of his stud farm, but now the stables stood empty. And all of that devastation was just after the *first* war. . . ."

In his family too many stories were told that ended with "and after 1918"—then came a deep sigh—or "after 1945," followed by a sigh, or more often by silence.

"You know, much happened to us, but we were always happy as long as we were together. Even then."

Martin knew what she meant by *then:* the time at the end of the war and the time right after, when they were together every hour of their days, walking east across Germany, every step taking them closer to Silesia. During the day they pulled a handcart and at night they slept wherever they could. He had liked barns best, but it wasn't often that a farmer would let them in.

"Until one day they told us that we weren't allowed to go back to Silesia." Maybe Mother knew what had gone through his mind.

He heard a sigh from Father's bed. Was he listening or sighing in his sleep?

"*Never.* That we would *never* be allowed to go back to live in Silesia," Martin added.

A helicopter clattered over their house, and he followed the sound dying away as though it mattered, as once the whirring of pheasant wings had.

"When we heard that our house had been burned to the ground, there was nothing left to hold us in Germany, because in West Germany we were strangers anyway and the time was right to go to America. They had taken our home from us and everything in it. All we had left was our lives."

The slamming of a car door woke Nini and made her growl. She was becoming heavy, and Martin twisted in the chair. Now that he faced the sofa, he was looking at the golden cardboard wreath with a "50" in its center. Martin had put it on the wall for his parents on their anniversary celebration, and his mother had never taken it down. The year after their golden wedding he had bought a single "1" at a florist shop and stuck it into the wreath in front of the much larger "0." Every year he changed the numbers. Now a cardboard "4" leaned from the wreath, as if it were ready to fall.

"But hasn't everything turned out as a blessing?"

The headlights of a passing car swept over the wreath and made the leaves shine golden above his mother's head. In the flash of the glare he saw her hand settling like a shadowy bird on his father's foot.

For a long time he listened to the rhythm of her breathing and hoped that she had fallen asleep. What blessing? A friend who had visited Polish Silesia had taken pictures of the garden that once had surrounded their house. The house was gone. All that was left was a grassy mound. A rusting pump, from which they had carried water for the garden, and the brick henhouse were the only things that survived. The fruit trees had been cut down in the garden, which was now overgrown with weeds. Travelers coming back reported that the bricks from the burned-out ruin of their house had been taken to the east, maybe even as far as Russia. That the stones had been used to build other houses had consoled him for a while, but not tonight. He wanted to be back in the railroad town that dreamed of being a garden city. Tonight he wanted to walk into the sunset across land flat as a slate toward the violet cone of the Zobten Mountain. He wanted to have his home back, the house of his childhood, the garden where he had run on paths bordered by wild strawberries, white and red.

He thought that he had accepted the losses and had made peace, but tonight the past stared at him, its bright yellow eyes undimmed by darkness and unclouded by time.

He saw himself standing in the snow, his head turned eastward toward the grumbling of the artillery that grew louder with every day. He stomped his feet, but the cold crept up his legs. His mother lingered with the house key in her hand. It was January, and so it was getting dark early. She couldn't bring herself to lock the front door of their house. Impatiently Martin flicked the cord of the sled as if it were a jump rope. He couldn't wait for the adventure to begin.

Now he understood.

On the afternoon of her thirty-fifth birthday his mother had gone into exile, once again, as she had done when she left her home in the mountains for their house in the plains.

Martin was sitting with his back to the night that was flooding through the window. Among the shadows of the living room he saw their home being eaten by fire. The flames were licking into the secret places until they reached deep into Mother's dresser that was hiding her amethyst and burned the violet gem to a yellow stone.

On the way to the railroad station they had passed the gray houses of the tailor, the druggist, and the butcher for the last time. They carried all they could, and then they waited on the same platform where Martin used to wait for the train that took him to school. Now their bundles were lying in the snow while they waited for the train that would take them from home forever.

Why bother to remember? Often Martin asked himself that question, but tonight he thought that he had found the answer. As long as they could remember, the row of houses between the drugstore and the railroad station would stand. His mother would buy toothpaste and soap, his father would stand tall as he was fitted for suits, and Martin could be poised with his sled at the top of the embankment of the road leading across the bridge. And only when the last one of them forgot or when death took their last body to be buried somewhere in the sunshine in America, only then would the gray houses crumble and, as if in a dream, fall silently and be dust.

"But we always sang." She began to hum a melody he knew from long ago. They used to sing "Come to the Vineyard" in the evenings, when the night stood across the road like a black wall and it was time to look for shelter.

"Come to the vineyard." She sang in a low voice as if she were murmuring an incantation. "Come all you harvesters arise. Can't you hear the trumpets blare? Soon it will be midnight."

She had stopped, but her voice kept hanging in the dark and again he saw them traveling east, clustered around the cart as if they were protecting their last possessions with their bodies. Martin pulled on the crossbar of the shaft, Mother walked on one side of the cart, Father on the other, and both of them leaned their shoulders into the load. Grandmother walked behind holding on to the tailgate. And they sang.

What will I do without them?

When they had fled farther west the previous winter, the driver who had taken them along from Waldenburg stopped for the first night out of Silesia. Half frozen, they climbed down from the back of the truck and carried their bags into a hall. It was as cold inside as it had been outside. Although people were sitting and lying everywhere on a thin layer of straw spread over the dance floor, they found a spot where they could set down their bundles. The family next to them were already wrapped up for the night, but they were still talking, except for one of them, who was lying like dead on the ground. The father of the family used a flashlight, whose beam happened to cut across the face of the still figure. With a start Martin recognized that it was a statue wrapped in an overcoat as if it were freezing like the human beings. Martin sat up and stared at the carved face. When the man saw it, he opened the overcoat wrapped around the statue and let the light play on it. "It's our Michael with his lance. We had to kill all of our cows and all the horses that we couldn't hitch to the wagon. Who would feed them? But Michael had always stood in our church, and our village is named after him. We couldn't leave him behind." Then the man patted the carved face of the statue and wrapped it again.

Martin's family turned up the collars of their overcoats and wound scarves around their heads, leaving just enough of an opening so they could breathe. Father, Mother, and Grandmother were lying pressed against Martin to warm and shelter him. Although he could barely move, before falling asleep Martin reached over to touch their faces where they were not wrapped. When his fingertips found their lips, he knew that he was still home.

Martin couldn't bear it any longer and he switched on the lamp, but only to its first stage.

In the pale light he saw his mother bent forward. With her eyes closed, she was humming while she stroked Father's foot. She had to keep his blood flowing through yet another night, so that in the morning she could present him once more to his son.

"Too early," Martin murmured.

"No, leave it on. I have to get up."

"I should go."

"Yes, get rest. You have to take good care of yourself. You are all that we have left."

Bending over the chrome rail, he kissed his father's dry, feverish mouth. A puff of his father's breath felt as if a small feather was brushing against Martin's lips.

"Until morning," Martin said. As if it were an answer, he heard a sigh rise from the yellow pillows.

Martin was standing in the open door with the dog at his heels, when he heard his mother half whispering and half chanting. "Soon it'll be midnight." But he did not turn back for a last look, because he knew that the song was not meant for him and that, once again, he was being shielded from what was about to happen.

Dogs of Autumn

The humming of the swimming pool pump bored into the heavy silence of fall like a cicada that had forgotten its time. In a garden down the street a dog kept barking.

"*Herbsthunde* . . . dogs of autumn," Ala said. "Their bark sounds different this time of the year . . . when it's nearly over." She closed her eyes to listen. "Last year, just before you shut down the pool, they were barking like that too." She took a strawberry from a green plastic basket on the deck and dropped it into her champagne glass.

"Do you want one?"

From a handful of strawberries she selected the biggest one and held it out to him.

The dog barked again.

"It sounds as if it comes from the Marcus house on the corner, but that couldn't be because their German shepherd died years ago." She sat down on the stairs in the shallow corner of the pool and leafed through the newspaper.

"The falcon died." She dropped the newspaper on the deck.

"One of the peregrines they are raising on top of the Hilton Hotel?" Martin asked. "I remember a color picture of the falcon perched on the yellow leather gauntlet of the hotelman's wife . . ."

"He has since become president of another hotel chain and I wonder, now that he is gone, if they'll keep breeding falcons on the roof of the Hilton."

"The picture showed the falcon in profile. A beak like my father's and my uncle's nose and a mustache like mine. His eyes, a perfect yellow *cocarde,* were fastened on me. *Kriemhild dreamt . . ."*

"She raised a falcon . . ."

"Strong, handsome, and wild. Did you read the *Nibelungen* in one of Paul Wyler's classes?"

"In the first of the surveys of German literature, but just the beginning, so that we would get a notion of the rhyme."

She had been a couple of years behind him in college, but had taken many of the German literature classes from the same professor, a man they both had loved and who had died too young.

"When I went on to Harvard, I had to take a year's course in Middle-High German from Bumke—you don't know him—and I really didn't do well in it, but I did learn a *Minnelied* by heart about another falcon. It's sung by a woman's voice, but you have to put up with mine: 'I raised me a falcon,' he began and then stopped pedantically or out of a teacher's habit, at the break in the middle of the line, before he continued, 'for longer than a year / but when he, as I wanted // was tamed by me / and I had prettily enwound // his feathers with gold / he rose up // to fly to a distant land.'" He stopped and shook his head. "I can't remember the second verse."

"What happened to them?" asked Ala.

"The falcon never came back. Wait, I remember the last line: 'God bring together those // who want to love each other.'"

They were silent. He saw the falcon rising from the fist gloved in yellow leather of the dark-haired woman, climbing and circling and finally stooping toward its quarry, its wings pressed against its body, hurtling toward the earth like a dive bomber toward its drop.

"The article said that the falcon died because it had fed on poisoned pigeons."

"Yesterday they wrote of the pigeons dying on Fremont Street. Cars were hitting the poisoned pigeons, as they lay kicking and twitching, their wings and legs broken. While they were dying, tourists were watching from the sidewalks. Now the falcon died and it was still so young."

"Falcons fly fast, like pigeons. If you fly like a pigeon, you die like a pigeon."

"I know that they are predators, but they can't help it."

"In German the peregrine is called 'wanderer,' like us."

"*Kriemhild dreamt* . . . and now the falcon is dead. Do you think it is an omen?" she asked anxiously. "I'm not going to read the newspaper today."

"You're not going to miss much," he said, although she always read the obituaries, and today's paper had half a page. Maybe because of the lingering heat. She didn't read the obituary out of morbidity but because she wanted to know where the people who died in Las Vegas had been born, always reading aloud to him the ones who were born in a town in Eastern Europe.

Ala began to rub suntan lotion on her face and arms.

"Tourists. I can just see them on Fremont Street with their paper cups of quarters, not knowing what to think about the pigeons in the street. Tourists. The last of the convention people left yesterday, and today should have been slow. After all, how many tourists come to Las Vegas on a Monday in October? But already I had seated eleven hundred for lunch and there still was an hour left of my shift. Thirteen buses brought up the count, mostly old people, jostling each other for baby back ribs at the carving station."

She paddled the white-and-blue lounge out of the shade of the roof overhang into the sunny part of the pool.

"My legs were hurting because I had to run so much, but now at two o'clock it was slowing down. Then I saw *her* waiting in line—a small old woman dressed in black—but first I had to seat a couple holding discount coupons. When I came back to the hostess desk, the woman took time to read my name tag. For all employees the hotel had made up plastic tags embossing first name and hometown. Since I thought that nobody would recognize my birthplace, my tag instead shows in gold letters the country where I was born. Even now people come up to me and ask, 'Honey, where're you really from?' When I've finished telling them, they still don't know.

"Holding her face close to my tag, she read, 'Alexandra Poland,' just like that, as if *my* country, well, the country of my birth, were my last name. Then she said, 'I . . . my family too is from Poland.'

"She looked up, wanting to talk, and did not hurry me demanding to be seated immediately, either by the window or away from the window, near the buffet or in a booth.

"'From Krakow . . . and . . . from another city.' She hesitated as if she were about to ask me for a favor. 'Lemberg?' She sounded timid and apologetic as if she was used to being rebuffed. 'You may know it as Lvov.'

"'But I was born there.'

"'Miss, miss!' Someone shouted from the line.

"'Just a moment.'

"'Their names were Schönfeld . . . and . . . Liebling. . . ?'

"'Miss!'

"'Let me seat you,' I said, leading her to a window table that was still being cleared by a busboy, but it was the only good table I had.

"Then I rushed back to the line. When I had a moment I took a saucer with three small cream puffs to her table, because people at a buffet grab cream puffs the moment the dessert tray is wheeled out from the kitchen. She thanked me and wanted to talk, but I had to get back to face the line and before I knew it she was leaving.

"'Schönfeld . . . Liebling,' she said again, the way people in railroad stations at the end of the war were repeating over and over the names of missing relatives to those who got off a train. Someone would hold up a sign with the name of the missing soldier in large block letters and an old photo glued to it that showed a young man. She looked so sad that I embraced her. When I held her frail body her heart pounded against me as if I were holding a bird. Dropping my arms I stepped back. I just had to let go of her. Then I saw that her eyes and her nose were red.

"'Will you be back?' I asked.

"'No.'

"Black and small, she stood a little longer in front of the large window that fit like a picture frame around the blue pool and the cluster of palm trees by the Polynesian hut with the hotel towers in back of her, as if she were posing for a postcard of Las Vegas.

"'Be well,' she said softly and walked through the lobby, black and erect as if she were crossing the town square on market day, walking past the Adonis fountain, across the whole square that always smelled of fresh vegetables."

Ala stopped the float by the stairs and got off. Without looking, she set down her glass, and its foot caught at the edge of the coping. Crying out, she cupped her hands in vain trying to keep the dark stain of wine from spreading.

"I'll get some more." He climbed out of the pool.

"For the gods," she said.

From the door he saw how she rubbed the spilled wine with her fingertips into the rough stone. She didn't mourn the loss of the champagne because it had cost money, but she believed that nothing should be wasted, that everything in life should serve its purpose.

"For the gods," she said again. He heard her voice clearly all the way to the door.

"It's not your fault," he said while he filled up her glass. "Watch, it's full," he warned.

"I followed her with my eyes to the escalator. Each step seemed to be painful for her. When she slowly disappeared downward, clutching the rails with both of her hands, I wondered why she had come to Las Vegas if it hurt her so. Maybe it was just another stop that she had to make.

"When I went to do my end-of-the-shift paperwork, it came to me that she must be as old as Mother when she had her stroke. As old as Mother. You know that I never really knew my mother's true age. By the time I was grown up enough to think about it, she, like the rest of our family, had been issued so many different identifications—new baptismal records in Warsaw and Vienna, passports and *Heimatscheine* along the way—that, somehow, through the chain of papers she had become younger. You know that I told the mason to engrave the most recent of her claimed birthdays on her headstone. After he had hauled the gray granite block from Southern California, I told him to write '1897.' It would have made her happy."

The dog barked, not in bursts but in a long, low howl that didn't seem to end.

"Remember that Sunday in New York at the old Broadway Central Hotel? It was September, and we were staying up on the fifth or sixth floor. Of course there was no air conditioning, and we kept the windows open. It was muggy, and all morning long a burglar alarm was ringing in one of the smaller buildings down below. Looking from the back window toward Union Square, we kept hearing the bell until we went out just to get away from it. It sounded like a school bell telling us class was about to begin and we were late. It didn't stop, just like that dog."

Reaching out with the long-handled pool brush, she drew the lounge over to her and climbed on. Wearing her dark glasses and sitting stiffly erect with her arms resting on the wide floats she looked theatrical, as if she were on a throne but wasn't quite dressed for it, like a queen in exile.

"That Sunday in New York we walked down to Wall Street," Martin remembered. "The buildings and the streets were deserted, the way they look in a De Chirico painting. Empty squares with a refugee train pulling out of the station. Sometimes I wonder what it would have been like to be the last one left in town. Everything would be yours and yet nothing at all. Our own people executed the mayor of our town because he wanted to flee with his family like the rest of us."

He remembered photos she had taken on her last trip to Poland of houses whose facades were still marred by holes from bombardments more than forty years ago.

"On the way back from school I used to stop at a seed store on our street, because its window was decorated with tin carrots and beets made of glossy red and yellow enamel. Sheet metal cabbages were strung across the back while shiny tomatoes grouped around a pumpkin filled out the front of the shop window. While we were living in the apartment on Bagatella, I dreamed that I could have a garden.

"On my last trip, I stood in the street and looked up at the old apartment."

Although he was used to the leaps in time and place of her storytelling, this time he wasn't sure in which city her mind had landed or in which decade of her life she had lived in "the old apartment."

"Warsaw," she added when she saw that he hadn't understood.

"Can you imagine what it meant to me, to be standing once again on that street and to be able to look up at the windows of our apartment?

"When we lived there during the war, it had expensive black furniture with beveled-glass doors. Every piece came from a Jewish household except the piano. That came from a spa where a relative of ours owned a sanatarium and was hiding some Jews. He sold the piano to us. It fit in nicely because it was black like the rest of the furniture. For years I felt guilty about the furniture and the apartment, that it had been taken away from Jews. But the piano cheered me, because it had been paid for by us."

"On July 18, 1944—just twelve days before the Warsaw Uprising—I stood in the same spot where I was now taking pictures and looked *up* for the last time at our apartment, while Boy, our wirehaired fox terrier, looked *down* from there. Since I never saw a fox around Warsaw, my mother told us that instead of foxes Boy could chase rats. Uncle Fredzio and Aunt Galina moved into our apartment. Neighbors must have wondered that one day we were gone from the house and on the next day a Jewish-looking man like Fredzio had been assigned by the German housing office to such a nice apartment."

"Jewish-looking? You mean, the police stopped him in the street?"

"Stopped him?" Ala laughed. "Traveling on a train late in the war, Fredzio was wearing a small, beaded Carpathian cap he had bought on a vacation. When the train stopped in the middle of a field, Fredzio stuck his head out of the window to see what was causing the delay. A German soldier must have mistaken Fredzio's cap for a yarmulke, because he took a shot at my uncle. But even Jews themselves . . . In the days before the Ghetto was closed, when they were still allowed to move freely around Warsaw, two men were sitting across from him in the streetcar speaking Yiddish to each other and then to Fredzio. When he didn't answer—he didn't know Yiddish—one of the men sitting across from him turned to the other and said in very formal Polish: 'He's ashamed of our language. That's the youth of today.'

"Aunt Galina kept Boy for us. The dog didn't like Germans. Once, during a downpour, my parents and I took shelter in a house entrance and two German soldiers rushed in out of the rain. Boy barked and snapped at them and didn't stop until the soldiers looked at each other, as if they had become ashamed of who they were, and walked back out into the rain.

"The Warsaw Uprising started on the first day of August 1944. It was after my parents had left Warsaw with Zofia and me. The SS led Fredzio and Galina, along with hundreds of others, out of the city. My aunt told me later that Boy ran along by the side of the road to Pruszkow, as if he were herding the people pulling wagons and carts with their belongings. Somehow the dog found bags of dry paint that had been dumped, spilling mounds of yellow dust on the shoulder of the road. He ran back and forth through the powdered paint until saffron dust covered his winter-white fur from head to tail. When the column of refugees settled down to rest by the road, Boy ran excitedly from group to group, barking all the time. He jumped on suitcases and bales, and kept barking until an SS man angrily turned on him and shot him in the head."

From beyond the hedges, the howling of the neighbor's dog rose up and then hung flat and straight above them like a vapor trail crossing the sky.

"Maybe the owners moved away and left the dog behind?"

"There is a proverb, *In der Fremde bellt der Hund sieben Jahre,*" said Ala. "I get *the dog barks* and *seven years,* but how does *Fremde* translate into English?"

"A place away from home?"

"How can a single word turn into a whole phrase and mean less?" Ala asked.

"In a country away from home the dog barks seven years."

"Why are words that mean the most to you, like *Fremde* and *Heimat,* the hardest to translate into a foreign language?"

Ala took a sip from her glass.

"Was that a Polish or a Ukrainian proverb?"

"It's Jewish. Jews know more about living in a place away from home. Maybe we ought to learn from them."

"What kind of dog do you think it is that keeps barking?" he wondered. "How big? What color?"

"King Sobieski had three small dogs," Ala recited in a singsong voice, "a yellow one, a black one, and a blue one."

"A children's song?"

"Don't know. Two lines are what I remember. Maybe if I said them in Polish, other lines would come back to me. Sometimes I am so between languages, as if I had sat down between chairs. In a dream I shouted at the devil: 'Let me be, Shatan!' My tongue, still heavy from sleep, made up a name for him that he doesn't have in any of the languages I know."

Martin remembered calling Ala on the first morning after she came back from Poland. She had asked him to call because she wasn't sure that she would wake up to be on time for work. When he called she was still asleep. He said a word in German to her and she sleepily replied in German, but, after a few words, she lapsed into Polish. He continued in German. She laughed in quick bursts, like someone coughing, and after a word or two in German, she slid back into Polish.

Later in the day she said, "You were angry with me." She had sounded ashamed.

"No, I wasn't," he replied, which was true.

"King Sobieski . . . Sometimes, especially during the hot months, we took the streetcar from Warsaw to Wilanow, where King Sobieski had built his palace."

"Did you like it there?"

"You know how I feel about palaces and museums. That's what Wilanow has become, a museum of Polish portrait art. Some of the paintings are of Jan Sobieski. In one he is dressed like a Roman, with a short leather skirt on the bottom of the armor covering his huge chest. The face of a caesar was painted on each of the leather tongues making up the skirt of his armor."

"What did *he* look like?"

"Round-headed, with a fierce mustache and black eyes staring at you."

"Were there dogs? Like in the Velázquez paintings of the Spanish court?"

"No dogs, but in one portrait the king rides a horse. With one eye turned to me, the king's horse smiled and winked, as if it was inviting me to be in the picture too. Only the horse and I knew that I should be in the paintings along with the other princesses with curly blond hair and silk dresses. Do you know that Zofia and I were the first two girls in our class who had our braids cut off and got a permanent? The other girls sneered and taunted us. 'Wait till you get to be forty,' they said. 'Then you're going to be bald.' But in a few weeks they all had their hair done. Father didn't object, because he didn't like our braids, calling them 'rat's tails.'"

"Who was Sobieski?"

"Jan III Sobieski, the savior of Vienna." She sounded as if she were reciting homework. "In 1683 he led the European armies relieving Vienna of the Turkish siege."

"I knew the Poles had been at Vienna, but I forgot who had been their king. Maybe I never knew." Martin shrugged. "After all, what did they teach us in school about the history of Poland?"

"You Germans . . ." She stopped as if she needed to catch her breath. Then she slipped off the lounge and stood in the water by the edge of the pool, near her glass and the basket of strawberries.

In all of the years since they had met in Europe, through marriage, divorce, and their friendship since then, he had remained a German for her. That had stood between them, like Silesia lay between Germany and Poland, because he had been not only a German to her, but also a Silesian.

"Although in most of the pictures Jan Sobieski is painted in armor, in none of them, at least not in the ones that I saw, does he wear the *ryngraf.*"

"*Ryngraf?*"

"A small shield that hung on a chain around the neck of the armor . . ."

"The gorget."

"Jan Sobieski had a picture of the Black Madonna of Czestochowa on the *ryngraf* on his chest when he rode into the Battle of Vienna."

Martin knew what the Black Madonna looked like because Ala had brought him an *oplatek* from Poland, a large rectangular altar wafer to be offered in small pieces to friends at Christmastime. Martin had never done that, because he would have felt strange breaking off a small piece of wafer—this one had two angels embossed on it hovering over the child in the manger—and putting it into someone's open mouth, as he had seen Ala and her Polish friends do. He had saved his wafer. Ala had told him that she had bought the *oplatek* in Warsaw at the cloistered convent of the Sisters of the Sacrament. The card that had been in the same cellophane sleeve showed the long-nosed Madonna, her face scarred by two gashes running down her right cheek like trails left by tears. He knew that the Madonna had different dresses that were slid before the painting for special occasions. He learned that the one she is wearing in his picture was called the Ruby Robe. Two angels hold her golden crown, as if it is too heavy for her, and two others carry the crown above the child in her arms.

"They say that Saint Luke the Evangelist painted the Miraculous Picture of Our Lady of Czestochowa, on cypress wood, on planks from the table at which the Holy Family ate in Nazareth."

"And who slashed the cheek of the Black Madonna?"

"All I know is that the monastery was ransacked one Easter Sunday. Swedes? Turks? At least Jan Sobieski made sure that the Turks never got into Vienna."

"The last time I took a cab from the Südbahnhof the driver was a Turk." He laughed. "So the Turks did make it after all into Vienna."

"There is something about the Siege of Vienna that has been scaring me since I first heard about it. Actually I *saw* it first in a coloring book. A rider in heavy armor, with a lance that was longer than the horse. What scared me was my father telling me that at the crucial moment of the battle Jan Sobieski brought in his lancers—just like the one I had begun to color—and they had iron wings."

"Wings?"

"The Polish lancers—hussars?—had tall metal wings mounted on the back of their armor, reaching high above the red plumes of their helmets. On the Sunday of Divine Providence they charged into the center of the Turks defending the green flag consecrated in Mecca. When the seven thousand riders charged, the wind howled and screamed in their wings, scaring the Turks into running away. The moment they turned their backs they were easier to kill. That night, while the Poles were plundering the Turkish camp, Jan Sobieski slept in the tent that the grand vizier Kara Mustafa had pitched in Saint Ulrich's parish."

The dead leaves rustled under the oleander bushes by the fence.

"Do you remember our picnics on the side of the Kahlenberg?"

"Sure." He smiled because he thought often about the first years of their marriage in Vienna. "You used to make lists . . ."

"Don't I make lists of everything, the good and the bad?"

"Then you made lists of what we could afford to buy at Meinl. . . ."

"I remember the moor's head that was the store logo."

"One hundred grams of cheese, four rolls, eighty grams of lemon wafers. We put the blanket in the big bag and take the streetcar, number 38 or was it 39? . . ."

"The slope where we spread our blanket? From there the armored riders began their attack. They had their weapons blessed at the top of the mountain before they screamed down the hillside into the Turks, spearing them left and right." She shuddered. "I took my brightest red crayon and made a chain of drops from the point of the lance running down to the earth under the hooves of the horse. First I had to draw the drops in pencil, because the coloring book didn't have any outlines for spilled blood." She shuddered.

"When we were sitting on the blanket and looking down on Vienna, why didn't you tell me about the charge of the winged riders?"

She shrugged. "Maybe I didn't want to remember. You had come from America and we were happy. Maybe I was hoping that the past would fade away."

"General Trommel woke up." Martin watched the tortoise push out of the shadows. He had found it wandering under the Spanish bayonets in a parched canyon near the California border. Since it had moved like a tank across the sand, he had named it after General Rommel, and since it had a large rounded shell, he had combined the name of the general with the German word for *drum*. That he talked German to the tortoise didn't have anything to do with its naming, because he also talked German to the cats in front of his house. Martin watched the tortoise march across the patio, stiff-legged at first, as if the earth was already cooling down at night. At the fruit basket behind Ala's back it stopped, its head poised like a snake's. Then it struck and struck again, opening up pink gashes in a large strawberry.

"I'm going inside. Do you need anything?"

She shook her head.

When he came out, he took a head of lettuce to the oleander bushes and broke it into chunks like he would with a loaf of French bread. The tortoise hissed when Martin lifted it up and then kept its head hidden while it was carried to the end of the patio. Why did he bother with such a mute animal and worry that one spring it might not come back from its winter tunnel? When he took it from a desert canyon he knew that he could never take it back, just as they could not move back to Europe.

After he set the tortoise down, it pushed its head forward, its beak still rimmed with red.

"General Trommel makes me think of our tortoise in Warsaw. Remind me to tell you about it."

"But what about King Sobieski and his three dogs?"

"For his victories over the Turks Jan Sobieski was rewarded with the beautiful palace in Wilanow. In 1970, when I was visiting Warsaw for the first time after the war, Galina took me to the palace. We had lunch by the river in a restaurant belonging to a famous lady of the theater. The waiter was dressed formally although his white nylon shirt had turned dingy yellow with time and wear. When I told him that I wanted vegetables because I don't eat meat, he pointed to cauliflower on the menu. I ordered a whole one. He looked me over and told me that in Poland, I couldn't afford a whole cauliflower. He was right, it was an expensive restaurant. Because of some regulation I was only allowed to exchange twenty dollars into zloty.

"Wilanow, the palaces of kings . . . I remember that sunny day in 1943, in September . . . on the ninth . . . the ninth of the ninth . . . Mother had taken Zofia and me to Wilanow and when we came back to Warsaw we were so tired from playing all day in the sun."

"How old were you?"

"Thirteen . . . but almost fourteen. On this day, *this* day, on this day."

She was speaking hurriedly as if she wanted to keep him from interrupting again while she was seeing the past.

"It was in the night after we came home from Wilanow that my sister lost her mind.

"That evening we had guests in our apartment. We were tired, but we smiled like good hosts should. It was hard work, that's why I remember. When Zofia and I went to sleep it was still light outside. Summer days are long in Warsaw. Even Mother was tired, and so she didn't keep her usual bomber watch. On other days she stayed up until midnight to be ready in case the sirens wailed the warning signal. Being already dressed she could shake us awake and get us faster to the cellar. If the bombers didn't come by twelve, the rest of the night was safe."

"Who came?"

"At night the Russians, during the day the Americans. A siren still makes my stomach heave up."

"You were going to tell me about your tortoise."

"Usually it went to sleep with its head on Father's leather slipper."

"What did you feed it?"

"Beefsteak tartar. We should have paid attention to our tortoise, because it never settled down when Warsaw was going to be bombed later in the night, no matter which part of the city was going to be hit. So far our area had been spared. On *that* evening the tortoise kept circling the radio stand, but we were too tired to understand what it was trying to tell us. Even Mother didn't believe what she must have seen, because she went to bed, although *she* should have stayed awake. . . ."

Ala glanced left and right, but he was sure that she wasn't seeing anything in the garden, the oleander hedge of alternating red and white bushes, which they had planted more than a quarter of a century ago, the olive tree, or the bamboo thicket by the shallow end of the pool.

"King Sobieski had three small dogs—one yellow, one black, and one blue."

With closed eyes he listened. Her voice rustled soft like the bamboo after the summer had dried it out.

"Suddenly it was light. So much brightness made me think that I had not slept at all, that it was still daylight.

"'Alarm!' Mother shouted. 'Alarm!'

"The apartment smelled of gas, as if someone had turned on a burner but had forgotten to light the stove.

"'Get out!' she shouted. 'Get out! The house is going to explode!'

"Running toward the stairs I looked down at what I had on, which was what I had worn to bed—a short muslin dress with sleeves so puffed that they looked like wings. When Zofia and I had outgrown our identical dresses and couldn't wear them anymore on the street, Mother had dyed them banana-yellow and now they were our nightshirts.

"Bagatella 13 with its seven or eight stories was tall for its time and it took a long time to get to the basement. Stumbling, falling and getting up, I bounced down the stairs like a ball, hitting walls and banisters until I tumbled—as if I had been kicked—through the front door. Numb and dazed, I walked under a small black crucifix adrift on a current in the red sky. I craned my neck at the circling black cross as if my father had called out, 'Look at that shooting star!' Sticks dropped from the crucifix and grew into bombs that fell toward me. Nearby a bomb burst, throwing me headfirst into the belly of a woman. I was a torpedo and she a battleship."

Ala took a sip of wine, and carefully, without spilling a drop, set the glass on the sloping stone.

"Did you even hear the explosion?"

She shook her head. "I stumbled into a house—not the one where we lived—but into the basement of Bagatella 11, which seemed a safer cave. People hovered around flickering candles. They said prayers that never got to amen, as if I had stumbled into an underground church. Even down here the crashing of the bombs was so loud that it hurt my ears. After a while our catacomb stank because people had made into their pants. Finally the stench made me sick and the prayers that ran around the rosary."

"Is this why you don't go to church?"

"I *do* go to churches, I *like* churches. . . ."

"You know what I mean."

She didn't answer.

"Each blast made the big house sway as if a storm was thundering over its roof and an earthquake shaking its foundation. When I couldn't bear it anymore, I walked through the door and not one of the praying people tried to stop me. Imagine, a thirteen-year-old girl walking out into an air attack and no one cared enough to hold me back. Stepping into the night I didn't recognize the street, and I kept turning around and around while the wind whipped my yellow dress. I was the orphan girl of the *Märchen* walking through the ghostly forest while the trees shook. . . ."

"And like the leaves had rattled on the linden trees after Siegfried's murder," interrupted Martin.

"I was trapped in a fall of icicles when shards of glass from the upper floors struck the pavement. Every step made glass squeak as if I still wore the new stiff shoes my parents had bought for us when we were small and that I had outgrown when we still lived in Lvov. Willfully we had twisted the heels of our patent leather shoes—*squeak, squeak, squeak*—until Mother screamed that we were driving her mad.

"The seed store's window was blown out, the tin vegetables flung into the street, carrots and beets screeching in pain under my shoes. I was walking through my own garden.

"When I found my way back, our house was still standing. With my head down I wandered through the deserted rooms, searching the floor for bodies or trails of blood. In front of a big mirror clouded with dust I happened to look up. Screaming with fright I jumped back from the strange face staring at me, its eyes bright yellow yolks while its lips had disappeared, leaving the mouth a black hole in the horrible face that was my own.

"That night my sister didn't come home. Not until the afternoon of the next day did I see Zofia again, her legs bleeding where they had been cut by flying glass and her banana-yellow dress spattered with blood. Our caretaker was so shocked that he fumbled with his keys until Zofia shouted, 'Open up!'

"Determined to find one of her shoes that had been torn off by the blast of the first bomb, she had kept walking through the streets covered with broken glass. She was from a different *Märchen* than I, she was the girl who has to walk up a mountain of glass so she can redeem her lost sibling. Later she noticed that she had lost one of her hair curlers. Our hair was still in braids, so all we had to curl were their ends. Wearing only one shoe, Zofia walked over piles of glass looking first for her shoe, then for her lost curler, not minding the bombs that were falling near her. Sometime, while wandering through the night, she came to a Jewish watchmaker's shop and later to a *Schilderhaus*. She said that she had hidden in one of the wooden sentry boxes at the garrison. Through their lookout holes I sometimes saw soldiers hugging girls. She never told anyone where she spent the night and most of the next day. Maybe she didn't remember.

"When she came home her face was blue. We asked the doctor about that and why my eyes had turned yellow after the attack, but he just muttered while he kept probing my sister's legs. On the following day we went by streetcar to Wilanow, to rest and get my sister well, but she was never quite the same. The night of the day when we came back to Warsaw, we were hit by another air raid, although not as severe as the one on the ninth of the ninth. . . ."

"What happened then?"

Ala didn't hear Martin because she had climbed out of the pool and gone into the house. When she came back she carried a plastic bag with LUCKY SUPERMARKETS imprinted in blue on it.

"These are some of the books that I brought back from my last trip to Poland."

He got out of the pool to dry his hands before he leafed through a book on Warsaw, and then one on Kazimierz filled with photographs of medieval buildings and a Jewish cemetery. A small yellowed booklet looking as if it had been printed on newspaper had no pictures and turned out to be a play.

"*Wielkanoc.*" He tried to pronounce the title but doubted that he had said it right. "What does that mean?"

"'Easter.' It's about the Ghetto Uprising."

"You were there, I know. How much did you see?"

"I remember eating in a restaurant with my parents. On the plate in front of me I had slices of meat and a mound of very green peas. Through the window I could see the sky, as yellow as the paper of that booklet, and in that sky I saw bombs falling that seemed no bigger than foil-wrapped chocolate eggs. Somehow it seemed appropriate, because it was Easter, Easter 1943. They fought for twenty-seven days. On Place Krasinskich they had set up a carousel, maybe a whole carnival, right by the wall of the Ghetto."

She was silent, and then she added, sounding apologetic, "I don't know about children. They care about what gives them joy or pain, but I don't know about their analytical thinking. I was just looking on, watching the bombing while I was eating. It was as if I were watching a newsreel about another city."

"When did they close the Ghetto?"

"Sometime in November 1940, maybe on the twenty-first, but

definitely in November. On the evening of the Ghetto closing we were moving to a new apartment that had been assigned to us. All of our belongings were on the back of a truck and we were sitting back there too, with the bundles and suitcases. The driver took the route through Warsaw toward the Ghetto, and when the truck slowed down I could see the sorrow in the faces of people standing on the sidewalk who thought that we had to move into the Ghetto.

"After its closure we could still ride the streetcar through the Ghetto, although it didn't stop there anymore. Every day I took number 22 for part of the way to school. The streetcars were always crowded, the ones that were reserved only for Germans had a big *O* next to the destination plate in front."

"What did you see?"

"I remember a poster, Jews, Lice, and Typhus. The last time I was in Poland, I saw something—not a poster but a slogan painted in white letters on a wall. No Hitler, No Soap, Too Many Jews. It wasn't hastily scrawled on the wall and it looked like it had been there for a while. I saw that slogan in another small town between Warsaw and Wroclaw. The letters looked official, like Post No Bills, which was painted on the same wall."

"Could you see clearly from the streetcar?"

"Oh, I could see clearly enough," she said, "so that I could see the diamond pinky rings sparkle on the hands of the Jewish policemen. In the Ghetto I saw a baby carriage heaped with books that a man was selling while another man was rummaging in the buggy, the way women reach in to caress a child. Loaves of bread lay in a bird-cage on the sidewalk. I don't know why. An elegantly dressed gentleman was being driven around the Ghetto on a bicycle ricksha. His driver wore an overcoat and a hat, as if he too were a business-man."

He wanted to smile, but didn't.

"Once when the streetcar had to stop I remember a corpse still wearing a cap on the sidewalk, placed exactly parallel to the edge of the house and the curb. Even his arms were parallel to his body, as if he were lying at attention. Other bodies looked not as tidy, as if they had been laid out at the curb hastily, on top of old newspapers, their faces shiny with what I took to be death sweat. . . . I saw other things. . . ."

"The day will never come," he said with great emphasis, "when you won't remember anymore."

"The day after the bombing raid, when my sister finally came home, her whole face was blue, completely blue. . . ." She didn't finish her sentence. "I will not give up one word, one picture of what has been, not until . . . until . . ."

A large drowned spider drifted by. With its legs splayed it looked like a black star adrift on the shimmering water. Taking an ivy leaf that had dried into a twisted brown scoop, Ala lifted the spider from the water and carried it over to the roots of the olive tree. From a nearby garden came the smell of burning charcoal.

"It must have been twenty-five years ago. I had already stopped eating meat and I was sitting by the kitchen window in our house in Salt Lake City and was looking out into our green garden. For some reason—I don't know why because then I had no connection to Warsaw at all, hadn't been there since the Uprising began—I wrote down on a sheet of paper all the streets of the Ghetto that I could remember. In Polish. 'Goose Street,' and Krochmalna, the 'Starch Street,' where Isaac Bashevis Singer was born and Janusz Korczak had his children's hospital, and 'Cold Street,' and . . . and 'Cool Street' and 'Iron Street.' I saw a picture taken from an upstairs window on the corner of 'Cool Street' and 'Iron Street' of a row of men who were being executed and who stood with their hands raised up as if they were surrendering." She stopped for a while. "These are all the street names that I now remember, but twenty-five years ago I knew by heart a dozen Ghetto streets and wrote their names down to save them, at least for myself. For years I kept seeing this slip of paper with the twelve street names in Polish, in one or another of my drawers until it yellowed and only after we moved to Las Vegas did I lose it . . . like so much else."

A wild dove called and they both listened. It cooed three times and stopped and cooed again three times, sounding far away, as wild doves do.

"For a while Zofia was with us, but not for long. In the last months of the war when we were in Austria, she left with Hubert, a sergeant in the German army who was an instructor in a basic training camp for the Hitler Jugend. My parents had stopped in a small town near Vienna. On Easter Sunday Zofia said that she didn't want to be taken by the Russians and that she would make her way as far west as she could. In the woods, on that day, they were executing boys that had run away. Hubert was involved in the shootings. Before the execution Zofia heard the lamenting of the boys."

Ala stopped and picked up her glass. Martin wondered that she would use a word like *lamenting*, which reminded him more than anything of Jeremiah.

"Then I didn't hear from my sister for a long time. She stayed lost until I found her in America. She had gotten her pilot's license and was really in love with a plane. Although it was in the late 1950s she had made herself into something from the thirties, sort of an aviatrix like Amelia Earhart, with leather jacket and men's boots. One night she and I were standing at an airfield outside of Miami. Tamiami, that was the name of the place. She was talking fast, as she always had when she was excited, and while she spoke she kept stroking the propeller of her small plane. That night she had plans, big plans, but nothing ever came of them. The other day I heard from her again. You know how she always was. Years went by and I wouldn't hear from her. She wrote that she was sick and was being evicted from the house she had been renting and that she had put everything she owned into her old car. She didn't know where she was going, she was just going to be on the road. 'Once more!!!' she had added, underlining her scrawl in heavy blue strokes."

He didn't answer nor did he ask about her sister.

"It isn't as if Zofia has dropped off like an old leaf. . . . She is a human being that breathes and who now lives in an old car with an old dog that smells bad. From time to time she checks into a motel so that she can take a bath."

Lost in her thoughts she shook her head.

"I didn't know her when we were young and I don't know her now and I'll never know how it is with her."

Martin swam to the diving board.

"I don't really want to hear from her, think of her, or have her share my life." She closed her eyes, tilting her face up into the setting sun.

"I'm going inside." Martin climbed out of the pool. "Do you want something to drink?"

She raised the empty glass. When he slid the door shut, he saw that she was bent forward in her chair as if her stomach was hurting.

When he came back he stepped down into the pool, poured, and dropped three strawberries into the wine. In silent toast she lifted her glass to him.

"This here is an island," she said, pointing down into the pool, and then at the edge, "with America beginning over there. When I talk to you America has vanished and the shore is by the concrete walk, the bamboo, the oleander bushes. They try to fool us, by calling this tree a Russian olive and that a Chinese elm, but it's America all right, over there—the hotels, the Strip, the city."

A large jetliner rumbled over the house as it climbed in a curve toward Frenchman's Mountain.

"Since they are already using the south-north runway for takeoffs we might be getting a storm."

"To our island." She lifted the glass. He nodded at her. "At Wilanow we were surrounded on three sides by the palace with its Roman gods on the roof. Hercules carried his club and had a lion skin slung across his chest, while Diana the huntress reached over her shoulder to pull arrow after arrow from her quiver."

He watched her drink from her glass, now red from the half-eaten strawberries drifting in the wine like pieces of flesh. Was she a hunter like Diana, stalking sorrows in the dark forests of her past?

From beyond the hedge drifted the smell of fat drippings burning on the coals.

"The clouds were massing behind the statues. They became black silhouettes and I couldn't tell if they were gods and goddesses or had they become a sentry line of soldiers pointing their rifles at us."

The leaves rustled under the bushes. Standing deep in the pool, Martin looked in that direction. Soon the tortoise was again on the march. At this distance and from that low angle it looked like an earth-colored tank advancing toward him. But then, then it had been night and he had never seen the color of the tank rolling toward his foxhole. He had cowered as deep down as he could when the motor roared above him and the treads ground dirt onto his shoulders and helmet.

A bark tore the silence.

"King Sobieski had three dogs," Ala whispered.

The legs of the tortoise pumped as if they were part of a machine.

Martin remembered a news photo of General Rommel, smiling from a tank. The goggles were pushed high up on his cap so that it covered the German eagle while he stood like a hero between the steel of the turret and the smoke drifting across the horizon behind him. Like a forward observer, Martin peered across the edge of a foxhole. He could clearly recognize the heavy horned pads protecting the front legs of the tortoise, like pebbled greaves on a knight's armor.

"Yellow, black, and blue," Ala sang.

Martin's eye caught the wobble, but not in time to stop the glass from splintering at the clawed feet of the tortoise. The crash made its head snap back while its shell settled with a thud on the concrete. At the sound of the glass breaking behind her back, Ala whirled around in a fan of water, her face distorted by fear. Breathing heavily, she watched the wine foam on the rough stone.

Martin couldn't believe that he had seen fear in Ala's face when the glass broke behind her. He had never seen her afraid of anything. It had been for only a moment, and maybe he had seen wrong. He picked up the tortoise. The flat bottom of its shell felt cold. While he carried the tortoise he looked down at it. With its head hidden, it looked as if it was a dusty helmet from an old war. Gently he set it among the red and white oleander bushes, and when its head appeared from beneath the sheltering rim, he reached down to scratch its ancient, wrinkled neck.

He took a tin can to the pool and together they picked up the shards. Then he slipped into the pool. Ala was rubbing the wine into the stone.

"For the gods."

"Soon the tortoise will go to sleep for the winter."

"The nights are getting cooler."

She climbed onto the lounge and drifted to the corner where the sun lingered longest. This was her cove. Big towels hung to dry formed a shelter against the wind that came up over the desert in the late afternoons. On the red towel draped behind her head, two rows of triangles were poised against each other like teeth.

The dog barked more insistently, then another joined in and then yet another. Their barking became an unending lament.

"A dog howls and someone is going to die."

She was wearing sunglasses, so he couldn't tell by her eyes, but her voice sounded tired, as if the telling of her story had drained her strength.

"Why don't you keep the pool going a little longer this year?" She tilted her head as if she wanted to say more, but instead she closed her eyes and floated in silence.

He knew that she was drifting into the past, but he didn't know how far. Lvov in the thirties? Warsaw in the forties? Vienna in the fifties? Was she traveling to find her sister under the trees of glass? But while she was searching, who was guarding the past, so that day after day she could act it out on her own stage of mirror-smooth water?

As he swam into the yellow spill of the late sun, his strokes broke the mirror and flung shards of light across the towel's savage pattern. Ignited by the dying sun, the triangles leaped as flames against the red backdrop of Ala's stage, and while she slept as once her mother had slept, behind her a city was still burning.

On the Road to Szkaradowo

". . . and blueberries with cream for me." Martin closed the heavy leather-bound menu with a thud. The waiter nodded approvingly and held out his hand for the menu, but Martin opened and closed it once more.

"Like a hymnal on Sunday. Aren't you going to have some blueberries too, Josef?" Martin looked questioningly at his friend. "Blueberries always remind me of home."

"You know what Thoreau said: 'You can't buy berries.' Besides, this blueberry thing may be true of Silesia, but in my part of the country, in Baden, everything was plums, plums from Bühl." Josef turned to the waiter. "I'll have a brioche with scrambled eggs and wild mushrooms."

"And ponds. Blueberries and ponds. In that part of Silesia—mind you, not where *I* was born but around my father's village—there were many ponds. They raised carp in them, tench, and even pike."

"If you want to know about ponds, you know whose book to read," Josef laughed.

"I did, but ponds aren't international. What's true in Massachusetts doesn't have to hold in Silesia. One Sunday afternoon friends drove me past Walden so that I could see it at least in the distance. The car window was rolled down, and even from that far away I could hear the radios from the pond. Remember when you gave me a paperback of *Walden*? For weeks I carried it around in the side pocket of my fatigue pants." Sitting with his back to the wall Martin stretched out his legs, smiling at his friend.

"And for how many years have we known each other? You are the one who calculates things, you're the accountant." Martin laughed. By now Josef had become much more than an accountant, but when they first met, he had still been in the middle of his accounting courses at City College.

"Just this June it was thirty-three years since that day on the troopship. I bet you don't remember its name."

"You're right! All I remember is that it was a Liberty ship painted gray and they were using it for transport to Europe. On the way over it was a ship called 'General Something' and on the way home—I mean, on the way back here—the identical-looking ship was now called 'Pfc. Somebody.' They were named after Medal of Honor winners, that much I remember. Thirty-three years ago." Martin shook his head.

The waiter poured coffee into their cups, thin china with red roses painted on them.

"And how long have we been coming to the Hotel Carlyle for breakfast?"

Josef shrugged.

Whenever Martin came to New York, he stayed with Josef, who, at first, had lived with his parents in the Bronx, on Morris Avenue, just below Burnside. One of his aunts lived in the basement apartment next door, another one upstairs in the same house. On nice days they took their aluminum lawn chairs outside and sat on the sidewalk. Then, trying to live by himself, Josef had taken an apartment in Yorkville. By then everyone in the family had moved away from Morris Avenue to New Jersey, and on his trips to New York Martin was now staying with Josef—who had married—in Oradell. His parents lived with him, in the downstairs apartment. His father, crippled with multiple sclerosis, sat in a chair in the corner of the family room.

For years Josef's mother had prepared breakfast for both of

them, insisting that "her boys" eat a hearty meal before setting out for the city. And so they ate omelets and toast and drank juice and coffee. As she grew older and "her boys" became more prosperous, she let them have breakfast in town and the Hotel Carlyle became a habit on Martin's visits.

He looked past Josef at the pale gray walls of the dining room, enjoying the silence of the room and the efficiency of the service.

The waiter brought melon for Josef and a deep bowl of blueberries for Martin.

As soon as he had left they switched back to speaking German, as they always did when they were together. Even during the Korean War, while they were stationed in Europe and both were wearing American uniforms, they had spoken German to each other.

"Look at those blueberries." Martin held up a spoon that was filled by three large berries. "They are the size of grapes."

"Even if you can't buy berries, as Thoreau said, you'll keep on trying, right?"

"The blueberries here don't resemble, not even vaguely, the little ones I picked when we vacationed in Militsch, near the Polish border. My father was born in a village close by. In Militsch they had cavalry—before my time, of course—and whenever I was out there I imagined them riding through the narrow street where my aunt lived, the drummer of the blue riders swinging his sticks high, beating out the pace of the horses on the kettledrums. Listen, even the Red Baron was stationed there before he took up flying. My grandfather had served with them—during the war of 1870–71—and as my father used to tell me, every first of the month the postman came out to the village and brought him a ten-mark gold piece as his veteran's pension."

Martin scooped up another spoon of blueberries from the cream. With deliberation he bit down on each berry. Josef laughed, as Martin popped them between his teeth.

"The small farm where my father was born lay in the village of Gugelwitz, five or six kilometers north of Militsch, which was at least big enough to be on the map. One time, when we went berrying, I remember *being* on a bicycle—*riding* wouldn't be telling the truth. I was just learning and I was scared that I would fall off. I wobbled along atop a narrow balk between two fields lying lower than the grassy strip dividing them. I was so scared that my front wheel would slip down into the soft earth and I would be pitched headfirst over the handlebars that I finally walked the bike, while my cousin laughed at me.

"We crossed the Bartsch River where it made a bend. To me, coming from a safe suburb of a big city, it was as if I had entered a forbidden world. The river flowed slowly, its water of such a dark green that it might have been very deep. I didn't know how to swim, and the water should have looked dangerous to me, but somehow it drew me near. Beyond the river we immediately entered the forest. It was as dark as a cloudy day after sunset. And in that darkness we picked buckets of berries." Martin laughed. "Sure, they weren't big buckets, but they weren't big berries either. People are always saying that things were larger and taller when they were children, but the American berries are so much bigger, almost as if they were a different species. And we picked them by hand, didn't strip them out with combs—that would have been illegal—but we picked buckets of berries and my teeth were stained blue for days."

"I wish I had seen the east, but no one in my family ever got out there. Except my mother, of course, when they sent her to Theresienstadt."

Martin knew that Josef's mother had been sent to a concentration camp, although she herself never talked about it to him. He looked at his friend in silence and nodded. When he spoke again, it was with a softer voice, making him sound apologetic.

"On other days we went into the forest to gather mushrooms. *Pfifferlinge.* For some reason I have never seen them in America, except in cans. Small wonder that you don't see them around, since there doesn't seem to be an Anglo-Saxon word for them. What kind of wild mushroom are you eating?"

"It's hard to tell." Josef stabbed with his fork into the side of the brioche.

"I remember *Pfifferlinge* as tasting peppery."

"They were the color of egg yolks."

"*Pfifferling* makes me think of whistling—the word, I mean. The sound of the word makes me think of whistling, although I'm certain that it doesn't have anything to do with it. And it makes me think of *pfiffig,* of being sly and cunning and artful. I can still conjure up their weird shapes, as odd as those you got from casting hot lead into water on New Year's Eve to forecast what the coming year would bring. Each mushroom looked different from the one next to it. I think of them as slyly making their living in a secret society in the moss under the big trees. *Chanterelle,* what does a word like that tell you?" Martin asked with disdain.

"Little cups?"

"Little cups nothing! Sounds much too innocent. With its fleshy indented cap, a *Pfifferling* looked like some genitalia Georgia O'Keeffe ought to have painted." Martin stopped and ate a few mouthfuls. "Those twisted yellow mushrooms growing among the tree roots and the dank moss always made me think of magic. Some even looked like mandrake roots, and you know what they say about how they grow."

"What do they say?"

"When the last spurt of seed of a hanged man falls on the ground, the mandrake grows at his feet among the roots of the tree while his body rots in the branches."

"*Guten Appetit!*"

"I'm sorry, but the past swirls around in my head and usually gets the better of me. On our vacations in Militsch, we threaded up the *Pfifferlinge* we had gathered and hung them in the open window like welcoming garlands. Or amulets. Not to scare away Silesian vampires—I heard nothing about vampires at all while I grew up—but to dry the mushrooms for the railroad trip home. Through the long eastern winter Mother used them in soups and sauces. Do I remember their aroma? Their fragrance?"

Martin raised his head and noisily sniffed the air as if he were an amber-eyed hunting dog tracing down the past.

"No, it's their *smell* I want. Listen to the sound, *fragrance.*" Martin had stretched the word and had pronounced it in an exaggerated French. "*Fragrance* sounds like 'Fragonard' and you expect everyone from the 'Fête à Saint-Cloud' to go mushrooming for *chanterelles,* of course. No, our mushrooms were different. Their *smell* would fill our room when we strung them across the windows. When I lay in my bed, the smell would come to me, a most peculiar smell of ripeness. Plums or maybe apricots, and earth. When I would catch a whiff of the dried mushrooms—even in the middle of January—I would begin to think about summer vacation and the dark forest rising beyond the bend of the Bartsch River. And then I would think of walking barefoot on the cool moss and the bed of pine needles."

"Weren't you afraid of snakes?"

"I don't know if I was scared of snakes or not. There were only two kinds of snakes I ever heard mentioned back home, *Blindschleiche* was one of them. Isn't 'to sneak blindly' a funny name for a snake? Could you be scared of a creature named like that? *Kreuzotter* was the other. In my whole childhood, I never saw a snake."

He stopped to think.

"Maybe Silesia *was* like Ireland. In other respects too, like growing potatoes, or in the way its people were religious—some might say superstitious—and how it was patronized by Germany in the western part of the country for being backward and primitive. Actually there had been Celtic settlements not far from where I was born. Maybe we Silesians aren't one of the lost tribes of Israel, just a lost Irish clan." He laughed.

"My biggest problem wasn't being scared of snakes but how to scrape the tree sap from the soles of my bare feet." He laughed again, but only briefly. "The silence was so deep that it scared me. It began when you crossed the bridge over the Bartsch. I stopped to look down into the water, which flowed so slowly—making no sound at all—that it might just as well have lain there, twisted and green, like the tail of a dragon lying in wait. On the other side of the river rose the dark forest. The branches of its pines didn't grow until high up on the tree, and so the forest looked as if it had been hollowed out like a dark, silent cave. I never really believed that I was allowed to pick berries and mushrooms in the forest. Someone could come, take away our tin buckets filled with blueberries and kill us. Someone or something. This forest was near the village where my father was born."

They didn't speak while the waiter filled their cups.

"Your father. How old is he?"

"He'll be ninety in April," Martin said proudly.

"And how is he?"

"It's like this: On a Sunday morning in the summer of 1917 in the

Champagne, an artillery shell exploded behind him. He was twenty-two. The blast didn't blow him down. He was left standing, and he screamed while the hot fragments punctured and seared his body. He told me that often when I was a child because I kept asking for that story. The surgeons at the field hospital found some of the fragments and took them out, but there were others they couldn't locate. When I was a child I used to look with awe at the scarred lips of the pits and hollows in his chest and back. Twenty-five years later one shell fragment had traveled through his body and was lodged at his liver. When it finally pressed against his liver, his whole body became infected and that old piece of steel nearly killed him. Maybe now another fragment is wandering through his body. . . ."

"We don't take Visa," the maitre d' interrupted apologetically. Wordlessly Martin slid another credit card across the tablecloth.

"I'll call you tomorrow, before I go to work. Since I'm flying out in the afternoon, I'll get in early enough to have a chance at sleep. Too bad that Flight 711—straight from Kennedy to McCarran—was dropped from the schedule. Now, if I want to or not, I first have to go to St. Louis."

"Kissinger sat where you are sitting," the maitre d' said while waiting for Martin to sign the credit card slip. "And Abba Eban."

"How is your father . . . *really?*" Josef asked again, even more gently than before.

Martin leaned his head against the wall behind the banquette. Without the voices of the eaters the dining room seemed darker to him. He felt uneasy in the sudden quiet, as if things were about to happen. The glazed lions guarding the door—or were they dragons?—whipped the air more alertly with their tails. And on the long buffet table to his right, the copper bellies of the food warmers gleamed in the mauve light like kettledrums strapped across the back of a cavalry horse.

"On to battle." Martin stood up. "I'll call you tomorrow, that's all I can say." Moving out from behind the table where world politicians had sat, he worried how his father was, *really* was.

Martin crossed the bone-colored carpet of the living room to the sofa that looked like a field of flowers and dropped the morning paper in his father's lap. Then he bent down and kissed him, stroking his cheek with the back of his hand.

"How are you?" he asked, as he did every morning. As always, Mother answered, "Fine." His father smiled, looking at his son with what Mother used to call "his great green eyes."

She went into the kitchen, separated only by a counter from the living room. He kissed her while she was pushing carrots into a rattling juicer.

"How did he sleep last night?"

"Wait, I can't hear you." She shut off the motor and began to slice a melon. "Now, what did you say?"

"Sleep. How did he sleep?"

"Monday he had a bad night," she whispered. "I didn't think that he would see the morning."

Martin felt guilty that he had been in New York during Father's bad night. But had he been here he knew that she wouldn't have called him either, unless things had been truly terrible, and even then he wasn't sure that she would want to disturb him.

"If I had asked you Tuesday morning how he had slept, would you have told me?"

She shrugged and carried the breakfast tray over to Father, pointing out to him the boiled egg, cereal, carrot juice, and the melon cubes.

"He is so *brav*," she said, patting Father's hand.

Brav, Martin remembered—that's what she used to say to him when he had finished his homework. Is that what Father is doing now, finishing his work?

When Martin drove up to the house of his parents, he saw his father sitting in the doorway. Since it was a windless day, Mother had opened both wings of the double door. Although Father's wheelchair stayed inside—so deep inside that the slanting morning sun reached only the right half of his face—he wore a tweed cap and a gray muffler that Mother had pulled up under his chin. The way his wheelchair stood, Father could see the bare flank of Sunrise Mountain in the distance.

"Here we have a mountain in front of our window. What a fine country we live in." Only then did Martin see that his mother stood in the shadows behind the wheelchair. "Not like Brockau, which was so flat." Both of his parents were looking in the same direction, at the mountain rising east of the city.

"Champagne country. Back home was champagne country," Father said. "You don't understand that." Father did not speak unkindly. But Martin *did* understand what his father meant. During the first war he had been in the northeast of France, and he often talked about the chalk caves of the Champagne region. It was there that he had been wounded. Now flat terrain reminded him forever of the Champagne.

Their home had been in flat country. When Martin was a boy he had thought that it was terribly flat. He remembered the walks he had taken at dusk with his father. Summers or winters, they passed the park of the Walter estate. Once they reached the fields, they continued along a dirt road furrowed by farm carts. On some days they walked as far as a row of birches. They would stop by the slender trees and on clear days watch the sun go down behind the Zobten, the only mountain on the plain. Martin would slide his hand over the smooth patches of birch bark. Like skin, he had thought. Sometimes he would go over to the machines that the farm laborers had left in the field. Pretending to be a farmer, he would stand on the harrow, hold the handles of the plow, or sit in the iron saddle of the tractor.

"Are you cold? Do you want to be taken in?" Mother asked.

"No, I'll stay a while longer." Father looked toward the street.

Although Father enjoyed being near his garden and he liked to hear the morning sounds of the birds, it was really the walkers he was waiting to see. Sometimes they came as early as dawn. They were a group of women he knew from the time when he still had been able to go to church. He gave them a courtly wave when they passed, as if he were a monarch on the balcony of his palace. Dressed in pink, blue, and red warm-up suits, the walkers rarely, and then only with caution, came up the driveway. Like shy birds, they never let their feet rest, even while they spoke a few words to Father. When they didn't come at their usual time, he kept watch in the darkness of the entrance, even after the sun had left his face.

Huddled under an oatmeal-colored comforter, Martin's father gazed past the television set at the palm trees in his front garden. When he had moved to Las Vegas—more than ten years ago—he wanted something green in front of his window. He planted a cluster of palms the size of shrubs. They had grown too fast and instead of fronds fanning in the occasional breeze, he now had to look at four scaly brown tree trunks stuck in his garden like the legs of a giant turtle.

"What do you see?" Martin asked this question so often that it had become part of their morning ritual. They would sit in the same places, his father in one corner of the bigger of the two flowery sofas and Martin in the corner of the shorter sofa. He would ask his question and his father would assure him that he saw nothing, sounding regretful that he had no report to give.

"What *do* you see?" This morning Martin asked a second time, which he never did, because today his father had a private smile, the way Martin's son Bert used to smile when as a child he had carried a secret with him. Martin felt it to be his duty to rouse Father and to keep him from staring into his garden, where he had loved to work.

"Last night I was back in Gugelwitz." Father raised up his face and smiled slowly at Martin. When he looked into his son's eyes, Martin felt how much of a great and painful effort this was. Martin could never get his father to smile like this when he took pictures for the distant part of the family that still lived in Europe. When he was being photographed for overseas he would try to look even more grave and dignified than usual, because he thought that was demanded of him as head of the family.

"Gugelwitz," Father repeated smilingly, as if he had achieved a secret triumph.

Why was he thinking this morning about the village by the Polish border where he was born almost ninety years ago and where he hadn't lived in over sixty years? It bothered Martin, it reminded him of dying. He didn't know why, but it did. Surely, thinking of one's birthplace had nothing to do with dying, but it was the joy he had seen in his father's eyes that worried him.

"What *did* you see?" Martin insisted. He was not indulging his father anymore. Now he really wanted to know what his father thought and remembered. Martin wanted to know about Gugelwitz, because he had been there, even though only on school vacations. He remembered going barefoot through the village and feeling the warm dust ooze up between his toes. They had walked between reed-thatched farmhouses that stooped low in fields that were mere patches, long, narrow slivers of brown earth that stretched from the houses to the woods. "The forest belongs to the Graf Maltzan." His father had shielded his eyes with one hand, and with the other he had pointed to the dense woods. They had stood in front of the house where Father was born, its walls washed white and its doorway a dark hollow in the shade cast by the low roof. Larger fields were crowding the narrow ones that the villagers worked for themselves. The big fields belonged to the count.

Martin also remembered the time when he had seen the ponds where the Christmas carp were being raised. One day he had wandered off by himself. Peering through a reed thicket, the pond had lain before him in the heat of the day, still and leaden as if it were not water but metal.

Some years ago Martin had become curious and had looked up the regions of Militsch and Trachenberg in the Brockhaus encyclopedia. It said that one-fifth of all the Christmas carp served on German tables was raised in the fish ponds around his father's birthplace.

"I saw the ponds again, shining in the sunlight, the water bumpy with fish." Then his father's voice faded into thought.

"You want me to remember?" His mother laughed. "For that I need to sit down."

He had asked his parents to jot down anything Father could remember that had to do with his village, its events, even descriptions of how things looked. Martin thought that it would be good for them to recall and organize their memories, as therapy to keep his father from staring into his garden. Home was a place where they couldn't go anymore, so they should remember and at least preserve it this way.

A few days later Martin had found two sheets of paper on the end table between the sofa and the love seat. One was a plan of the village, with numbers next to the squares drawn to represent houses, and the other sheet listed numbers and names of the owners and renters.

Martin began with the outlying houses and the names of their owners. There was a Dörhaus family far away and, to his surprise, even a windmiller named Schrinner. He couldn't remember that he had ever seen a windmill around the village. Then came a large body of land. The domain of the Maltzans.

"What is this little thing in the middle?"

"Let me look at it."

"Oh, that—that was the village pond. There was not one fish in there. When it got down low, we let some water run in from the ditch, and in the winter, when it froze over, we would go sliding on it."

"Did you skate?"

"We were too poor for skates. One of the boys had a single skate, and he skated as best as he could on his one skate, but I slid on my shoes. I'm sure it didn't do them any good."

Martin looked down at the plan. Next to number 4, it said in Mother's handwriting—he imagined Father dictating impatiently—"Nightwatchman Urban. Not married. The watch hut stood close by his house with a peephole cut into its door. While he was making his rounds through the village, he whistled." Then he found another paragraph added under the same number. "Gruttke, the village barber, rented a room from Urban. He also was unmarried. He had no legs and his knees were capped with leather. With the help of two short sticks he walked on his stumps along the village road. I saw him often on his way to the tavern. Those who wanted their hair cut by Gruttke had to go to his room, the one he rented from Urban, which also served as his bedroom."

Martin looked down at the plan of the village.

"There is no cemetery."

"My own mother, whenever she talked about the time of dying, she would say, 'When I'll lie in the birches.' To us it sounded like a threat. When she felt that, she would repeat, more gently, 'When I'll lie in the birches.'"

On the way to his parents' house, Martin stopped at Marie Callender's to buy a blueberry pie.

Father was sitting in his wheelchair by the window, and he kept looking over at Martin and Mother, who both stood behind the kitchen counter. Martin was lifting the heavy pie out of the box while his mother reached for the good cake plates in the cabinet above the refrigerator. She cut three small wedges of pie, carefully sliding the remnant back into its cardboard box. Then she sat down in Father's wicker chair, which he didn't use anymore.

Martin had decided to buy the pie when he was flying home. He didn't have anything to bring back from New York, and he thought that when they tasted blueberries again, they might think about home and reminisce about Silesia.

"This is a delicacy . . . hmmm," Mother proclaimed after only a small bite, smacking her lips slightly to show how delicious the treat was. When she lifted another tiny piece of pie to her lips, she did it with such concentration, as if it were part of her religion. On the white plate in her lap the pie filling looked as if it had been spilled from a jar of grape jam.

"Isn't it good, Papa?" she asked.

"Yes," he nodded, "it's very sweet."

"But this is America," Mother defended the pie, "everything is sweet. Maybe it's something in their soil."

"Maybe it's so sweet because it isn't just plain blueberry sour cream pie, but it also has apples in it," Martin explained. "They didn't have any blueberry pies without apples."

"It's something *extra*," Mother said. Martin knew that she wanted to say "something special," and he kept telling her about that word, but she forgot.

"It's very good," she insisted. "Just like home."

But Martin knew that it wasn't like home. The pie was too sweet, too big, too fluffy and at the same time too heavy, and too rich. It was just another store-bought pie from a shop on the corner of Sixth Street and Sahara.

These days he didn't look anymore for berries, and if he found some he might not eat them, because they would be dusty and might be poisoned with some chemical. The finding of blueberries came back to him every time he found a coin. When he found one—usually a penny—he picked it up and slipped it into one of his loafers. If someone watched him, he would laugh and say, "If you walk on a penny for a day it brings you luck." Sometimes he even found a dime, but hardly ever a nickel. He believed a little in the luck part, but mostly he felt good about finding the penny. The found berries from the woods at home had been tarter than the

American ones raised on a berry farm, but it was the joy of finding blueberries that had sweetened them.

"Isn't it a blessing to live in such a country?" Mother asked, smacking her lips again so that her son would know how much she appreciated his gift pie.

I guess she's right, Martin thought. Be grateful, anyway, be more grateful than I am. Why am I not happier here? The only person with whom he shared his doubts about living here was his friend Josef, never his parents. They had made so many sacrifices to bring him to America that he could never tell them how much it meant to him just to be able to walk down a street in Europe. When he was depressed he would ask himself, Why would anyone live here voluntarily? Even Mother, who always said how glad she was to live here, asked, after hearing Jerry Lewis mention to his telethon audience that he was living in Las Vegas, "Couldn't he have found a better place?" Since it didn't sound at all like his mother, Martin decided that he must have heard wrong, but he didn't ask her.

The truth was, if it hadn't been for the war, they wouldn't have been here. It had been good to come here, but the country was using them up, like in a western. A string of graves across the desert, that would be the end of the line. Neither of his parents would ever say anything pessimistic like this, because even such a thought would be a sacrilege. If it was not his mother, then it was his father who would remind Martin that it had been God who had led them to this country and that it had not been mere human desire for wealth or comfort.

But they were dying out. His mother's mother had been buried under a big tree in the Elysian Fields in Salt Lake City, and Father, he would be buried here.

When Father was still driving the gold-colored Toronado, he had taken Mother to North Las Vegas, to Eden Vale, so that they could select their grave sites together. Three times, or it might have even been more, they had asked Martin to go with them, but he had answered with irritation that this was no way to talk, because they surely would live forever. Martin couldn't face the idea that when he drove to North Las Vegas, past the baseball stadium, past a park where Mexican families celebrated Cinco de Mayo, past the oldest adobe house in the valley, he would also be driving past the graves of his parents. So they went without him, and when they came back they showed him the contract they had signed. "We'll be buried, one on top of the other, one facing this way, the other that way, under a big shade tree." Although Martin didn't say that he approved of the purchase of the cemetery plots, he felt relieved that it had been done without him.

"By the way, I finished ironing your shirts."

"You shouldn't . . ."

"Shhh, I brought the ironing board into the living room so that he could watch me. I couldn't sleep anyway. The shirts are hanging in the hallway."

Martin looked over at his father, still sitting in his wheelchair by the open door, slumped forward with fatigue.

"Do you want me to help you put him to bed?" Martin asked.

"The walkers didn't come this morning. He's still waiting."

A little while later, while she was fixing Martin's tray, she said, "When he dreams he always dreams so beautifully." She sounded as if she were in awe. After a while—Martin was already eating breakfast—she said, "The mountains look so beautiful in his dreams."

"You haven't worked hard enough during the day when your head can still feel the buttons on your pillow at night." Father sometimes spoke like that.

None of Martin's pillows had buttons anymore, but he remembered when he had been put to bed as a child, that he would sometimes bite the buttons, chewing down to the flat metal core of them.

"All of us worked in our family. Herding geese was my first work as a boy away from our farm. Right there"—he pointed at the map they had drawn of Gugelwitz—"number 23, next to the schoolteacher's garden, that's where I herded geese. I was still going to school. Geese were mean. The gander stretched out his neck at you, always attacking. When we had goslings, the Poles from across the border drove their horse-drawn wagons into the village and bought up the little geese. They raised and noodled them—force-feeding them—to sell them later as the famous Polish geese. Very fatty, much too fat."

Martin remembered that at home there had never been a Christmas goose like in other people's houses. At Christmas Mother served duck, and when he asked about it he was told that geese had too much fat.

"At fourteen, when I was out of school, I worked as a carpenter's apprentice for the Graf von Maltzan. Andreas, was that his name? Yes, at that time it was Andreas von Maltzan. I worked on the expansion of his palace, which lay in the middle of a beautiful park in the bend of the Bartsch River flowing toward the Oder. The count was the patron of the Lutheran Grace Church in Militsch, which was also used as a garrison chapel for several *eskadrons* of the uhlan regiment 'Emperor Alexander III of Russia.' They fought at Sedan, Le Mans, and were in on the siege of Paris. But that had been in '70–'71. My Uncle Karl served in that unit as an orderly to an officer, and now and then he came, galloping on the officer's horse into our village, with a large dog running by his side. When he was discharged he hung his saber over his bed, crossing it with its scabbard. They called the uhlan regiment the 'Bosniaks.' Why, I don't know and I don't know what it means. The regiment, the First Uhlans, had been named in honor of Czar Alexander III, and they had his signature embroidered on their epaulets. Of course, this was before Russia became our enemy in 1914. The first of the czars named Alexander actually came through our area at the time of Napoleon. The Russians then happened to be friends with us, the Prussians, and were as determined as we were to defeat Napoleon. Although they were our friends, they were still Russians and had been here before. The townspeople remembered that and were afraid. Our citizens' rifle guild marched out in force to impress them. They even flew their flag. Very handsome, white and gold with the coat of arms of Militsch embroidered on it: Saint George, riding to the left and lancing at the same time a dragon curling up under the belly of his horse. When the Russian soldiers saw the flag, they crossed themselves, fell to the ground and prayed, because Saint George was their national saint.

"We were proud of our church, a grace church of which there were only seven in all of Silesia, so named because they were the first churches granted through a sovereign's grace to us Lutherans after the persecutions of the Thirty Years War. When I was fourteen I was confirmed in that church. People then were still of the same religion as their sovereign, we believed as the count did, who believed as Luther had. But going into Poland was different; there they were Catholic."

Martin listened and tried to see clearly what his father was telling him.

On Sundays before the war, Father set out for work in Poland, shouldering a bag with his clothing and food for the coming week. He had trained himself to take steps of exactly one meter, so that he would be able to pace off the length and width of a house or to calculate the size of a room.

The road took him first to Szkaradowo, where a procession with crosses and church flags moved slowly through town. Walking, he parted bluish bands of incense that hung as fragrant ribbons across the street. Voices that he didn't understand called out to him, as men and women prayed and sang by the wayside. When the crosses in the procession passed by, people flung out their arms and toppled into the dust, as if they themselves were crucifixes heavy with flesh. Bells tinkled as Father stepped—a meter at a time—between limbs and over bodies lying in the dust, on his way to build houses somewhere in Poland.

That was before the war, the first war, when Father walked Sunday after Sunday through Szkaradowo, while the smoking censer swung back and forth as it ticked out his time.

Standing on the patch of green outdoor carpet that covered the front steps, Martin turned toward the window. His father wasn't looking at him but toward the east across his garden bordered by the severely cut hedge that hid the narrow street from his view.

What did his father see? The mud-colored flank of Sunrise Mountain stood out in hard edges and ridges against the bright blue American sky, like a plow forgotten in the field. From where he stood Martin could not see his father's green eyes—faded by time to a shade that he knew his own eyes would finally be—gazing steadily at a point in the greatest distance imaginable, across as many time zones as the number of decades his life had lasted.

Hoping that his father was back in his village, Martin pulled the door of his car shut as softly as he could. Once again his father might be setting out for a job of work somewhere along the road beyond Szkaradowo, carrying bread, cheese, and sausage in a sack slung across his shoulder. Martin saw him stride past blue ponds rippling with fish, saw him turn and wave with a smile, promising that he soon would be back home.

Martin did not yet start his car and waved instead, through the rear window, although he knew that his father did not see him.

When Martin came that night and opened the front door, his father was waving his right hand above the pillows piled on the hospital bed.

"He's so restless tonight," complained Mother, dragging her wicker chair to the foot of his bed.

Martin bent over the chrome rail. When he kissed his father he felt how his mouth moved impatiently, shaping and pushing words against his son's lips.

"For weeks . . ." he stopped to fight for breath, "all of this labor has been done . . . with the wild game. So much work was done. Hundreds and hundreds of wagons have been brought together . . . now they are waiting on the line." Gasping, he grasped Martin's sleeve.

Worried, Mother bent over him from the other side of the bed. "Maybe he remembers Gugelwitz." Although speaking to Martin, she didn't take her eyes off Father. "Maybe he remembers Graf Maltzan's hunts. . . ."

"No, no!" Father interrupted, squeezing Martin's forearm harder while still waving his right hand. "You don't understand! No! Graf Maltzan's hunt had been only one day . . . but now . . ." He was drawing in air. Martin slid his arm under his father's head, lifting it quickly from its hollow in the pillow. Mother motioned for Martin to be careful, and after she had turned the pillow over, he eased his father's head back down. His father sighed with relief when he felt the coolness of the pillow against the back of his head.

"It used to be just a small hunt, but now . . . now there are hundreds of wagons hauling away the dead game."

Martin stood silently by the bed. Although his father's great green eyes were shut at the bottom of their deep hollows, he was not at rest. He lay still, but the fierce thrust of his hawk's nose pulled his gaunt face forward, as if—at any minute—he would rise and walk.

"Sit down, Martin." His mother pointed to the armchair where he sat every morning since his father didn't leave his bed anymore.

Martin leaned back and closed his eyes. He too remembered the farm wagons rumbling back from the hunt bringing home the kill. Body hung next to body, hooked to steel rods crossing the wagons: hares or pheasants and other fowl, depending on the season.

"Martin, you look so tired, why don't you lie down in the bedroom, nobody is using the big bed anymore."

"Thanks. But I need to look after my place."

Once more he leaned over the hospital bed. His father's head was now turned to one side and lay flat against the yellow of the pillow, like a gray sail before the late-afternoon sun.

Martin stood by the door without saying a word. Like a goodbye at the railroad station, he thought. The luggage was stowed away, *Auf Wiedersehen* was said, and you stood at the open window. The other person nodded and smiled mutely as if the window had already been pushed shut. There was nothing left to say, and you waited for the stationmaster in his red cap to raise his signal staff and blow the whistle. Finally, when the wheels began to turn, grinding slowly at first, only then would you begin to wave.

Martin knew that at the foot of the bed his mother would hold her watch through the night. In her long silence the living room opened out into the Champagne country at dusk, stretching flat beyond the row of birches toward the lone mountain that rose like a shadow from the plain. And in that same silence, time, that for so long had kept them from going home, ceased to hold them back anymore.

Sitting at the window by the front door, Martin looked out into the garden. He was watching the tree trimmer, who was cutting the row of cypresses. Twice a year, whenever he felt that the time was right, the trimmer drove his truck north from Arizona. Although one of his hands had stiffened into uselessness, he could clip a cypress with nothing but a pair of hand scissors into a smooth, conical shape. Martin watched idly because there was something familiar about him that he couldn't spot. Then, with a start, Martin saw that the tree trimmer was wearing Father's hat. Martin turned around to his mother, who was looking through the window with him. She was smiling one of her smiles that Martin knew so well, when her gaze was not directed at anything that could be seen. She must have recognized Father's hat immediately, while Martin had not. Then he remembered that after Father's death she had given his things away. They were still good, she had said.

One morning, four weeks after the funeral, Martin sat with his mother in the living room. The hospital bed, now covered with brown and beige throw pillows, had been pushed against the back wall. "One doesn't know how soon it's needed," Mother had said and had not given it away. From where he sat Martin could see the four holes the casters of the bed had dug into the carpet. Although the bed had been moved, the wicker chair, from which she had massaged Father's foot that had grown colder and colder under her fingers, had stayed in the middle of the room.

"I have seen him since he died." Mother looked at Martin as if she expected him to challenge her.

Martin nodded, not knowing what to say.

"There." She pointed at the television set. "He walked right in front of it. He was so handsome and he walked with such energy. Then he sat down where you are sitting right now."

Martin put his hands on the armrests. This was one of the two high-backed chairs that his parents had brought along when they had moved here to Las Vegas to be with their son, from what was to have been their retirement home. His hands gripped the armrests as if by holding them he could keep whatever was left of his father.

Peering through the window in the front door, Martin could see that the living room was still dark. Not even the kitchen light was on. As soon as he had let himself in, his dog, whom he had brought along to cheer up Mother, ran to the sofa, snuffling at a dark shape. Martin turned on the light by the door. Mother lay on the sofa, buried under blankets. He had left her there last night, just after Angela Lansbury. The television was still on, but its sound was off. The dog jumped up on the sofa and lay down across Mother's feet.

"Mama?" Martin called softly.

The blankets moved.

"Oh, is it morning already?" She sat up with a groan. "And I wanted to have breakfast ready for you."

"It's all right. We're in no hurry."

She tried to stand, but halfway up she sat down heavily, almost falling back onto the sofa.

"I dreamed of scrubbing laundry on a washboard."

"It's been a long time since you've had to use a washboard."

She shook her head groggily.

"I saw my mother eating a margarine sandwich."

His grandmother had died years ago. In a flash Martin remembered the brassy taste of wartime margarine.

"Was *he* here?"

"Both of them were here." Her voice had steadied.

"What did he do?"

"He came up to me—you know the way he walked, so quickly that it was almost like running?—and then he busied himself around me." She sounded proud.

Martin clearly saw his father's movements prescribing a swift circle around Mother. Every one of his movements would be thought out as he methodically tried to create order within a space given to him. "Creating order" had been one of his favorite expressions.

"I ran to make a meal. I kept looking for the can of sardines. You know the one we've had for a while?"

True, Martin thought, the one that I move out of the refrigerator again and again, telling her that unopened sardines don't have to be kept cold.

"The can you put from time to time on my dinner tray?"

"Yes, the same one. Then I hung up many socks."

She was silent and Martin didn't interrupt her as she slowly rose from the hollow pressed into the sofa where she had sat under the golden cardboard wreath of her fiftieth wedding anniversary. In the middle of the living room—she was already halfway to the kitchen to make breakfast—she turned around and spoke in very formal German, as if she were giving testimony in church, back home in Silesia where they had still understood what she had to say. "These events did not happen in a known locale."

On another morning Mother told Martin that once again she had dreamed of Father. In this dream they had met in a railroad station, as they so often had in their life together. While she was talking to Martin she stood in the doorway to the back bedroom where she slept if she didn't stay on the sofa. After Father's death she never went back to the big bed in the master bedroom, which they had added on to the house after they bought it. Although he couldn't do the work himself anymore, Father still had designed the addition.

"He arrived on a train and stood on the platform. Everything was gray, it must have been all that concrete. His briefcase stood on the ground next to him. Then someone from another train took Father's briefcase. When he left, it was on a train going in the opposite direction from the way he had arrived."

Then, after some thought, Mother spoke again. Her voice was not sad, as he had feared. She spoke almost cheerfully: "I understand now that he doesn't want me yet. I'll stay with you for a while."

Martin could have told his mother the meaning of the stolen briefcase in her dream, but he didn't want to break into her thoughts. When they were fleeing from Silesia and had been on trains for a long time, Martin couldn't remember when last he had slept in a bed. Every one of the four—Father, Mother, Grandmother, and the boy—had been assigned pieces of luggage to guard. Martin's task had been to watch his school briefcase, with two glass jars of duck meat. Father had slaughtered them on the chopping block of their garden when, just ahead of the Russians, he had gone back for the last time to their house in Brockau. Martin had cared for the ducks since they had been brought home from the hatchery. The ducklings had wobbled after the boy on the garden path, toppling over when he walked too fast. When the train finally stopped, somewhere in Bavaria, he had been so sleepy that he had forgotten the school briefcase, or someone had stolen it during the last night. But it had been his task, and he had been responsible for the loss.

"That was a good lesson in Sunday school today," she said. "I like the Old Testament." They were still dressed for church, sitting next to each other on the sofa. Martin was bent over his lunch tray, which stood on the hassock before him.

"The angel of the Lord went out and smote . . . right now I have forgotten how many Assyrians."

"It was 185,000, I think." Martin was slicing a tomato for his sandwich.

"I've got the Bible right here. I'll look it up." She leafed through the Luther Bible that she always took to church, following the lesson in German.

"You're right—185,000. *And when they arose early in the morning, behold, they were all dead corpses.*" She slipped the envelope of an electric bill as a bookmark between the pages of 2 Kings and closed the Bible.

"During the night when Father lay dying, I summoned the angel."

Martin slowly laid his knife across the plate and turned toward his mother.

"*Es ging nicht mehr.*" Twice she repeated that it couldn't go on anymore.

Listening to her, Martin thought carefully about her words. She was saying, that she had summoned *the* angel—not *an* angel, not the *dear* angel of childhood prayer and picture, but *the* angel. Had it been the same angel, he wondered, that smote the Assyrians? And finally she had not pleaded for him, but had *summoned* the angel.

"'It is enough,' I said. He had suffered so much pain. 'Enough!'" Her voice was not loud, but the imperative sounded to Martin just as strong and final as when she had called him into the house from playing in the garden. Darkness was falling over the garden and the boy was but a shadow when her voice would call him for the third time.

"This didn't make it easier for Father. 'It is hard,' he said three times during the night. 'It is hard.'"

"'Enough!' I said." His mother's voice faltered. "'Enough,' I said." Although she was tired, she spoke to her son with the voice of a woman who had finished the work that needed to be done, the washing was done, the ironing done, and once more her family had been fed.

Father had died in his sleep at sunup.

He had died in the first week of September and the mornings were cooler now, but, out of summer's custom, the walkers still passed early by the house. They were the first to be with Mother. He later imagined them standing around the bed, their feet moving not with impatience but out of habit. With their heads turned to one side, they looked down at Father's body with the unblinking amber eyes of wary birds ready to take flight.

When Martin drove up, he saw that both wings of the front door had been thrown open. Maybe it was an Old Country superstition to leave the doors open to let the soul fly away, he thought as he stepped on the landing with the green carpet. He was already through the door and he could see his father's body, before he shook his head and said to himself, "No, we don't believe that."

Mother stood quietly by the bed. While the men from the funeral home prepared to lift the body onto the gurney, Martin led his mother to the bedroom in back. He kept her there until one of the men called out that they were ready to leave. Martin was walking in front of his mother through the dark corridor when she touched his sleeve.

"I forgot his wedding ring. I would like to have his ring." She spoke humbly as if she were asking a favor.

Later in the morning Martin sat by the window where Father had sat, staring unseeingly at the glass dome of the year clock. The four golden balls of the torsion pendulum twisted back and forth in the sunlight. At every turn they flashed brightly into his eyes, but he did not blink.

At the funeral neither Mother nor Martin cried, not during the service in the chapel or at the grave.

When they arrived at the cemetery Mother pointed to a spot under the broad branches of a mulberry tree—the fruitless variety one saw everywhere in the valley—and whispered to Martin: "This is where we bought our plots. This is where we wanted to be buried. They promised us." Instead the grave had been dug close to the fence and by the noisy boulevard. Martin talked to the funeral director about it, but was told that a mistake was impossible because the salesman had been an old and reliable employee. Martin turned away and went to stand with his mother at the open grave. A canopy of green fringed canvas had been erected, and as they stood in the bright September sun, the men were dressed in dark suits and he felt as if he were part of a delegation to an exotic land, maybe the coronation of a foreign king.

He looked down into the grave, beyond the sharply outlined rectangle that had been cut into the thin layer of turf covering the straw-yellow desert sand and the caliche underneath.

During the war their newspaper at home had printed many black-rimmed announcements by families of soldiers killed on the battlefield. Often these words were used: *buried in alien soil.*

To any new place Martin had ever gone with his father, he had always picked up a handful of earth and had crumbled it between his fingers, rubbing, feeling, and sniffing it. Would he think this to be worthless dirt or would he say, "This needs more humus" and go to bring his spade?

During the prayer Martin kept his eyes open, looking at the boulevard across the spray of roses lying on the lid of the coffin. Homeless men, one after another, were walking down the street—some carrying bedrolls and plastic shopping bags filled with their belongings—toward the old supermarket that was now serving meals to transients.

While the family and some people from church sang at the grave, he remembered that, as the funeral cortege had traveled to the cemetery, the only person who had paid attention to the passing of the cars was a wild-haired young Mexican, wearing earrings and gold chains. He had stopped suddenly by the roadside, as if someone invisible had pulled him back from the curb. Then he had crossed himself and waited while the white limousines rolled by.

On the evening of the funeral Martin had thought about his father's village. The watchman whistled in the clear starry night while Gruttke hobbled along the road, dodging in and out of the moon shadows of the thatched roofs.

"What happened to Gruttke's legs?" Martin had asked his father.

"He lay for a night in a roadside ditch. By morning his legs were frozen off."

"Didn't anyone hear him calling or see him during the night?"

"You know how the winters were back home."

Martin nodded, but when he thought of Father's village, he always felt the sand of summer between his toes. Now, even the thought of the harsh eastern winters made him shiver.

"It happened on the road to Militsch," Father added.

"Militsch. I always wondered what the name meant."

"Silence."

"Silence?"

"In Polish."

"And Bartsch? What does that mean?"

"Mud River. In Polish."

Finally Martin called Josef to tell him of Father's death. While they talked there were long silences on the other end and he knew what went through Josef's mind—Josef, whose own father sat dying in the corner of the family room. Neither of them wanted to hang up and they talked again about the time when they had met, two or three days out of New York, on the deck of a troopship heading for Europe, and how they had come back as veterans.

He laid the receiver on the telephone sitting on the carpet and slid down in the club chair. In the silence after speaking and listening for so long he tried to think and remember. The paint of the troopship had been dull gray, like the leaden waters of the pond where gape-mouthed carp raised their heads in rippling waves. What had been the name of the troopship? They were all named after heroes, but since then they had been cut up for scrap iron.

He walked to the bedroom and sat down on the edge of his bed, looking at a wooden Christ that stood by the lamp on his night table. The simply carved figure was nailed to a green wooden base, that had been faded by the strong afternoon sun. The figure, clad in a white robe, was covered by a bright red cloak, which was also fading. His hands were folded and manacled in front of him. Instead of a scepter he held a long reed stalk that crossed his upper body as if someone had called "Present arms." The carver had driven a nail through the reed stalk into the navel of the figure. The cloak was trimmed with gold. Martin thought that it must have been the only good paint the carver had, because the golden stripes were the one thing that had not faded.

The round head—a simple face with flat features—sat squatly on the trunk. The cheeks were as red as the cloak—from scourging— and the eyes were large and black, much bigger than the face could bear. Green wire had been twisted around the nails that the carver had hammered into the head of Christ to form his crown of thorns.

When a friend from home had visited Martin, she had said that the statue looked very Slavic. He had told her that it had been carved in a Polish village, but had not mentioned that the Polish village was in what once had been *their* Silesia, where they all had been born.

Deciding to write to the European relatives, he went to his desk. The pale blue sky over the red and white oleander bushes was scored and furrowed by clouds as if it were a washboard. After a while he stopped writing and looked down at the paper in front of him, with its salutation at the top and a dryly factual announcement of his father's death in the first few lines. This is what I do and I don't even do that well, he thought. I make lines twisted into hasty hints of letters—mere approximations of letters, he corrected himself—like the clothespins his mother left on the wash line. Father had kneed down wood and sawed it along straight lines. He could hammer with either his right or his left hand, as demanded by the work space. When his father heard a nail sing that he was driving squarely into solid wood, he would laugh and say to the boy watching, "This one's drawing," and then he would hit the nail again.

Martin wondered what it was that *he* made. Letters? In his mind he used the German word for "letter," *Buchstabe.* Does the word really mean "beech stave"? Doesn't that also make him a woodworker?

With his pen hovering over the paper he looked down at the white star on the top of its cap. His fountain pen came from the same company that had made the pen his father had carried every day in the left inside pocket of his jacket. Martin capped his own fountain pen, laying it across the pad of airmail stationery before he went to the other room. After his mother had given him Father's writing set, he had never opened it. Slowly he pulled back the flap of the old leather holder and saw that both pen and pencil had been tucked in an orderly fashion—still by his father's hand—into their compartments. He knew that the pencil would contain spare lead and that the pen would be filled with ink. Feeling as if he had pried into his father's desk, he slipped the leather flap through its loop.

As he turned the etui over in his hand, Martin noticed that a small hole had been worn through the leather where his father had carried it closest to his heart. He looked at it for a long time and then took it back to the other room. Standing in the doorway, he thought of the hole in the leather, worn thin as skin, and that a fragment of the artillery shell fired on a Sunday morning more than sixty years ago had finally found its mark.

Following the Nun

Martin had crossed Bonanza Road and was passing the buildings of the baseball stadium that lay scattered in the dark like a played-out toy set.

"We're *not* going to the cemetery tonight," Ala said with exasperation sounding in her voice. "Did you forget Jozefa?" She was looking straight at the road, as did the dog who perched on a pillow between them.

Angrily Martin made an uphill U-turn. He had driven deep in thought and he *had* forgotten. She was right. What a day. Already in the morning he had been unhappy for the first time when Ala had told him that she had invited Jozefa. Why did Ala take for granted that he had nothing better to do on Christmas Day than to drive her and her friend across town?

As always, Martin had trouble finding Jozefa's house, and Ala was of no help. He thought that since he picked up Jozefa only once or twice a year, he could be excused for not remembering in which of the low one-story cubes of public housing she lived. Driving slowly, he finally recognized her apartment, but only by the silhouettes of the many small figurines in her windows. He knew that most of them were statues of saints from Poland, but in front of the bright lights of her living room, the figures looked more like pent-up animals crowded onto the windowsill.

Ala walked over to Jozefa's house while Martin kept the motor running. It was Christmas Day, and even in Las Vegas December could be cold. Wiping the condensation from the side window, Martin watched the two women walk toward the car. Ala was wearing denim pants and one of her battle jackets, as he referred to them because they reminded him of the Ike jackets he had been made to wear in the army. Jozefa was festive in gold lamé pants and fur coat. Martin wondered if the golden pants had been handed down from Ala, because on occasion she gave Jozefa things to wear. She walked unsteadily toward the car. Nini growled, and when Ala pulled her seat forward so that Jozefa could climb into the back, Nini barked and would have lunged at Jozefa if Martin hadn't clamped his arm on the dog's neck.

"It's me, baby," Jozefa spoke soothingly to the dog. Martin was surprised that Jozefa spoke English to Nini; usually she addressed Martin and the dog in broken German. "It's me, baby."

Ala said something in Polish to Jozefa and then sat down in the passenger seat. "I told her that the dog was barking because Jozefa was wearing a fur coat. Nini must have thought that she was a bear."

"Nini is good dog, like dog in Old Country. There dogs work and bark." Without paying attention to the dog's growling, Jozefa reached across the seat to shake Martin's hand. She looks so different, he thought, and wondered what it meant that her face was now shiny and translucent as if it had been cast from wax.

"*Wesolych Swiat!*"

"Merry Christmas to you, too." Martin had guessed at that because the only seasonal greeting in Polish he had learned from Ala was the Easter one, *Christos woskres*. She had told him how people greeted each other in the street on Easter Sunday and the days following with "Christ is risen." He enjoyed thinking of such scenes of greeting on the streets of a city that he had never seen. From one of her trips back to Eastern Europe, Ala had brought him an Easter card that showed Christ standing in front of a huge red egg decorated with the yellow cross of the Orthodox Church, which he recognized by its second slanting bar. An angel with wings so large that they scraped the ground knelt before Christ and waved a palm frond. Christ's face was yellow, as were the halo and the rays of light, sharp as spikes, that beamed in all directions. The scene was enclosed in an arch of letters that still was a mystery to him. Thinking about the card with its Cyrillic letters, he suddenly remembered that the greeting *Christos woskres* was Russian and not Polish at all. So he hadn't even learned this much of her languages.

"*Wesolych Swiat,*" Jozefa said once more, while giving an envelope to Ala. She opened it and pulled out something small, looked at it, and handed it to Martin. It was a star made from straw.

"To hang on Christmas tree," Jozefa said proudly. "From straw grown in Polish field."

Or from a field that the Poles took from the Germans, Martin thought. He certainly wouldn't say that, and even his thoughts weren't angry as they had been years ago, whenever Ala had talked about her relatives from Lvov who—after 1945—had been settled by the Russians in the same Silesian city where Martin had grown up. He still was thinking about it but not with as much bitterness as he used to feel. Turning the star over in his hand he admired how carefully the straw rays had been pinked at the ends, bundled, and tied in the middle with a double yarn that—at home—had been called *Zwirn*. The tips of three rays were broken and jagged. How long had she carried the straw star with her?

"Here." Jozefa held out a small package to Martin. The car's dome light reflected from its silver foil wrap with its red, green, blue, and orange polka dots. Weighing the present in his hand he guessed that it was some kind of cologne. Last year she had given him an Avon bottle of "Spicy After Shave," topped by an American eagle perching on a golden ball. She told him that she had found it at a swap meet. He had looked through the translucent label of George Washington at the pale amber liquid but he had never unscrewed the eagle and the golden ball to open the bottle. He *did* like the word *Avon,* although it didn't make him think of Shakespeare, but of birds and of the island of Avalon, the earthly paradise in the western seas.

At one time he had met Jozefa quite accidentally at the Broad Acres swap meet, pulling a handcart into the wind and straining against it as it blew dust and paper across the lot. When he hadn't seen her for a long time, he thought of her as a tiny woman, thin and plain as a stalk, with a head surrounded by fine white hair like the plumed fruit of the lion's tooth when its seeds are ready to spread in the wind.

The envelope of last year's Christmas card she had addressed to him in a shaky hand, and as Ala had translated for him, her address had meant "To the Honored Gentleman."

"I forget your name." Jozefa tugged at his shoulder and pointed to the green envelope glued to the box, which she had left blank.

"You don't have to give me presents." Martin was embarrassed that once again she had given him a present while, as always, he had nothing for her.

"For driving me." She leaned back into her corner as if she were about to ride in a limousine.

He felt guilty, because whenever he drove her Ala had to shame him into it. Once she had given him a present, an unassembled travel lock. "So you can lock up something in your hotel room." He tried to put it together, but since she had lost the paper with the combination he could not even open it. Finally, on one of his drives to the cemetery he dropped the lock into a collection box at a charity in North Las Vegas. Maybe somebody there could figure out how it worked.

Martin was playing a tape with Italian Christmas songs, and Jozefa began to hum along. He drove with his left hand on the wheel while his right arm was around Nini, not only to keep her from biting Jozefa but also because he liked to stroke her. Sitting on the console made her as tall as the two human beings on either side of her. The dog's shoulders strained against the crook of Martin's arm, as she twisted her neck to stare into the corner of the backseat, where Jozefa hummed the foreign melody.

Martin pointed to an old brick church on the right.

"Sometimes I drop Ala off at the Polish-American Club."

"Not for a long time, but I really don't want to go anyway."

"I know," Jozefa said. "Polish Clubs the same the world over. All they do is argue. Red-faced men drinking and shouting Hell and damnation, I'll never talk to him again. Argue over nothing: ham sandwich, pennies, or who should be president over next meeting."

Before turning off Maryland Parkway they had to wait at the

traffic light by St. Anne's Church. Its narrow-chested gable was taken up by an illuminated window that showed not human figures but colored glass that looked as if it had splintered and now was bursting apart. Some of the light from the window fell on the concrete center, which showed shadowy female figures, one standing—Martin assumed her to be Anne—who was bent over another woman, surely Mary, who was holding a child.

Ala looked over at the church. "Too bad Father Lapi died."

"Good death," Jozefa said.

"He died sitting in his chair," Ala told Martin. "The cook had waited for Father Lapi to say what he wanted for dinner. Since he didn't feel like eating a meal he took only a bowl of cereal to his room. He must have fallen asleep in his favorite chair and then . . . then just kept falling."

Nobody spoke and in the silence Martin listened to the children's choir singing "ding, dong, dong," and a girl's voice wishing everyone "Buon Natale." Then the choir sang a Christmas song that they recognized as "Silent Night."

Jozefa was the first to hum along, and then Martin. Ala didn't join in because, as she had said so often, she didn't like group activities. While Martin hummed, he thought that Ala might just be too shy to sing with them.

"Father Lapi saw the pope," Jozefa said cheerfully from her dark corner. "Two Poles gossiping," she chuckled.

"Although he had spoken to the pope, he *still* liked my painted Easter eggs," Ala said. "Already in January, when he came to my house to write with his consecrated chalk K + M + B on my doors . . ."

"Kaspar, Melchior, and Balthasar," Jozefa interrupted. "At Mala Vigilia."

Then she leaned forward so that Martin would know that she was talking to him. "You revealed your only Son to the . . . aliens," she said triumphantly.

"Gentiles," Martin corrected.

"Gentiles, yes." She laughed. "The Three Kings were Gentiles, but aliens, that's us. The kings wouldn't need green cards."

The two women laughed together.

"Father Lapi was still putting away his chalk into the silver tube he carried it in, and already he reminded me of Easter—'You won't forget my *pisanki* this year?' Of course I wouldn't forget and I never have. Every Easter I make him a special basket, each egg painted differently from all the others."

On Oakey Boulevard Martin angrily cut across the double yellow line to pass a dawdling driver. He accelerated on the wrong side of the road, saw a black-and-white police car drive directly at him and quickly swung to his right, in front of the car he had just passed. In the rearview mirror he watched the police car as it slowed down but continued in its direction.

"Do you think the policeman saw you?"

"Of course, I was driving right at him. Maybe the only reason he didn't turn on his siren and come after us was because it's Christmas."

"I doubt that," Ala said, while trying to see the police car in the mirror on her side. "People around here are less sentimental about Christmas than anyone I know, except Communists."

Martin didn't ask if she had meant Las Vegans or all Americans. In the rearview mirror he saw that the car he had passed so impatiently was turning very slowly onto Eighth Street. Angrily he banged his fist on the steering wheel.

"What an idea, to call a miserable two-lane road a boulevard. Baron Haussmann would turn over in his grave."

Jozefa hummed, oblivious to Martin's comments and his driving.

He was still a block away when he saw the glow from Ala's house. Every elm, palm, and mulberry tree, the privet and pyracantha bushes as well as the eaves of her house had been strung with lights. A woman and a small child stood by the oleander bushes trimmed to a hedge, admiring the Christmas decorations.

"I'm already scared of this month's electric bill. But what do I spend money on? I don't go out and gamble, playing video poker every night like Pat. Anyway, I *have* to put up the lights, I don't have any choice."

Martin drove into the carport. Even that had been decorated with stringed lights shaped into branches. Ala was rummaging through her bag for the house keys. She had brought the leather bag from a trip to Poland and every day she turned it upside down looking for her keys while he waited and wondered if he should shut off the motor. Finally he heard a muffled rattle from her bag. Holding the keys, Ala tilted her seat forward for Jozefa. The dog again tried to lunge at her.

"Nini is hunting the Carpathian bear!" Ala took the arm of the older woman and guided her along the path. After a few steps Ala turned around. "Aren't you coming in?"

"I'm going home."

"I've lit the fireplace."

Martin shook his head.

"Then pick us up no later than nine. I have to go to work in the morning."

Backing out of the driveway, he told himself that he was making them a present by not going in. The two women wanted and needed to speak Polish to each other, especially Jozefa, who, after all her years in Canada and the States, still spoke English haltingly, although she understood more.

When he stopped at the Yield sign, her lights shimmered on the hood of his car. There was no traffic on the street, and so he idled on the corner. Years ago he used to help her hang the decorations on the higher branches, but not anymore. He remembered that she never put them up according to a plan. It wasn't like her to arrange them in straight lines like a neighbor down the street who had framed the eaves of his house in flashing blue lights. Ala wouldn't criticize him—she liked anybody who tried to put lights up—but it wasn't her way. Something else she didn't like to do was to put reindeer, Santa Clauses, or angel figures in her yard. Once, she had shown him the outline of an angel among her lights. It was there quite accidentally—and you had to stand in a certain place to even see it—because her lights grew organically out of the branches like a harvest of berries.

As he turned into St. Louis Avenue, Martin still hadn't consoled himself about having to crisscross town on this holiday as if he were homeless. Why am I doing this anyway? he asked himself. She's my *ex*-wife and I don't *have* to do any of this. He could think of it as a good deed, but he knew that he had ruined that chance through his anger that had burned all possible spiritual benefits to smoke and ash. He felt so bad about his lack of charity, that even a question of semantics had become cause for anger. Why doesn't the English Bible clearly and directly ask for love and not for charity, a word that didn't even have enough power to summon human beings to his mind, only organizations?

He slowed down and let the car roll to a stop across the street from the Trinity Temple. In the three lighted upstairs windows stood Christmas trees, looking so identical to each other that they had to be artificial. Through the large windows he saw how orderly and empty everything was. There were no people. As he was driving off he saw that the large lighted sign on the lawn had been altered. TRINITY TEMPLE, it used to read, but now the church had changed its name to TRINITY LIFE CENTER.

He drove faster. If Ala had not run into Jozefa at yesterday's Polish midnight mass he would not have to be driving on Christmas Day. At the last minute Ala had decided that this year she was going to mass. The year before she had wanted to go, but when it was time she had stayed home, saying that there was no one to bring her back and, anyway, she was tired because she had worked that day.

That had been last year. On this year's Christmas Eve the fireplace had been lit and the family sat by the tree when Ala had picked up the phone to call St. Anne's parish.

"At what time does the Polish midnight mass begin?"

Martin's son had chuckled and then whispered to his father, "It's a Polish joke." Martin hadn't said anything.

"At nine o'clock?" Ala had confirmed. "The Poles have to be out of the church so that the Americans can have their midnight mass at midnight." Ala had looked pointedly at her son. Maybe it was the result of that gaze, but quite unexpectedly he had decided to take his mother to midnight mass. This morning Martin had heard about it when he took Ala to work. Not only had their son and daughter-in-law driven Ala to mass, but they had stayed throughout the service, although they are not Catholic. Maybe it was a Christmas miracle — they were not very close to each other.

After midnight mass Ala had spotted Jozefa dressed in her fur coat and gold lamé pants and had invited her for the next evening, knowing that it couldn't happen unless Martin would pick Jozefa up and take her home.

Christmas hadn't always been like this. When they had been a real family, when his father had still been alive and had sat at the head of the table, it had been different. He remembered the drive home from his parents' house after dinner on Christmas Eve. In the back-seat, the boys giggled, covered up to their necks in piled-up boxes of toys and presents so that they could barely look out.

The thought of the children in the backseat under all of the presents made him feel better about Christmas. Ala did ask him to come in. He could have brought Nini and like two old dogs they could have warmed their backsides in front of the fire. But, as always, when she asked him to come in he had said no to her. After their divorce a shyness had grown on him like a second skin that protected but also separated Martin not just from her but the world. He did not want to see the inside of her house so he would not think about her in the rooms that now he could imagine. So, for many years he had refused to enter through her dark-stained door. When he finally did—reluctantly—it had been an emergency. One of her dogs had died and she needed him to dig a grave in her backyard under the elm tree.

It wasn't that anything in her house offended him, but he felt like a nonbeliever in a cathedral, who concentrates on the artwork so as not to be affected by the spirit of the church. Church is right, he thought. The wall facing her fireplace was covered with icons that she had brought from Poland and Ukraine. He liked to look at the medieval faces that stared at him from paintings sheathed in metal carapaces of gold, silver, copper, brass, or pewter. Only the sacred flesh of Mary, Christ, or one of the saints was left uncovered. Squinting from far back in her living room, he saw her icon wall as a shimmering pond of metal on whose surface swam severed heads, legs, arms, and the tiny white flecks of the toes and fingers of the Christ Child.

One of his favored icons had a chased-silver covering. In his left hand Christ holds an open book. The fingers of one hand curl around the edge of the metal pages, while the other hand is raised in a blessing, with the thumb forming a circle with two of the fingers. His dark face stares out without emotion from under a raised metal halo that looks as if it was crocheted from silver filigree.

"What do they say?" Martin had asked, pointing at the open pages of the book, covered with what he thought were Cyrillic letters.

"I can't tell right now," she said, without even looking at the icon, as if she didn't have her glasses handy.

"But they are big letters." Martin pointed at the writing.

"Not now!"

That means *never*, Martin had thought, and indeed the icon wasn't mentioned again. But Martin didn't give up and kept pointing at the foreign letters in the metal book, certain of their importance because they were so large and had been engraved so clearly.

When she saw him standing once again in front of the icon, she muttered while walking by, "It's unreadable Old Church Slavonic."

Sitting in his study, he tried to compose a late Christmas letter to Europe, but he stared across the sheet on his desk at the objects on his bookshelves. On the left stood a small black vase that the potter had shaped into a woman's face. He had been very young—twenty-one—when he had bought it in Assisi. Next to it stood a broad-browed lion's head with verdigris patina highlighting the folds and creases of its face. Then came a statue of a kneeling priest that a friend had brought from a trip home to El Salvador. He had said that it was Saint Francis, but when Martin turned the carving upside down, he read on a handwritten sticker that it was Cayetano, a saint about whom he knew nothing at all. He told his friend to find out what he could about this saint.

Martin went into the other room to look for the letter that he had received in reply. Saint Cayetano had worked in the hospital in Venice, he read, and then in Rome as one of the founders of the clerics regular—the Theatines—and with the poor in Naples, where he had established pawnshops to help them. Then came two sentences that had startled and moved him when he had first read them. "This order was dedicated to helping those sentenced to death to go to their end in peace. From there stems the custom to ask San Cayetano for 'a good death.'"

He looked across his unfinished Christmas letter at the statue. Since its head was bowed the black-rimmed eyes looked humbly at the ground, but never at him. Cayetano's left hand was raised to his heart while his right was stretched forward and curled as if it had been carved to hold a banner or a flower. Not wanting an empty-handed saint, Martin had taken a slender wooden crucifix that Ala had brought back from Warsaw and had whittled it to a point the way his father had sharpened the pencil stubs he always carried in his pocket to mark the wood he was about to saw. After he had fitted the Polish cross into the hand of the statue, he felt as if he had grafted a shoot into the cleft of a wild fruit tree. His father had taught him that as a child but after they had fled from Silesia, Martin had never done it again.

Glancing at his watch, he realized that it was time to take Jozefa back to her apartment. His Christmas letter would have to stay unfinished. Maybe writing a letter wasn't enough anyway. Ala had told him that she would rather have "a single living word than all of that letter writing." She didn't write often to her relatives and friends in Europe, but when she did, her sheets were soon crowded with large letters and written with such energy that the lines looked ready to take flight. Even the addresses were written so boldly that it left barely enough room on the envelope to glue the many stamps necessary to send a thick airmail letter to Eastern Europe.

As he drove up the ramp to her house, the branches of light reached out from her carport to embrace whoever entered. He opened the door, but the ivy covering the wall had grown so lush that he could barely squeeze out of the car. In front of Ala's door a white cat stood by a bowl, and Martin heard how she crunched the dry cat food. He stopped at the big living room window covered almost entirely by ivy that had grown in scaly vines from the brick planter to the roof of the house, where some tendrils had shot above the eaves. Although large leaves covered most of the window, he could look in between two vines as thick as a woman's wrists. Jozefa was sitting on the sofa, her child's face turned toward the Christmas tree that Ala had decorated with so many strands of bulbs that the green was almost hidden so that the fir had turned into a shiny cone.

Ala was dressed in a tunic made of a nearly white material whose stand-up collar, cuffs, and placket were trimmed with bands the color of oxblood. Martin remembered this peasant blouse that Ala had brought back from a trip to the Ukraine. In the same folk art store in Lvov catering to travelers from the West she had bought the Y-shaped bead necklace she was wearing now. On the lappet—three fingers wide—that hung onto her chest, the blue and yellow beads formed a geometric design of triangles and squares that he had seen on Eastern crosses. Although tunic and necklace were familiar to Martin as souvenirs from a faraway place, tonight they seemed strange to him, as if the bright lights had transformed them into parts of a priestly vestment.

Candles flickered everywhere in the room, on the windowsills, the hearth, the top of the television set, even among the dinner dishes cluttering the low table. A black one-eyed cat, the latest of Ala's strays, wandered among the candles, and Martin worried that the cat's swishing tail might catch fire. Incense drifted in thin layers over the table crowded with red borscht bowls, glass jars with gefilte fish in jelly, smaller dishes with red beets, a jar of horseradish that was also red, cake plates, and a bottle of vodka surrounded by a set of small thin-walled tumblers that Ala had carried in a suitcase from Poland without breaking a single one.

Through the pane he could hear Jozefa's thin voice singing along with a record, a Christmas song he recognized by its march step. He had learned it from Ala, remembering only "Do Jezusa i panienki," to Jesus and the Lady. Ala had told him how she and her sister had marched behind their father around the dining table, singing that they were on their way to Jesus and the Lady. For years he had imagined the *thump thump thump* of the shoes of the girls on the parquet floor. Then, although he couldn't believe his ears, he heard Ala's deeper, darker voice join Jozefa's high-pitched singing.

Shifting his stance so that he could see better, he suddenly became aware of how this must look to anyone walking by. Standing among the ivy by the window he felt as if he were Actaeon, who did not take his eyes off Artemis bathing until his fifty hounds tore him to pieces.

The music ended, but the women kept singing to each other in a tongue that after so many years was still foreign to him. Now it didn't matter anymore; he knew it was too late.

On the concrete landing he tapped out the march step of the little girls and hummed the melody from the record that had stopped. Then he felt something brush against his legs. It was the white cat wanting to be let into the house. Stepping back, he upset the bowl of food Ala had put out, which she had heaped especially high with food because it was one of the magic nights between Christmas and the feast of the Three Kings when every animal and every human being should celebrate.

When Martin saw the two women walking toward the car, he put his arm as a precaution around Nini's neck, but she lay peacefully with her head on his thigh and stayed that way while he drove to the housing development.

"We will have to see each other very soon, Jutta," Ala said.

"Jutta?" Martin wondered. "I thought your name was Jozefa."

"Jozefa, Jutta, Jozefina, Josephine. When you move around . . . They have to make an extra big gravestone for me so that all my names fit on it."

Ala pulled her seat forward to let Jozefa climb out. Nini didn't growl and only lifted her head to look sleepily at Jozefa.

"Good night, Old Country dog."

"You know that she is the only real American among all of us," Martin answered.

"Nice Old Country dog," Jozefa said as if she hadn't understood Martin.

The two women walked arm in arm across the parking lot to Jozefa's door. When Ala came out she carried something heavy, but it was too dark to see what it was. When she came closer, Martin saw that it was an old typewriter.

"The kings of Sheba offer gifts," she said.

"Let me help you." Martin got out and took the typewriter to the trunk.

Driving out of the dead-end street, Martin rolled down both windows so that they could wave to Jozefa, who stood in the lighted doorway. He could still see her in the rearview mirror when he turned the corner to Bonanza Road. From there he drove slowly through the empty streets, as if he were looking for an address, until they reached Las Vegas Boulevard.

"Why did she give you the typewriter?"

Ala didn't answer for some time. "She says—now don't laugh—that she wants me to be her heiress. And this is one of her great treasures."

"The old manual typewriter?"

"She used to write poems in Polish—never publishing anything—and this typewriter has a Polish keyboard. This is why she wants me to have it. But you know how I am with anything mechanical."

"That's why you don't drive."

"I am doing everybody a favor by not driving. Nobody would be safe with me behind the wheel. Machines and I are enemies."

"What did you two talk about?"

"Her life."

"How old is she now?"

"Seventy-three. But didn't she seem older tonight?"

Turning right into Fremont Street, he drove toward the Plaza Hotel.

"It's hard to imagine the old one-story railroad station that they tore down for the hotel."

"Do you remember when Mother came to live with us, how she looked when she stepped from the Salt Lake train? She was smiling and carried a bouquet of roses as if she were a bride on the way to her honeymoon."

Last night, before dinner and the opening of the presents, he had driven Ala to Woodlawn Cemetery, to her mother's grave. Ala had lit candles on top of the headstone and around its base, so that throughout Holy Night the grave would be surrounded by light. On the way back to the gate, when they had driven between rows of elm trees whose branches had grown together over the road, they couldn't see a single light in the dark graveyard.

"Heathens," Ala had chided. "They have forgotten their dead. When I was visiting Wroclaw on All Souls' Day I went to Aunt Lola's grave. It was ten, maybe eleven o'clock at night. I was walking through fog and it was so quiet that now and then I heard a leaf fall. The whole cemetery glowed with orange lights as if the earth itself were afire, while through the fog I heard the glasses cracking like shots from the heat of the candles burning all around me."

"You remember, Christmas Eve two or three years ago, when we took Jozefa with us to the cemetery?" Martin asked.

The three of them had stood in the darkness by the grave, while at their feet the candles had flickered in ruby-red glasses. The women had toasted Ala's mother with vodka while a music box played "For Elisabeth." A bisque angel was trying to turn on top of the music box, but the mechanism was broken and the angel only twitched.

Driving along Fremont Street between the light walls of the casinos flashing red, green, blue, and gold onto the empty sidewalks, Martin turned left. His car dipped into the darkness of a side street lined with railroad cottages built in the early years of the century. In spite of the darkness on both sides, the lights of Fremont Street were still flashing in his eyes, especially the yellow ones, as if they had burned themselves onto his eyeballs. Since there was no traffic on the street, he drove slowly to rest his eyes in the darkness.

The small houses on both sides of the street stood in yards strewn with sofas and chairs. Some were abandoned, their doors standing open as if their inhabitants had hurriedly fled, while others were still occupied, judging by the old cars that were pulled up onto the dirt in front of the doorsteps, where once lawns had been.

"What was that?" Ala called out, pointing to her side of the street.

Martin backed up, remembering now that out of the corner of his eye he had seen something glitter. Then he shifted forward and drove even slower than before. The headlights picked a tree out of the darkness, a short tree growing on the narrow strip between sidewalk and curb. The tree had been cut back so that its branches were nothing but stubs. Martin stopped by the tree. Beer cans stuck on the ends of the black stubs made them look like drummer's mallets. The cans were red and white and it had been their silver bottoms that had glittered in the beams of the headlights.

"I've never seen anything like it."

"Maybe that's all the man had handy when he wanted to decorate the tree," Ala said.

Martin tried to imagine who might live in the dark house next to a pile of car parts. He drove slowly on and then turned onto the Strip.

"Slow down. On the left we should be passing the house where Jozefa had opened a Polish restaurant, although that may be too big a word for her food business."

The building was dark, its windows boarded up. Martin pulled up to the curb without turning off the motor.

"It still looks like the root beer place it used to be, maybe because of the hat-shaped roof. Jozefa couldn't have changed very much on the building before opening it up as a Polish restaurant."

"They didn't have money to change anything. She was in it with a partner, but it was *she* who lost her money."

"What did she put on the menu?"

"Pierogi, borscht, *bigos, golabki,* the usual for such a place."

Martin looked up and down the empty street. "To whom did she hope to sell? Kids from Las Vegas High School?"

"No, she wanted to cater to the office workers from the Federal Building. Besides, it *is* on the Strip and with all the cars driving by . . ."

"How long did it last?"

"One day when we were passing—we must have been going to Mother's . . . to the cemetery—I saw a handwritten sign in the window saying Closed and next to it a bigger, printed one, For Rent."

The whole area on this side of the street looked so deserted that a tourist might doubt that anyone ever walked here.

"All of these blocks are supposed to be torn down. A Japanese developer is planning to put up an office building, the tallest in town, right along here somewhere."

"One day, while Jozefa was still selling *golabki* and pierogi, she asked me if she didn't look younger than her age. Her partner—a young Polish refugee—was the cook, who I don't think brought anything into the partnership except that he cooked and was young. Jozefa grandly named the restaurant Kraków, after the city where once Polish kings were crowned. Jan Sobieski, the victor over the Turks at Vienna, is buried there in the Stanislaw Cathedral on top of the Wavel. With such a name for the restaurant people may have expected more than a place the size of a hot dog stand."

"But then, the kind of people driving here, would they have known what Kraków meant to her . . . and means to you?"

"I can't remember if the cook was twenty-eight years old or if she lost $28,000 in her Polish restaurant, twenty-eight was in there somewhere. It really is a shame that she lost all of her savings."

"How did she scrape that much money together?"

"She always worked as a maid. I first met her at the old MGM Grand Hotel. I was a hostess at the deli upstairs—you remember the pictures of the movie stars on the walls?—when I heard her speak Polish to another maid in the help's hall. While she was working there, she was also buying jewelry from people who had lost all of their money in the casino. She bought, just now and then, when she could afford it. Then she retired, got the union pension, but kept on working. Her last job was at Caesars Palace. Whenever they needed a maid to fill in, they called her. On most such days she took the bus to Caesars, but sometimes, to save money, she walked for a day's work from where she lived in North Las Vegas all the way to Flamingo and the Strip. She invested all of her hopes and everything else she had in the lunch business of her Kraków. Close to downtown and with so many law offices around her restaurant, she had a chance, she had a real chance."

Martin turned east on Charleston Boulevard and then again.

"Where are you driving?"

"I'm looking for Christmas lights."

In the darkness of Sixth Street, among the old homes that already had been converted into law offices, his headlights picked out a glittering tree, waiting by the curb for the next morning's garbage pickup.

"How can people do that, put out a Christmas tree on the same day, as if suddenly everything is over. *The moor has done . . .* how does that go?"

"*The moor has done his duty; the moor can go.*"

"In Poland we kept celebrating Christmas all the way to Three Kings on the sixth of January."

"And kept the tree up until the beginning of February." He laughed. Every year Ala clung longer to her Christmas tree. He would remind her to take it down so that people who walked by her house and saw the lighted tree in her picture window wouldn't begin to think of her as a weird, lonely woman. She would answer by saying, "Today is only Russian Christmas" or "*Now* it's only Orthodox Epiphany," and keep the tree as long as she could.

"Christmas ends on the second of February. In the Orthodox Church, that is. Nobody celebrates anymore that late, but it's nice to keep the Christmas things around the house."

"Does a special saint's feast fall on that day?" Martin asked.

"No, Christmas just ends. Do you know that the Three Kings are the patron saints of travelers?"

"Maybe they should also be the saints of immigrants who keep on traveling."

"*We saw his star at its rising*—I can't remember how it goes. Now that Father Lapi has died, when Epiphany comes, who is going to chalk the initials of the kings and the new year on my door?"

"Who replaced him at the midnight mass?"

"They brought a Polish priest from Cedar City."

"That's a long drive—four hours each way—to come every Sunday, and who knows what the roads in Utah are like in the middle of the winter."

"They don't have regular Polish services anymore at St. Anne's. They now celebrate mass in Spanish."

On Oakey he crossed the Strip and then the railroad tracks.

"The last time I was in Poland I brought back a calendar for Father Lapi, with a different icon for each month, and some *oplatki* that the nuns had baked and were selling at the shrine of the Black Madonna in Jasna Gora. I put off bringing him the little presents, I didn't have a ride to St. Anne's parish house, *you* didn't want to go . . ."

"Now it's my fault that he died without his calendar?"

"Or I was too tired after work to walk over there or even to talk to anyone. I kept telling myself that he could have enjoyed the calendar already through October. Although the calendar was for the new year, he could have looked ahead of time at the icons. When it got to be the end of January, I told myself that it was too late to bring a calendar, although there always would've been those dark icons for him to look at. And when I heard that he had died, then it really was too late."

"He might have come over to pick up his calendar, if you'd just phoned him."

"I am not a telephone-*Mensch!*" She spoke with such emphasis— almost anger, he thought—as if she could not understand that he, of all people, should not know this about her.

He didn't say anything.

"*Panowie mówia,* that's what that is. When we were children, small children, my parents had a crystal set radio. When my father was listening to the crackling voices and we were laughing or talking, he would admonish us, '*Cicho, cicho, panowie mówia,* Quiet, quiet, the gentlemen are talking.' Whenever he said that, I imagined the gentlemen as busts like Marshal Pilsudski on a postage stamp. Later, after 1960, when men wore longer hair and mustaches, I still imagined male callers to look like the men-busts of my childhood.

"You know that I can talk to friends on the telephone, but with strangers. . . . To talk to someone on the telephone I have to know what they look like. Sometimes I ask people what they are wearing. The other day I talked to Eudora on the phone. 'What are you wearing?' I asked her. 'This isn't television,' she replied. 'I'm just grubbing in the garden.' But that isn't me. If I can't imagine the person on the other end of the telephone, I have problems."

In silence they passed through high walls into streets named after towns in New England. Marblehead turned into Nashua, Fall River wound to Gloucester, and Provincetown curled into Methuen, all coiled like passages in a maze. In front of each house stood two olive trees strung with a few chains of blinding white lights.

Having driven into a cul-de-sac at the heart of what in the New England town might have been the commons or the town green, they were facing three houses at the far end of the turn circle. At first the windows of the middle house looked as if they had been decorated with large Christmas cards with a bear motif, but when they came closer he could see that tableaux had been set up, the largest being a Santa's workshop in the picture window of the living room.

Martin switched off the headlights and slipped a cassette of Polish Christmas songs into the player.

"No. Too rambunctious for tonight. Play the Italian songs again."

Martin pushed the Eject button and reached into the backseat for a handful of cassettes.

"Jozefa didn't have an easy life. She told me tonight that she had been raised in an orphanage. When she was a small child one nun in particular was looking after her because Jozefa had problems with her legs. Although she couldn't walk well, all day long she kept following the nun, and at night she even slept in the same bed with her because the other children didn't want her around. Then, one day, she was taken in by a farmer . . ."

"Why?"

"The institution gave the orphans away. The farmer had nine children of his own and his wife died on the ninth one . . ."

"Heh, look!"

Slowly, as if they were awakening from a long winter's sleep, the bears began to stir. The one who was bent over the workbench raised and lowered the hammer tied to his paw, while the saw of another bear was gliding through a piece of wood, and a third one kept lifting a big needle with a bright red piece of yarn. All three shook their heads while they were working.

"Maybe somebody in the house saw our car and turned on the mechanism," Martin said.

"They probably took pity on us for having missed the show."

"Any moment now I expect to hear music from a calliope and to see a carnival wagon with puppets who blow their horns and beat on drums while one of them waves a baton."

"As a child I didn't like those puppet musicians with their waxen hands and faces," Ala said. "They scared me when I saw a calliope at the carnival. First they looked as if they were dead, and then they twitched around and looked as if somebody had sent electric current into their fingertips."

Martin started the engine and began to drive back. Even while he was turning onto Oakey Boulevard, he could see that down the street the railroad crossing light was flashing red.

"This was not the nineteenth century with orphanages out of a Dickens novel. When was she born, anyway?"

Ala counted the years aloud while he pulled up to the barrier. From the right he heard the rumbling of the train.

"1914."

"That's not far from the nineteenth century."

"She was put into the orphanage during the first war. Someone left her as a foundling with the sisters, her name written on a note pinned to her diapers." Ala was silent for a while. "Was she born Jewish? Maybe a Jewish woman had brought her to the orphanage."

"Why do you think that?"

"What the baby wore wasn't of poor quality. The nuns kept it and later showed it to her. And she wasn't naked. She had diapers, which was something."

"Where was she during the next war?"

"She didn't tell me much about that, only that at one time she was doing forced labor in Germany. Before she moved to Las Vegas she had married a gambler and lived with him in Canada. This is how she must have come to Las Vegas, moving down here with the gambler."

With its horn blaring, the engine pulled the train very slowly across the street. Sealed freight cars were followed by boxlike container carriers. Then came a row of flatbed cars with tanks on them painted in desert camouflage colors of sand and olive.

"Maybe it's just the National Guard going on maneuvers." Martin's voice trailed off. "So she was taken from the orphanage to the farmer?"

"In the meantime they found what had been wrong with her, the reason why she couldn't walk. In the orphanage they had left her shoes on. Can you believe that? She doesn't know whose fault it was, but her shoes stayed on, day and night, although her feet kept growing inside of the shoes. She was taken to the doctor . . ."

The end of the train came into view, a two-tiered railroad car loaded with new automobiles painted electric blue. The light of the streetlamps made them glisten as if they had been hosed down. Martin pushed a button and, as the window on his side slid down, the car filled with noise and cold air.

"What are you doing? It's freezing!"

Martin raised his arm outside of the window and waved when the caboose rolled by. The brakeman waved back. When Martin pushed the button, the window closed and suddenly the car was silent again.

"How was her life with the farmer?"

The red-and-white barrier was not raised quickly enough and the cars behind them honked.

"And a Merry Christmas to you too," Martin said as the car bumped across the tracks.

"The farmer already had nine children and his new wife wanted a child of her own and Jozefa didn't fit into her plans. So they sent her out to herd cattle and whenever the cows damaged the crops or ate vegetables in the garden, Jozefa was beaten for it. She was beaten until she was twenty-one years old. After one terrible beating she knelt down, in front of everybody in the farmer's living room and swore by the Virgin Mary that she would set fire to the house."

Crossing the Strip at the Olympic Gardens he read aloud the red plastic letters of the lighted advertising sign: DREAM GIRLS OIL WRESTLING COMING JANUARY 6.

"What a shame. That used to be a nice Greek restaurant. Why did they have to go and ruin it?"

"I guess that's where the money is."

They drove the last part of Oakey in silence. Already from the Stop sign on Tenth Street he could see the glow from her Christmas decorations, as if her house and the trees around it had been turned into a cloud of light.

"Your house is beautiful this year."

"Oh, there are still not enough lights. Some strings went out in the storm and from the beginning I should have put up more lights."

He pulled into the carport and turned off the motor. He knew how she worried about her Christmas lights, spending every year more and more time and money on them.

"I feel as if I really ought not to ask, but what happened to Jozefa at the farmer's?"

"He left her alone for three years but then he beat her again."

"Did she set fire to the house?"

"No. That night—Jozefa remembers the date exactly, but I can't—she slipped out of the bedroom window and left forever."

"That was saintly of her not to burn the farmer's house down."

Ala opened her handbag and began to rummage through it. Martin sighed impatiently when he turned on the spotlight focused on the passenger seat. But when she finally withdrew her hand from the bag she didn't have her house keys, as he had expected. From an envelope with large colorful stamps she pulled a white altar wafer. The letter must be from Aunt Cesia, who sent *oplatek* in her Christmas letters to Ala. She broke off a piece of the wafer and motioned for him to open his mouth. First she put a piece of the wafer on his tongue and then a small piece on her own tongue. "Merry Christmas!" With great care so that the fragile wafer wouldn't crumble, she slid the unused portion back into the envelope with the large foreign stamps and put it in his hand. "For New Year's and Three Kings."

With the tip of his tongue, he tried to taste the wafer stuck to the roof of his mouth, but to him it had no particular flavor. He drove slowly so that in the rearview mirror he could see Ala's lights as long as possible. By stringing wires with tiny bulbs over and through trees and bushes, she had transformed her house into a chapel of light in a dark neighborhood. Maybe she had felt that it was her duty to bring forth light as an outward manifestation of her underground church. She might have seen herself, although he doubted that she would think of herself in such terms, as a missionary building a chapel somewhere in the jungle.

When he stopped in his carport he kept the motor running to keep the heat on and then he pulled the wafer from its envelope. By the pale dome light he saw that a Christmas scene had been baked into the surface of the wafer, the Adoration of the Magi. Ala had broken off part of the manger, but the mother and the baby lying in the feeder were safe under the roof overhang, while on the right two kings knelt by their gifts. He wondered where the third king was. Was he looking into the stable through a hole in the walls, an outsider, as he had been at Ala's celebration? Shaking his head, he broke off a small piece of the stable's roof and put it on his tongue. Reaching into the backseat for Jozefa's present, he noticed that the black upholstery in Jozefa's corner was covered with short white hair from her fur coat. Smiling at the thought of the Carpathian bear shedding, he leaned back in the driver's seat and closed his eyes. Finally he began to feel peace. He was resting when he saw Jozefa tottering after the nun in the orphanage, saw the child clutching the sister's grayish-brown habit whose hem was sweeping along the cold stone floor. And then, in a fierce Polish winter, he saw the orphan child burying its face in the rough folds of the nun's habit, breathing deeply the smell of saintliness.

He weighed Jozefa's present in his hand and decided to keep it the way she had given it to him: the green envelope uncut, the card unread, the box unopened.

"Come along, you Old Country dog," Martin said, and with Nini trailing after him, he walked through the empty house to his library. At the shelf across from his desk he pushed things to the left and the right to make room for Jozefa's present. Holding the brightly wrapped package to his ear, he shook it gently and listened to the faint sloshing. The apple trees of Avalon, the island of the blessed, he thought, as he set the package between the lion and the kneeling saint.

It was then that he remembered the typewriter. At first he wanted to leave it in the car till morning, but then he thought, no, it is a present and for another hour or two it was still Christmas. When he came to Ala's house she was still outside, hanging up a chain of lights that had dropped from a branch. He offered to take the typewriter out of the trunk, but she insisted on carrying it herself. With the bulky typewriter clutched against her body, she walked heavily, the way she did at the end of her shift with the hours of work weighing on her shoulders. He watched her pass through the corridor of lights blinking and flickering on both sides of her path and then he backed down the incline of her driveway. On the other side of the hedge he stopped again.

"These are the best lights ever," he called out. He couldn't see her, but from the deep shadows cast over the doorway, her hand waved briefly like a white bird rising.

The Pilots of the Rose Trellis

"Your grandmother was such a gentle woman," Lottel said. "Why is it that you call her *Urn*? For me, of course, she was always Frau Jung."

"When Bert was small, he couldn't pronounce such a difficult word as *great-grandmother,* so we shortened it for him." Martin smiled when he thought of his grandmother together with his son.

"Your grandmother was so protective of you. When she brought you down to the garden, she didn't want to go away. She would stand by the white fence and watch over you. When she finally did leave, she would come back after a while and wave to you so you would stop playing, because she feared that you might wear yourself out and catch pneumonia."

"I remember when we were fleeing from the Russians. She was standing outside a refugee train—maybe the last one to leave town—waiting for me to catch up. But I couldn't run very fast because I was wearing two of my father's suits, one over the other. Urn waved and waved for me to get on board before the train pulled out of the station."

"I still see her by the fence, her round, gentle face creased with worry as she calls you, '*Kummock! Kummock!*'"

"I was never allowed to say words like *kummock* or anything else in Silesian dialect. The other children around me spoke it, at least those in grade school. By the time I went to prep school, the others spoke High German like my parents had made me do. If I wanted to say *come along,* they had me say *komm doch,* rather than allowing me to use Urn's homey mountain Silesian *kummock.*

"Still, even though she was the oldest of us, Urn was always the most forward-looking of our family. It was she who bought the newest electric appliances, like our first radio or a heating pad to use instead of hot water bottles in the cold eastern nights. She always went ahead of us, so when we came to America, she was the first one of our family to die here."

"Talking about your *oma* has made me think about your family's garden." Lottel leaned back and, to her surprise, sank deep into the sofa.

"Don't worry about it," he said. "There's been something wrong with that sofa since my parents bought it. It's comfortable, though, isn't it? With the flowers printed on it, it looks as if you've sunk into a bed of roses." Martin smiled and sat back into the corner of the love seat. "You know, I think about our garden, too."

She looked at him briefly, as if she wanted to make sure he was serious. "I don't really believe you when you say that you spend much time trying to remember Silesia."

She must know that I remember, Martin thought. She has to know, and since she does know, every such question is really just one more accusation that I turned my back on Silesia and its cause.

"For me, America is the land of forgetting," she said. "Did you become an American? A citizen?"

"Yes, I was naturalized."

"What does that mean?"

"You take some tests . . ."

"No, I mean the word *naturalized.*"

"I don't know, I really don't. *Naturalized* makes me think of something entirely different from swearing an oath promising not to overthrow the government. Before Bert got married . . ."

"How old was your son?"

"Young, very young. A child groom or so I thought then."

She laughed. "So were you when you got married."

"When he was still living with me, we often drove into the desert. One day, after we had parked Bert's truck, we were hiking up in a dry riverbed. Scanning the banks for interesting debris carried down by a flood, I saw a book among the creosote bushes, a book that looked to me like it had been read by the wind. Really. It had been fanned open and its pages had been abraded by the grit of the desert wind. The edges of the pages had been rounded until it looked less like a book and more like a head that had been scissor-cut and blow-dried."

"What kind of book was it? In stories like this it would have to be something meaningful like a Bible."

"Don't scoff! No, it wasn't anything as obvious as that, but a paperback copy of *Dr. Zhivago*. What it was is not the reason why I am telling you this. That didn't matter anymore, because the wind had turned whatever it had been before into a natural object, looking like a rock or a small dusty cactus. To me, that is what the word *naturalizing* means, to turn something back into nature."

"You didn't seem to have turned into a small dusty cactus. What happened?"

"We were just talking about my grandmother. When she came to America, she thought—and she always had her own way of thinking—that learning all of the words to 'America the Beautiful' would help her to become an American citizen. She learned them all, from 'Oh, beautiful for spacious skies' to 'from sea to shining sea,' although she never managed to learn English. Then Mother, her true daughter, decided to learn the same words. I have always wondered how the foreign words telling of alabaster cities gleaming undimmed by human tears helped her when she went to work every day in the casket factory, a job of work that drove her to the edge."

"Was it that hard?"

"It nearly did her in. I mean, she had to force herself every morning to go back. She knew that she had to keep the job, because she and Father needed the money. And I couldn't help because I was in school. I seem to have always been in school."

"Do you remember the rose trellis?" she asked.

Behind their gray-stuccoed block of apartments, the tenants had gardens, each with a small wooden house different from all of the others. The garden house of Martin's family was larger than the others, and it had been painted pale green, the shade of linden leaves. It was large enough to hold not only spades and shovels, wicker baskets of various sizes, rakes and hoes, but also a table and chairs and sufficient room for a handful of people to find shelter from a cloudburst.

Once, the children from the apartments had held a summer festival in and around Martin's garden house. They wore costumes made by their mothers, sang songs, and drank lemonade while Chinese lanterns glowed huge and yellow in the night above them like August moons on a string.

Next to the summerhouse and under the branches of a peach tree had been Martin's sandbox. Father had hired a carpenter to build the sandbox from the best wood and then—before it was filled with the finest sand available—he had ordered the wood painted with creosote to ensure that it would never rot. Why had his father ordered a sandbox built so that it would withstand the years? Martin was an only child, born late in his father's life. Why then had Father built this sandbox to last for eternity? Did he believe that his son would stay a child forever?

"The rose trellis always looked so big to me, maybe only because we were small. When Mother told me about the Israelites and how they suffered in exile, even though Babylon had such beautiful gardens, I imagined the gates of Babylon to be very grand, like our rose gate. There *was* something majestic about it, although it was no more than a rose-covered arch guarding a walkway to a wooden house that my father had painted linden green." Martin paused to think. "You know, that was really *our* garden, not my family's, but your and my garden. Ours."

"We used to sit up there and tell each other that we were going to fly away into the wide world."

"You sound sad about it, but all of us did leave home, even if it was against our will."

"The roses were growing up the sides of the trellis gate, but they were still so young that we weren't stuck by their thorns when we climbed up. They didn't reach all the way to the top, so we could sit up there on the wood grating and be happy."

The rosebushes were as young as the apartment house, as young as Martin. He was the first baby born in the house, in the bedroom of one of the two apartments sharing the second-floor landing. He remembered how polished the wood had been between the two doors. One night, Martin heard loud noises coming through their apartment door, voices shouting and then dishes being smashed on the floor and then more shouting. This had scared him so much that he still remembered it. Kneeling behind the door—which to him was as safe as Urn's lap—he kept listening to the noise until everything was quiet once again. Then he slowly pulled open the door a crack and put his head down on the threshold. He peered along the polished floor, which was now littered with shards of porcelain and crockery. The flat planes of broken dinner plates looked like ice floes on the Oder River, while standing above them—and that had horrified him even more—were broken cup handles, which to him looked like cutoff ears.

When his mother found him, she tried to soothe his fears by telling him that what he had heard was nothing more than *Polterabend,* an old folk custom of breaking dishes on the eve of a wedding. The violence had frightened him so that he would not believe his mother's assurances that it had all been in fun, and he certainly could not believe that it meant good luck.

"Sitting up there on the top of the trellis gate, one behind the other, we pretended to be fliers in one of the old planes of the first war, when the pilots still wore leather caps and goggles. Did you know that Manfred von Richthofen was born in Breslau?"

Martin nodded. "But so was Angelus Silesius, the mystic, who also went to Elisabetschule. Not at the same time, with me, of course. *'If you blossom like a rose unwithered, even under suffering, cross and pain, blessed you will be.'*"

"Sitting up there," Lottel continued without paying attention to his quote, "we would look across the top of the board fence that separated the gardens from the fields. Sitting on top of the rose trellis we could see quite clearly all the way to the Kaisergraben."

That about sums up Brockau, Martin thought. A place with nothing of importance, its highest point the railroad bridge. Only such a place would name its ditch after the emperor.

"When we were the pilots of the rose trellis, we played that we would fly off into the great wide world." She lapsed into silence and leaned back on the sofa amid the big flowers.

"How old could we've been?"

"Six, seven, at most eight years. After that you moved away."

"I was nine when I was sent to prep school, Elisabetschule in Breslau. That was when we moved into the new house on Winkler Allee. The garden of the new house was bigger than all of the apartment gardens put together, and instead of one summerhouse, it had two, one on each end of the garden. But I had to play there by myself. I liked our new house. My room faced into the crowns of the linden trees lining our street, which was so grandly called an *Allee*, as if Brockau could support something like a Parisian avenue. Sometimes—and always toward evening—I used to stand by our living room window in the new house and look across all the gardens toward the gray block where you lived. The sun setting over Zobten Mountain dyed the windows of your apartment house copper and gold. But somehow I couldn't see the garden where you and I used to play. It was too far away, although it was just around the corner. The only way I could even guess where it might be was when I could locate the top of the pear tree growing in the middle of our old garden."

He leaned his head back and closed his eyes for a minute. "I just remembered something. Once you and I were in the meadow by our new house. It wasn't a large meadow—more like a greensward by the side of the *Allee*—and we were lying there pretending we were on vacation in the Riesengebirg Mountains. We picked blowflowers, as we called the dandelions—do you remember?—and watched their white feathery seeds float away on our breath." Martin stopped to think. "This must've been when we were new in the house. Why didn't we ever play together after my family moved away?"

"I *knew* that you don't remember the past. You're just faking it!" Lottel said triumphantly. "We didn't play together anymore because it was wartime and the schools had to double up."

"I knew that," countered Martin.

"My school had the morning shift, and yours—I don't even know to which part of Breslau they shifted the Elisabetschule boys after the war broke out—you had to go in the afternoons."

"I hated—no, I feared—school. What I hated was when I had to go in the afternoons. I never liked school much anyway. All morning I would keep thinking that I would have to walk to the station to catch the train that would take me to the two o'clock class. My whole day was ruined because I could never really feel free. During the mornings I had to do homework—and I wasn't very fast at that—and by noon I was already trudging to the railroad station. When I came home, it was dark."

"See, this is why we never saw each other," Lottel continued, "except during vacations. After your family moved away, we never again sat on top of the rose trellis."

Years after the war, he had gone back to Silesia. He had gone just this once, but even that had taken all of his strength. On that journey, which he had to prepay in dollars with all the arrangements being made by the Polish tourist agency, he had to stay in one of the state-owned hotels in Breslau. It was new and built in a style thought of as modern according to western standards. It wasn't far from the main railroad station, from where he had once walked to school six days of the week and on the seventh had walked to church with his parents.

Now he looked down from his seventh-floor room into a huge parking lot, and he tried to remember the houses that once had stood where the asphalt stretched over what must have been blocks of buildings. Tour buses were parked where he once had walked between rows of houses that had been shot to rubble during the siege.

The hotel was occupied by Germans like him, who had returned to visit their old *Heimat*. When he went up to his room, two women shared his elevator. He was still deep in thought, having seen the railroad station again where once he had spent so much time waiting—which was actually all he remembered—and walking through streets that had been his way to school, so he was paying little attention to the excited female voices. That is, until one woman raised her voice until it became too loud for the small enclosure: "Breslau is now firmly in German hands."

Only when the woman's voice rose above a murmur had he become aware that she was speaking German. Her words and intonation were those of a news announcer reading a communiqué from army headquarters. Martin imagined her brisk voice coming from the black Bakelite radio Urn had bought. Sitting in front of the radio and looking at the illuminated dial shaped like a lemon wedge, he had listened to voices like hers reporting the war as it was being lost, but sounding strong until the very end.

It was not until much later that he realized that the two women in the elevator had talked without a trace of Silesian dialect in their voices.

After breakfast, he went to the lobby to exchange money. A taxi driver who had been waiting with others to be hired by a foreigner walked over to him while he stood at the bank window. The man was dressed in a suit and tie and looked like a person one could trust. He offered a much better exchange rate from dollars to zlotys than the posted official one. Martin knew the transaction was illegal and that he could be arrested, but he felt he could trust the man. While they were changing money in the cab, Martin asked the driver if he knew a place called Brockau. He nodded. "Not much there," he said as he pulled out of the hotel parking lot. As they drove through the city, which looked unfamiliar to Martin and yet close to him, the driver called out each of the streets they were crossing by their old German names. The driver never used the word *German,* instead he phrased it diplomatically, as, that is what the street was called before the war. The driver spoke German as well as English, because he claimed to have once lived in Chicago but that his American adventure somehow hadn't worked out.

When they passed over the railroad bridge into Brockau, Martin's heart was beating faster because he recognized so many buildings. It was as if nothing had changed, except that everything had aged. There had been no transitions for him, no occasional visits home from university or stays at home at Christmas, between when he had left Brockau at age thirteen and now. Things had aged too suddenly, like children do who act out growing old in a school play in which they look ludicrous but still make the audience feel an uncertain horror. To calm his unease, he tried to make himself imagine the journey as part of a time-lapse photography study. By means of this ruse, he could concentrate on solving imaginary technical problems and thereby keep himself from feeling. But when the car slowed to turn into the street of the house where he was born, his thinking failed to help him and he couldn't do anything except feel. He still made an attempt, a pretense at best, to be an observer who had come from far away, a foreigner protected from all evil by his passport.

When the cab had completed its turn, a single glance was enough to let the panorama of the street snap into place. Coming from the direction where once the Lutheran church had stood, he could see that every house on the left side of the street had disappeared, including number 42, where he was born. The gardens in back had grown into a wilderness without fences or summerhouses, and the pear tree that had always told him where he lived and where home was had been cut down.

The car rolled to a stop, but Martin didn't even reach over to open the door. Instead, he leaned into the corner of the seat and closed his eyes. Looking at Martin in the rearview mirror, the driver might have thought that his passenger was saying a silent prayer over the past.

After a few minutes of silence, Martin sat up straight. But instead of gazing across the rubble-filled foundation at the wilderness that once had been the gardens of his childhood, he leaned his forehead against the side window. Looking down at this steep angle, he didn't expect to see more than the crumbled sidewalk. He imagined it crushed by the steel treads of tanks. Out of the corner of his eye, he caught sight of a small metal rail running a foot above the ground. It surprised and cheered him to see that the fence between sidewalk and lawn—the children had not been allowed to play there—had somehow survived. It had been sturdy enough so that you could walk on it. With your arms outstretched, you could be a tightrope walker.

With his forehead resting against the pane, he tried to remember the men and women who had lived in this apartment building, but he couldn't, not even the children who had played with him. He recalled the children only as a singular blur, a running, shouting, whirling group dressed in white. He remembered more clearly the paper airplanes they had made, which had swished through the air where now the taxi stood on the broken sidewalk.

The car had no radio, and the driver didn't speak to his passenger. Martin was thinking of the planes they had made by tearing pages from school notebooks and then folding the lined or checked paper according to a method and pattern passed on in the street and strictly observed by everyone. When they had made all of the necessary creases—sharp and straight—their planes would circle like white birds before settling into the green grass on the other side of the metal bar. One day, a boy pressed pebbles into the center crease of the triangular wing as if he were loading a bomber, but instead of soaring on an upwind to the second floor—where Martin had been born in a dark-blue bedroom—the paper plane dived hard onto the sidewalk and scattered its toy bombs across the cement.

When Martin touched the driver's shoulder, he let the car roll forward with the leisurely pace of a buyer inspecting a piece of real estate. He turned around at a small square where Martin's mother had shopped. Soon they were headed back in the direction of the Lutheran church, which had been dismantled and taken east as if it were a factory and part of the war reparations. Old gentlemen used to walk on the promenade and then sit together on the shaded benches. They would clip their straw hats to the lapels of their linen jackets so that their hands would be free, although they had nothing left to do.

Martin pointed to the right, into an *Allee* defined mostly by its linden trees, since the buildings had all disappeared. He imagined that the Russian T-34 tanks had taken the same way, around this corner, their guns lowered like dogs' noses sniffing a trail of blood. The linden trees left standing looked stunted, as if their crowns had been chopped out by artillery fire. He remembered that his father had admired the sweet-smelling linden trees so much that he had bought a house on Winkler Allee.

No more than a hundred paces into the street, he told the driver to stop. This time Martin left the car, although he had seen at a glance that the lot was empty. All that was still standing was a brick chicken house and a rusting pump. As he stood by the wire fence and looked out across the weeds, a thought struck him. In the other street he had seen that the place of his birth had also been destroyed. The gray building that had enclosed—as a chest cavity holds the pulsating heart—the bedroom whose dark-blue walls had been splattered with his mother's blood during Martin's difficult birth was gone. And gone was their new house, plastered with its proud bloodred stucco, which Urn insisted was "the red of the Lord's blood, like velvety roses." No trace was left that he had ever lived here. Other houses in town had survived the bombings and the artillery barrages of the three-month siege of Breslau, but both of his houses had been destroyed. No trace, he thought, no trace of me is left. The birds had eaten all of the bread crumbs, and there was no way out of the forest.

Maybe somebody was cleaning up after him, putting his toys on a shelf, picking up his clothes and wiping away the smudges that his hands had left on the walls. And finally, as the last part of the cleaning, the walls themselves had been taken away, as if his childhood was a drama that had played its run and now the stage had to be cleared for another company of actors and a new play.

"To flee, like my family, or to be driven out, like yours, doesn't count as flying into the wide world, the way we had dreamed. It should be easier for you, because you do still live in Germany. Even if Bremen is different in a thousand ways from Silesia, it *is* part of Germany."

Martin pointed to a gingerbread house made from thin cardboard. "Take one."

Lottel opened the side of the house and took out a chocolate-covered heart.

"It's from a delicatessen that carries some goods imported from Germany."

Lottel took a bite out of the *Lebkuchen* heart. "For me, Bremen never became what Silesia had been. It doesn't matter that I was married there, that my son was born there, and that my mother and brother are buried there. I have always felt like a stranger, and as I get older it gets worse. We, the girls who went to school together in Breslau, meet twice a year, coming together from wherever the war carried us. The terrible thing is that we don't sound alike anymore. One of them had the nerve to say that I was speaking as if I were a woman from Bremen. Can you believe that?" Lottel shook her head. "But I got even with her. 'And you sound like a Bavarian,' that's what I told her." She laughed, but just as quickly she became serious again. 'And yet, once upon a time, we were all Silesian girls.'"

"Right now you're on vacation in America, and you should enjoy the pleasant winter weather we're having."

"It *is* nice here." Lottel looked out through the kitchen window, and Martin's eyes followed her gaze. His father had planted bamboo on the strip by the side of the house, and now the breeze was stirring the narrow leaves until they flicked in the evening sun like fishing lures.

"This is an exotic place, all right," Martin mused, "but not what you and I dreamed about when we were dangling our legs from the rose trellis. Our wide world had jungles, mountains, and deserts. We wanted to explore Africa, the South Seas, cross the Gobi, or travel to whatever else we had read about, in *die Ferne*. Here, I never even talked to anyone about our dreams. How could I in America? What we wanted, *die Ferne*, translates only clumsily into something like *faraway places*, which makes you think of nothing more than tourism or a 1930s song. What these words don't give you is that *die Ferne, the far*, is next to infinity. It's like the last mountain range you can make out in a Caspar David Friedrich painting of a moonrise. Neither you nor I—although I traveled more—ever went that far. *Die Ferne*, what did it mean to us when we were still on the rose trellis? How far was far to us then? The farthest we could see was to the city gas works, where we could watch how the huge cylinders of the storage tanks rose or fell."

"But I, I was the one who stayed home, and you, you flew away."

Brockau, plain, gray and green, had been home, but the world as he imagined it to be—wild and exciting—had been his only when he read books or drew maps. Thinking back, he saw himself endlessly drawing maps—usually of Africa. Hunched over the table in his room facing the linden trees, he would select different colors for the independent countries—there weren't too many on that continent—or if the puzzle-shaped pieces were colonies, he would color them in the shade of England or France, who owned most of Africa. There was only one part he didn't like to draw, the large dun-colored spill spreading across the belly of Africa that was the Belgian Congo. He had read bad things about that colony in more than one of his books, and he grew to dislike it, until he thought even its shape and color were ugly.

He remembered that once when the family was visiting Militsch, a town close to the Polish border where his father was born, he was bored and there was nothing to read. He must have been ten years old or even younger at that time. Walking around, he had found a church and had asked the pastor for something to read. Impressed, he lent Martin books about the missionary effort of the church. Fired up by what he read, Martin told his parents that he intended to become a missionary in Africa. A Lutheran missionary, he added with great passion in his voice. His father reminded him that there was war everywhere, and that besides, neither Martin nor his parents were Lutheran. After they went back home to Brockau, his father never mentioned it to Martin, who, once more, happily drew maps of Africa.

"I was just thinking about Africa. I've been there, in the north of it, anyway. Tangiers, Casablanca, but heading toward Marrakech I got sick."

"I didn't know that."

"It doesn't matter. It wasn't *die Ferne* either, like we imagined on the rose trellis."

When the war ended, they were walking back home across Germany from the place where they had fled, close to the Swiss border. In a town halfway home, they had to halt, because his father had been told that the family, being Germans, wouldn't be allowed back into Silesia. Through all the months when they were on the road, Martin had been pleased that he didn't have to go to school, but after they had to stay in Erfurt, his father insisted on schooling. Now was the time to tell his father that he needed an atlas at school. It wasn't true, but it was the only way he knew how to go back to drawing maps. None of the bookstores had an atlas in stock because there was no merchandise of any value whatsoever to be had. Finally, his mother went to a black market street and traded the family's meat rations for a used school atlas. The boy may have felt guilty at that time—Martin now hoped that he had—but he knew no other way to go back to his dream. Coloring maps made him happier than any of his travels ever did.

"Fleeing or being driven out is not the same as leaving home as an explorer." Lottel spoke again after a long silence.

"No, it isn't," agreed Martin.

"At least you made a place for yourself and your family in America." She sounded as if she begrudged him that.

That certainly hadn't been part of the plan of the two children, who thought that Brockau would be their home forever and the world was to be only looked at. Dressed in flying leathers, they would see the world. If the sun was shining brightly, they would put on pith helmets.

"I tried to make a life in America." He didn't tell her how much he had given up.

"You even became an American."

"I thought that I could fit in enough to be one of them. But maybe it isn't really possible to become an American. Not in one lifetime anyway."

"Why not?"

"For one thing, they won't let you forget that you're not one of them. In their customarily friendly manner, people ask you—I'm sure for entirely innocent reasons—'Do I detect the trace of an accent?' And there you are, a foreigner all over again, green card in hand, grateful for the first job washing windows. The terrible thing about this is that they usually mean well. Americans are the most well-meaning people in the world.

"But there is something else, and it has to do with me. I can't just slip into a new life as if I were a confidence man gluing on a fake mustache. I still have memories."

He fell silent, and for once Lottel didn't say anything about remembering.

"I like newspapers, and I always read advice columns. Here in America, there are twin sisters who answer questions that people send in. Some of these questions are sturdy perennials, such as, 'What am I supposed to do about a spouse who keeps letters and pictures of an old love hidden in a closet?' This is how it is with America and me. I still hide memories of an old love. I admit that I often forget about them, but they always come back to my mind. The older I get, the more the memories keep coming back. It is as if I never honored my pledge to forsake all others."

Lottel reached over to the Christmas plate on the table and took a cookie. "I even named my son after you."

"And then I went and changed my first name!" Martin laughed.

"This isn't funny! Did you have to do that?"

"No, but I wanted to be friendly, and I thought it would be friendlier to have the name of a saint than that of a Germanic warrior. Besides, it made it easier for people to pronounce my name when I was looking for a job."

"You could have stayed who you were and spoken for Silesia."

There it was again: he wasn't sufficiently Silesian for her taste. "At least, I must have cared enough for Germany to fly to Berlin to be there for the first election after the Wall came down."

"Did you come to Berlin to vote?"

"Of course I didn't!" he replied angrily. "You know very well that I can't vote in Germany."

"Maybe you came because you wanted to write about the election."

That hadn't been it, but Martin didn't correct her.

"Why don't you ever write about Silesia?"

He didn't answer.

"Why do you write in English?"

"Nobody in Germany cares about my writing."

"Be serious!"

"But it's true! I don't fit in over there. Most of the German writers are on the left, and you know that I am not."

"But you certainly aren't on the right either! Certainly not when it comes to our cause of getting Silesia back from the Poles!"

"I've never been interested in politics." Martin's voice was low, and he sounded tired, as if he were an actor who had said the same line once too often.

"I don't remember enough English from school to be able to read your stories, not even when I use a dictionary."

"This is too bad, because you are the one person who would have understood what I am writing. You might not like what I write, but at least you might have understood. This is how it is: Some people read you because they know you and they're as curious as cats what your stories will reveal about you. Others just read a little bit of a story and then get lost among all the foreigners. Then there are those who tell you that they are saving your story for that special evening when they will have a block of time to savor your fine writing."

"If you just wrote in German, I could read you." Lottel laughed as if that was merely a small favor she was asking. "From what my son tells me, your stories are set in all sorts of places, Russia, the Ukraine, Austria, even in Poland, but never in Silesia. Why don't you write about home?" she pleaded.

He took time and thought how to answer the question. "I don't want to lose the memories."

"How would writing about Silesia make you lose your memories? I would've thought that writing would make your memories stronger."

"I know of another Silesian living in Las Vegas, a lady working in an office tower near here. Not long ago, there was a newspaper article that mentioned that I am from Silesia. When the article came out, she called and said that she too was from there, from a place near the Kynsburg Castle. You remember that my father always used a walking stick, and on it he carried an oval silver badge impressed with the outline of this castle. When I was a child, I had even been to the castle ruin. In spite of all that, when the time came to talk to this Silesian woman in person—as I had promised her on the phone—I couldn't. I protect my memories as if they are something sacred—and they're nothing more than one man's recollections of his childhood—because I don't want their power weakened or even lost by talking to someone else about the past."

"That is sad."

"It's the only way I know how to write about Silesia, which is now lost forever, as if it were Atlantis. When I write about something from long ago, I have to force myself—as hard as I can—to haul up everything possible. Like a coal miner. Then I sift through what I brought up and write it. A year or two may pass—sometimes it's even longer—and finally it'll come out in print. By that time it has stopped being part of me. When I look at the journal or the book in my hand, it feels like a strange object. At the end of the war, when the American fighter planes were strafing Mengen, the little town in the south of Germany where we had fled, the shells from the machine guns were ejected and fell to the ground. After the raid, when the all-clear was still being sounded, I would run to the places

I had seen being hit, and if I was quick in getting there, the shells I grabbed would still be hot from the explosion in the chamber of the machine gun."

"This was a weird thing to do," said Lottel. "No, it's a terrible thing to do. The shells could have come from a shot that killed somebody."

"It's really not so strange. You get used to everything, even being shot at, especially when you're a child. When we were still at home, I would go to the end of the street, past the meadow where you and I used to sit."

"Once, maybe once we sat there. Not often."

"And from there I would turn into the small path that ran past the *Gasthaus.* On windy days I would wait under the big trees for the chestnuts to fall. When the spiky green balls hit the ground hard enough, they would split open and the shiny chestnuts would lie sleek and moist in the dusty footpath, and I would pick them up. That's how the brass shells would lie heavily in the palm of my hand, a piece of the strange world, as if I was holding a fragment from a meteor. The plane, of course, really was another world: Everything in it was American. I was craving anything American, and that is how America came to me when I was a child, I was either looking up at the bomber formations flying overhead on their way to a city, or I was dodging fighter planes shooting at me. But those brass shells in my hand made me feel the way I do when I hold anything that I have written and that has been published."

"How can that be?"

"From the moment something I've hauled up from the past is between covers, it fades and falls apart. The story from childhood is like a flower pressed between the pages of a book—you touch it and it crumbles to dust. My family has almost nothing anymore of what we brought from Silesia. For a while we still had a spoon from home, but now there are only a few snapshots and my memories, and when I write those down, they too will be lost. I want to have something survive from Silesia. *We* want to keep something from home, my mother and I, the last of our family. Can it get any smaller and still be called a family?"

"But you have a son."

"True, but for me *family* means those who were walking with me when my father, my mother, Urn, and I were pulling and pushing a cart across Germany toward a home that we would never reach. Through the years we searched for a new home, and that's why we came to America. Of these four people pulling the cart, now only two are left."

"But you have a son, just like Horst and I do."

"Bert is a good boy."

"Boy? He has to be around forty."

"Yes, he is. But every time somebody asks me, I have to stop and add up the years. After that newspaper article appeared, Bert called me later in the week and said, 'By the way, I'm forty-one and not forty.' That tells you how close we are." Martin picked up his glass and took a sip as if his mouth had become dry. "A good boy," he repeated. He cleared his throat, but his voice still sounded hoarse. "I never had to worry about him. But then he has never been part of it."

Lottel didn't ask what he meant by *it*, but she nodded in agreement. "Our son also is a good and respectful boy. He went with us to Silesia on one of our visits, because he wanted to see where his parents had once lived. Nowadays a lot of sons wouldn't have cared, but he still does."

They didn't speak. From a garden down the street they could hear a lawn mower.

"Winter grass," Martin explained.

"But you are right," Lottel said, "the young ones aren't part of the whole thing anymore. You know that we go to the meetings, every year in the summer, when the Silesians get together."

"How many are there?"

"Maybe a hundred thousand are left, but they are getting so old that the group dwindles and you can see that every time. One year the meetings will just stop because there won't be anybody left. They are trying hard to reach the next generation. They hold meetings with topics that might interest the youth, they have them march around the stage with flags. It's like my church trying to keep the young ones."

"Your church didn't even manage to keep *you*." Martin laughed, but Lottel didn't laugh with him.

"It didn't work for the church either," she continued.

"The young aren't part of the whole thing anymore, and they stand off to one side. Adam and Eve's children must have felt that they weren't part of something big anymore whenever their parents began to reminisce about their lost paradise. 'What did you do when you were in paradise?' one of their children might ask."

"And surely not with great interest," added Martin.

"And then Eve would tell her children about life in paradise, how they had picked flowers all day long and how, in the cool of the evening, the *Herrgott* would walk through the garden to look at His trees and His humans. Maybe the children listened to the stories their parents told, maybe they merely nodded politely and muttered *aha, aha,* but only if they were good children like our boys."

"*Ja, ja,*" murmured Martin.

"Gone and lost. We'll never get Silesia back from the Poles. The government in Bonn."

"It's now in Berlin."

"Don't joke. *That* government wrote off the Silesians, like a corporation would that has kept a debt too long on its books. They wrote us off and gave up any claim to Silesia. What right did they have to do that? Sitting by the Rhine River and not the Oder where we used to live at the other end of Germany, what right did they have to give up our land and our claims to that land? They gave up our land so they could trade with the Eastern countries." She stopped to catch her breath. When she continued, her voice dropped to a resigned murmur. "No, the young aren't part of it anymore."

Martin thought he could understand Lottel's anger and even her despair, but he had grown to feel and think too differently from her. Although he had known her longer than almost anyone else, there were some experiences he could not share, even with her. Would she understand what had really happened to him on his return to Silesia?

After the cab driver had taken him to the first house and they had turned into the street of the linden trees, Martin had seen a man digging just on the other side of their old property. He got out of the cab and walked with the driver along the sagging fence that marked the boundary of their property. By the side of their big garden had always been many small allotment plots worked by railroaders in their time off.

As they came closer, Martin could see that the gardener was a white-haired man who was spading close to the fence line. Martin nodded and smiled in silent greeting. Then he asked the driver in German, "Translate that I use to live over there," while Martin pointed across the fence.

Listening to the Polish words of the driver, the man's face grew somber. Did he resent a Silesian coming back? Martin wondered. When Martin asked if he could take a picture of him, the man shook his head and crossed his arms over his bare chest. Had this request insulted him? Martin looked to his interpreter for help.

"No, no," the driver translated the gardener's reply. "I am not dressed for photography." Martin smiled with relief, and the man lowered his arms. Again, through the driver's voice, Martin told how his family had to flee from the Soviet army, to which the man nodded in sympathy. He introduced himself as Jan, a retired railroad man who had been born in Lvov when the city was still Polish. After the war, when the Russians took Galicia from Poland, Jan along with many other Poles were resettled from Lvov to Silesia, and he was not even allowed to visit his birthplace. Now it was Martin's turn to nod sympathetically.

Jan went to his garden house, and when he came back he had put on a long-sleeved shirt and had brushed his hair. With a smile he pointed at the camera. Martin took pictures of the trees and shrubs but mostly of the gardener spading the dark-brown earth. Martin had helped his father dig beds for potatoes, carrots, beets, cabbage, asparagus, and much more than he now remembered, in the same earth, but on the other side of the fence.

Jan led them to a bower in front of his garden house and brought out a bottle of wine and three small glasses. When Martin pointed at the plain bottle without a label, Jan took him to the shrubs growing along the fence. Martin recognized the bushes at first sight as red currants. "*Johannisbeeren!*" he exclaimed, while Jan stood by his side and smiled the smile of a gardener.

Looking at the bush, he said "*porzeczka,*" and pointing to his glass he explained, "*porzeczkowe wino.*" Martin repeated slowly the Polish word "*porzeczkowe.*"

Time seemed to stop that morning as they sat in the shade of the vine-covered bower. They toasted each other with "*Na zdrowie!*" and "*Prosit!*" and drank wine that had been pressed from fruit grown from *their* soil. It was soil that Martin and his ancestors had worked since the seventeenth century, and that Jan and his sons and daughters would keep working.

The driver was with them, and yet he was not. After the first toast he had quietly walked away and settled into a chair outside in the sun. Martin and Jan were sitting shoulder by shoulder on a bench gray with age. Together they looked out from the shade toward the linden trees shimmering in the sunlight. Peace settled on the two men. Without a man in the middle, they were talking with gestures, slowly and bashfully at first, as if their hands were shy to be put to such a task. Now they understood each other and how alike they were, two men who by life had been taken far from home and who were trying to live as best they could.

And then they clinked glasses in a last salute. "To Lvov!" Martin said. "To Brockau!" Jan replied, giving the name its German pro-nunciation.

The driver asked how to get to the old highway to Breslau, and when he closed the door of the car behind Martin, Jan reached in to shake hands with his visitors. Through the rear window Martin could see Jan waving after them. On their way they stopped at the mouth of a narrow lane, because Martin had seen from his window that the old chestnut trees of his childhood had survived the war. He stood under the trees remembering, and when he turned around, he was surprised to see Jan walking toward him, leading his bicycle. He had taken a shortcut because he wanted to say good-bye once more. The two men beamed as if they had been away from each other for a long time. Seeing this, the driver brought the cam-era from the car and began to line up a shot. Jan pointed to his bi-cycle and insisted that his friend sit on it as if it were his own. Just before the camera clicked, Martin put his arm around Jan's shoulder and hugged him.

Back at the hotel, Martin asked the driver to return for him at six in the morning and take him out to Brockau before he had to catch his train. Then he went to the foreign currency store and bought a bottle of the best French cognac, handsomely boxed.

In the early light, they drove through a city that now looked even grayer than it had been in his childhood. When they crossed the bridge into Brockau, they began looking for Jan's address. He had told them that he lived in the back of one of the old railroad houses. Knocking at Jan's door, they heard a commotion on the other side. They waited and when the door opened, Jan had a towel wrapped around his waist and was dripping water. A large zinc bathtub was set up behind him in the middle of the cramped kitchen. He began to apologize for not being dressed, but Martin pressed the red-and-gold gift box into his friend's free hand. Then he told the driver to translate, "My present is not as good as *porzeczkowe wino,* but this is all I have to give." They quickly said good-bye to each other with tears in their eyes.

When Martin came back to America, he enlarged the picture of him sitting on Jan's bicycle and hung it over his desk. Whenever he looked up, he could see the two smiling men embracing each other, while behind them, under the old chestnut trees, the sandy path of his childhood ran deep into the distance.

Lottel had sat in silence, not telling him whatever thought went through her mind.

"You ought to ask yourself this—" Martin said. "Would you want to move your family out there, just so you could say, 'Once more I'm living in Silesia'? Would any one of us move back?"

"But the injustice!"

"A woman once said that if you really want justice, you ought to go to Hell, because you'll find justice only there. In Heaven there is mercy, and on Earth—as you and I have learned—injustice reigns. Yes, what happened to Silesia was against human and divine law, but no one spoke up loud enough or long enough. But we should've learned early. Every day when we walked from the railroad station to school, we saw the coat of arms of Breslau. Do you still remember what was on that shield?"

"Of course I do! The black Silesian eagle with a silver . . ." She motioned across her chest, and then she stopped to think.

"A black eagle," Martin spoke as if he were quoting from a book, "displayed, with a silver crescent whose upturned horns reached from wing to wing and which bore a cross. The eagle's legs and tail were splayed, and his raptor's head was turned west, not east."

"And a lion."

"Rampant."

"And I remember an angel or woman saint—Saint Hedwig or Saint Elisabeth?—bearing a crown."

"But what was in the middle of the shield?" asked Martin.

"A cutoff head."

"The head of John the Baptist. You didn't see Salome carrying the bloody head and giving it to her mother, but you always knew that. We should've learned from that picture instead of all the historical dates and the ballads we had to memorize in school. That should've been our real lesson. Every day we saw that picture of John's head. Wasn't it even on the sides of the red-and-white street-cars? It doesn't matter. We should've learned about injustice from that head on the platter."

"What injustice?"

"A double—no, a triple—injustice. One, John shouldn't have been killed, because he was a good man. Second, without having been given a trial, he should've never been executed in prison. And third, he was beheaded, which was against Jewish law."

"Ah, but that's just a symbol of a city."

"No! It's more than just that. I tell you, we were born under John's bloody head, under a sign of injustice. We could've learned the lesson on how to accept and bear injustice when we were young, but we never did. You didn't, and I didn't. Our feelings make us look for justice in different directions."

"I'll never forget," said Lottel defiantly.

"I'll never forget either," said Martin, but in a much softer voice. Even that surprised him, hearing himself say this sentence at all. "There are things you just can't forget, and it isn't just the bad, the evil, the unjust. Like this: On the night of St. John's, boys used to climb up into the trees on our street to pick the sweet-smelling linden blossoms and stuff them into white bags slung over their shoulders."

"Linden blossom tea, if it's picked during the night of St. John's, is supposed to cure many a sickness."

"The boys sang while they picked the blossoms."

"They say that during that midsummer night, the ones from the other side are very close to us."

For me the dead are always near, Martin thought, but he didn't say it. "The fires, there would always be fires on the night of St. John's. In the mountains they would light fires on every peak, until the fire rose like pillars into the sky."

They sat in silence.

"Did we ever even look at the roses when we climbed up the trellis to our perch on top of the gate?" Lottel asked. "Do you remember their color?"

"*Roses, white and red, blooming amid the thorns, so like my blood-bridegroom, my Lord.*"

"Really red and white?"

"No, I was just reciting Angelus Silesius."

"Too bad. I wish that one of us could remember."

"They might have been red and white."

"They might have. To flee or to be driven out. Why did it happen to us Silesians?" Lottel asked.

"The Russians came and swept us away. We were blasted with the east wind, as the Bible says."

"Why us?"

"It was our fate."

"But nobody asked us."

"That is what fate is, when nobody asks you. Back home when we played catch, someone had to be 'it.'" Martin reached for a glass dinner bell on the table and began to shake it.

"Do you remember the rhyme we chanted when we counted one of us out before we played a game of catch?"

She shook her head.

"*Blim, blim, blim,*" he sang, gently shaking a tinkling sound from the bell in time with each *blim*. Obeying the same rhythm, his pointing finger sprang back and forth between the woman and him. "*The train goes, blim, blim, blim, to Africa. Blim, blim, blim. Who comes along? Blim, blim, blim. YOU come along.*" While singing the last line, his voice rose steadily until at the end his finger pointed at himself as he loudly said, "*You!*"

After a while, Lottel straightened her back.

"Let me help you up," Martin said as he reached for Lottel's hand. She stood facing him, small and stout, as if she hadn't grown at all since he had seen her during that last winter in Silesia.

"How will it go with you here in Las Vegas?" she asked.

Looking over her head into the night, he could see the lights of the Stratosphere Tower. On a quiet day, he could hear the shouts of the tourists in the roller coaster running around the top. "What Las Vegas is, America will be, and Germany will become. Those who insist on remembering will die out, and everyone who was in the war will finally be gone. Those who remember will be replaced by those who forget, with the promise that life will be infinitely easier for them than it was for us."

Whatever else he knew would happen, he kept to himself. What reason was there to mention it? Already the axe was laid unto the root of the trees. What was to come would be less than what had been. Those who want to keep things will finally lose against those who invoke progress while calling for the bulldozers. The cheap will beat the good, the young blood will be prized higher than wisdom and memory.

He didn't tell her that he would fight to remember as long as he could. It would be a lonely task, because his mother would be gone by then. She was the last to really know, because she had lived as a grown-up in Silesia, while he had been only a child. Already he could feel that he was no longer a reliable witness to the grit and glory that had been his Silesia. Finally, he thought of the garden where he had played under the rose gate of Babylon, which had risen high but now lay crushed and burned to ashes. Babylon is fallen, is fallen, but he knew that the August moon would still be floating above, like a Chinese lantern over a children's feast.

He embraced her and said good-bye.

"What will you do?" she whispered.

What would he do? Go on as he had always done, until Urn would call out to him, "*Kummock!*" She would smile and wave at him, with her fine white hair rising above her head as if it were about to take flight like blowflower seeds on a breeze. "*Kummock!*" she'll call, now more urgently, because the last train was waiting. *Blim, blim, blim.* He would know that the time had come to follow her to wherever she had found a new home for them all. *Blim, blim, blim. You* come along.